CH00547459

GORDON'S GIFTS

Dear Jenny,

With love and Blessings,

Sally Petch

x

March 2005

In memory of Rosie who gave me so much joy

GORDON'S GIFTS

SALLY PETCH

TESSERA PUBLISHING

First published in Great Britain in 2004 by
Tessera Publishing
PO BOX 3183
Littlehampton
West Sussex
BN17 7WN

British Library Cataloguing-in-Publishing Data

A catalogue record for this book is available
from the British Library

ISBN 0 9539865 7 8

Cover design printed by
RPM Reprographics
2-3, Spur Road, Quarry Lane,
CHICHESTER
West Sussex PO19 2PR

Printed and bound in Great Britain by
Biddles Ltd.,
24,Rollesby Road.
Hardwick Industrial Estate,
KINGS LYNN
Norfolk. PE30 4LS. UK.

So many gifts, from so many people, in so many ways. My life has been truly blessed by my Mother and Father, my family, my partner, my friends, my clients and my animals. Thank you all from the bottom of my heart.

GORDON

CHAPTER ONE

Gordon Sinclair knew it was bad news when he saw the consultant rearrange his face into an expression of suitable gravity.

'I'm afraid it's not good news, Mr. Sinclair.'

In moments of truth, Gordon had known it would not be. He had had too many tests, including this morning's scan. However, now that the moment was here, he wanted to delay it. Just for a few more minutes.

He stood up abruptly and walked across the small room. He started to cough.

'Won't you sit down?'

Gordon was aware of the nurse lightly touching his arm and allowed himself to be steered back to the chair. The consultant was watching him, his fingers steepled in front of him.

'Mr. Sinclair, I'm afraid there's no doubt. You do have advanced lung cancer'. He paused, making a pretence of eyeing his notes. Eventually, he looked up. 'We'll start you on a course of chemotherapy next week.'

Gordon heard him continue, but the words just floated around the room, bypassing him completely. He noticed how crumpled his trousers looked, as if they had already given up. He unstuck his tongue from the roof of his mouth and interrupted, 'You mean I'm going to die?'

The consultant glanced at the nurse. 'That is what I've

been trying to explain to you. Your cancer is terminal. It is too far advanced to operate. All we can do is try to slow it down with the chemotherapy. And, of course, give you full support in pain management.'

'So there's nothing you can do?'

It may have been his imagination, but he thought the consultant looked slightly irritated. He saw him glance at his watch. Then he leant forward and spoke in a voice you might use to a child.

'Look Mr. Sinclair, this is obviously a huge shock to you. Why don't we…'

Gordon stood up abruptly, collected his coat and rushed out of the room. He heard his name being called, but hurried on. He was dimly aware of bays full of people, of coloured dots on vanilla-coloured, shiny floors, of a shop with soft toys and 'get well' helium balloons anchored to a bucket of sand. His shoes made a slight squeaky noise, which punctuated the word beating in his head. Dying. Dying. Dying. Information finally penetrated the fog of shock in his brain. It was quiet around him. He had come into a little used part of the hospital. He sat suddenly on a window ledge, the metal edging cutting into the back of his legs. The corridor smelt of decay. His lungs were settling after his frantic dash and he just sat, looking at his feet. At his brown brogues, at the turnups on his trousers. The numbness in his head was beginning to clear and he could feel a rawness in his stomach area. He folded his arms around himself as he realised he had started to shiver. The consultant's face reappeared in his mind, but he pushed it away. Not yet. He needed to get away from here. To be in familiar surroundings.

Gordon drove home on automatic pilot. He waved

absent-mindedly to his neighbour, Sid, who was hedge trimming, before he parked the Jag next to his cottage. The smell of the leather in the car had quietened him a little, comforted him. But he knew his world was changed forever. He let himself inside, went straight to the cupboard where he stored his drink and poured himself a very large port. There he sat by the kitchen range, huddling aginst it for warmth and let it all filter through. He was shocked at the tears that came and he sobbed, hunched up as his emotions pulled at his insides.

'For God's sake, man,' he said aloud, 'it's not the end of the world.'

His laughter bayed out into the room as he realised the absurdity of what he had just said. It had a hysterical note and he wondered if he was going mad. Tea, that was what he needed. Tea brought sanity and safety. He was just taking his first sip when Sid's face appeared at the window. For one frantic moment, Gordon wondered what he looked like, but it was too late. Sid had opened the top of the stable door, his ruddy face beaming.

'Good, you've got the kettle going. Would love a cup. Wondered if you wanted your hedge doing, seeing as I've got the cutters out.'

Gordon busied himself with teabags and milk. 'That would be great, Sid, save me a job.'

'What I thought.'

Gordon knew it was really an excuse for Sid to avoid his wife for a little bit longer. Maisie, large, plump, a real gossip, drove her husband to distraction with her chatter, never stopping to listen to the answers to her questions. Sid could be out in the garden and it would be a little while before she even realised. Gordon admired Maisie from afar, but was glad he did not have to live with her. He handed Sid a mug of tea.

'Been anywhere special?'

The question hung between them for a fraction of a second before he decided.

'Just been out to look at another car.'

'What, thinking of selling one of your two? Getting a little run-around?'

Gordon's extravagance with cars was often a source of conversation between Maisie and himself.

'No, no, it was another Jaguar. But I decided it needed too much work.'

With that lie, the moment of truth passed. He quashed the rising panic inside him. Not now, not now.

'Don't know why you don't get something sensible. Can't see how you get all your gardening stuff in the back of that flash car.'

'But the boot's huge, Sid. Besides, I don't want a small car. After all, not long on this earth.'

He could not believe he had just said that. He took a gulp of tea, which scalded his mouth and made his eyes water.

'Ah well, you know best, but I don't know how you can afford the petrol. What with you being retired.'

It was as if Gordon's brain was functioning on two levels. Here he was, in his kitchen, supping tea with Sid and chatting as though they had all the time in the world when the other side of his brain was in turmoil. The other side knew he had no time.

The phone rang. Gordon looked at it as if it would bite him. He saw Sid glance at him and picked it up.

'Lowesdon 476.' He'd never got out of the habit of answering like that.

'Mr. Sinclair, it's Mr. Brown's secretary from St.

Moorcrofts. We were rather concerned about you earlier and felt you should make another appointment so that Mr. Brown can discuss treatment with you.'

It was here, in the kitchen. Brought in through a wire. Inescapable. Death. He waved a hand at Sid who was disappearing out of the door.

'Mr. Sinclair?'

He realised he hadn't answered. 'Er, yes, perhaps I had.'

They managed to fit him in two days later. He had to go to the Oncology Department. A word that hadn't been in his vocabulary until now.

He went with a heavy heart, unwilling to tread the vanilla lino again. He sat in a numbered bay and waited. He tried to keep his thoughts on his garden. He had even brought along the new David Austin rose catalogue as there was a new rose he had seen at Chelsea. But one little sentence kept infiltrating his thoughts, 'What was the point?' In six months' time, or a year, he would be dead. Would be lucky to see even this season's blooms.

His gaze wandered around the waiting area. Most people were in couples. There was a family group, the husband holding on tightly to his wife's hands, the children close by, the youngest leaning against his mother, thumb in mouth. Gordon felt he did not belong here amongst the sick. He should be out with his beloved cars or in his rose garden or having a pint in his local and felt a surge of anger at the injustice of it all. He watched the nurses come out and call a name, scanning the faces for a match. He wanted to be amongst people who knew him, who understood him. Here, he was just a hospital number. He resolutely went back to his catalogue, forcing himself to concentrate on it, reciting names like a Mantra, 'Roserie de l'Hay', 'Mme Isaac Pereire', 'Belle de Crécy', over and over again, as if they would ward off his 'turn'.

But they did not and once again, he was ushered into Mr. Brown's room, sat in front of his desk and listened to his choices. Only they were not being delivered as choices. On Monday, he would start his chemotherapy. He needed to come in every day that week. Then he would have a week off. The consultant's voice droned on, explaining side effects, naming drugs as though they were items out of a shopping list, his tongue familiar with the names. Gordon could not get 'Roserie de l'Hay' out of his mind. He could almost smell the strong scent, could feel the velvet petals against his nose. He loved the deep colour. He was startled out of his thoughts by the consultant leaning forward and asking rather shortly,

'Mr. Sinclair, do you have any questions?'

It was obvious from his tone that this was the second time he had asked. The words formed and were spoken without any conscious effort.

'Do you grow roses in your garden?'

The surgeon's eyes narrowed slightly. He realised his patient had hardly taken in a word he had said. He sighed. Shock affected some of them like this. His tone, when he spoke, was gentler.

'No, I don't believe we have any. We had our garden designed and I wasn't really that involved in the planting decisions.'

Gordon thought that he did not even know what was in his garden and he didn't really care. Those perfectly manicured hands were involved in other business. A surgeon with dirt under his fingernails really would not do. 'So Mr. Sinclair, if you've no further questions, we'll see you on Monday.'

Gordon shook the outstretched hand and meekly followed the nurse.

'If you'd like to wait in Bay 4, Mr. Sinclair, as we need to run a few tests before Monday. Won't take long.'

She flashed Gordon a smile, pointed in the direction of Bay 4 and was gone.

Gordon did as instructed and sat on an orange chair, connected to all the others in the row.

'Why?' he mused. 'Were they so desirable that people would actually steal them?'

He tried to go back to the rose book, but now felt thoroughly unsettled. A door opened across the corridor and a young woman came and sat opposite him. She was beautiful. Fine bone structure, high cheekbones, but Gordon's eyes were drawn to her bald head. She saw him look and grinned.

'Glamorous, isn't it? I wear a wig normally, but couldn't be bothered today. Last day of chemo, so I'm feeling a bit jaded.'

Gordon, not naturally inclined to talk to strangers, struggled to find anything to say. Panic was rising in him rapidly. A feeling of being out of control. He stood up, aware that his legs were trembling and he touched the woman's hand briefly. 'I'm sorry about your hair.'

He left quickly, before he could change his mind. The idea, which had been lurking in the back of his mind, had pushed its way forward. Why bother to prolong the agony? What difference did it make if he lived for 6, 9 or 12 months? He was still going to die. Now if they could do something about that, then he would stay. Would try anything. But the consultant's words kept repeating themselves in his brain. 'I'm afraid your cancer's terminal ... terminal ...terminal.' Another little voice whispered to him, 'Yes, but what if they did keep you alive for another 6 months and found a cure in that time?' But he knew, he knew it was a hopeless dream. He was dying. Best face up to it, get it over and done with.

CHAPTER TWO

Over the following week, Gordon became obsessed with not seeing or speaking with anyone. That way, he would not have to answer people's, 'How are you?' This was said time and time again and the expected reply was, 'I'm fine, how are you?' He was guilty of it himself. It had become a habit with most people. He could visualise their faces when he replied, 'Oh I've got cancer and I'm going to die. How are you?'

So he stayed in and ignored the ringing of the telephone. It was towards the end of the week when a persistent visitor repeatedly rang the doorbell. In exasperation, he marched down the hall and flung it open. For a moment, he did not recognise the man on the doorstep, but then he saw the stethoscope. It was Tom Lander, his GP.

'May I come in, I'd like a chat with you.'

Gordon stepped aside to let him in and then led him into the kitchen where it seemed he spent all his time. He cleared a pile of car magazines off a chair so that the GP could sit down.

'Tea? Coffee? Or something stronger?'

'Tea would be good, thanks.'

Damn, the bloody man was planning on staying. In defiance, Gordon poured himself a large glass of malt whiskey. The tea made, he sat down opposite the doctor, turning his glass round and round in his hand.

'So, Doc, to what do I owe this honour?'

'I've had a letter from Mr. Brown, the consultant On-cologist at St. Moorcrofts. They're rather concerned that you've not had any treatment and I just wondered if I could get to the bottom of it.'

Gordon took a sip from his glass and looked at the doctor steadily. 'Doc, will I die whether or not I have the treatment?'

The GP looked a little taken aback by the directness of Gordon's question. He sighed, 'Yes, yes, I'm afraid you will. The cancer's very advanced as they told you in the hospital. I'm surprised you're not showing more obvi-ous symptoms.'

'So if I'm dying, why waste time, money and effort in chemotherapy?'

'Well, we would hope to give you an extra six months or so.'

'For what? So I can go on holiday? Write a novel? I think, if it's all the same with you, that I'd just rather get it over and done with.'

The GP sat in silence, looking at his patient before standing up. 'OK, Mr. Sinclair. But as the disease advances, you will need some pain control. I would like you to come in at least every fortnight so we can assess you.'

Gordon nodded, 'How long have I got. Realistically.'

'Six months, I'd say. No longer. I'm sorry.'

Tom let himself out and got into his car. He leant his head back on the rest and thought about his patient. He secretly agreed with him and hoped that if it ever hap-pened to him, he would be that brave.

Gordon felt anything but brave as he downed the rest of the malt in one. He had no sooner washed up the glass when there was a further knock on the door.

'Blasted doctor back I expect.' he grumbled to himself and he flung open the door.

'Alice.'

'Gordon! Whatever's wrong? I've been calling and calling you. A piece of furniture came into the shop that I know you were looking for.'

Alice Stamp was in her seventies, but was as bright as a button. She edged past Gordon and went on through into the kitchen, removing a large home-made cake from her bag and plonking it on the table. Gordon had followed her resignedly. Alice, quite at home in his kitchen, bustled around making tea, cutting the cake, arranging it on plates and talking nineteen to the dozen. Finally, she stopped.

'Well, you're a bit quiet today.'

Gordon groaned, 'Can't get a word in edgeways.'

Alice clucked at him, her hands on her hips, ignoring his jibe. 'You look a bit peaky. Are you eating properly?'

'Yes. Now sit down and drink your tea.'

Alice Stamp had been fussing over him for years, ever since he had offered her some shelf space in his pine furniture shop. She had put in bric-a-brac, pretty stuff that complimented the pine. They had been a good team until he had retired and sold up. Alice had long given up selling her bits and bobs, but still helped out in the shop occasionally.

'Anyway, why I came round was to let you know that Mr. Simmons has brought in a really nice meat block - just like you were looking for. Not cheap, mind, but nothing is since you've gone.'

She still begrudged him retiring and she always insisted she had never really got on with the new owners.

19

'So you'll be in to look at it then?'

It was the perfect time to tell her, to tell someone. But he could not. Did not want to. He did not want their pity.

'Er, yes, probably I will, Alice.'

'Well don't seem so keen.'

'Well, it's just that I'd decided that I really don't need any more things around the house.'

'Don't need any more things. Do you mean to say you've stopped collecting, then?'

'Well I suppose it does, really. In fact, I'm having a sort out and getting rid of the clutter.'

'Oh well, you won't be needing a meat block will you, not when you've already got a perfectly good chopping board.'

She drank her tea, an uneasy silence settling around them.

'Alice, I'm really grateful to you for taking the trouble to come round. It's just that I'm … downsizing.'

The word just came to him. He had read about families who had sold up their house and dramatically reduced their need for material possessions. He had always quite envied them.

'Downsizing'. What sort of new-fangled expression is that? What you mean is you're having a jolly good sort out. And not before time, too.'

She gave a quick glance around the kitchen, at the dressers covered in china and nick-nacks. The window ledges were cluttered with things that Gordon insisted might come in useful. Two demi-johns sat by the range, despite Gordon not having made any wine for years.

'I'd be glad to give you a hand, if you like. There's a Scout jumble next week.'

She looked as though she was about to roll up her sleeves and get stuck in. 'Still,' Gordon mused, 'not a bad idea to start sorting stuff out. Save someone else doing it.' To his utter dismay, he felt his eyes fill with tears. In his embarrassment, he knocked over his near empty teacup. Alice fussed around clearing it up and he thought that she really had not noticed. He would have to be careful where his thoughts led in future. The trouble was, almost all his thoughts led to the same place. He was putting his cup on the draining board when his eye was caught by a pretty little Spode teapot on the dresser. On the spur of the moment, he picked it up.

'Actually, I wonder if you'd like this. I know it's always been a favourite of yours.'

'Oh, I couldn't, it's too valuable.'

'Oh nonsense. Take it. It'll be one less thing to dust.'

He took the teapot away from the speechless woman and wrapped it in a few sheets of newspaper.

'Look at it as payment for clutter clearing.'

Alice did not look convinced, but accepted the gift. They settled on a day in the week to start and she left. Ideas were racing through Gordon's head. It had given him real pleasure to give the teapot to Alice. What if he really started to sort out his affairs before he died?

His thoughts went back to the time after the death of his father and the anguished sorting out which had been necessary. His father had died suddenly of a heart attack aged 55 and had had no warning.

Gordon had helped his mother to sort out his father's belongings. She had seemed to cope with it, but Gordon had found it painfully difficult. With each drawerful of clutter, he had felt as though he was prying. He had flatly refused to sort through his father's papers and journals, leaving them for his mother to do. She had seemed equally as reluctant and in the end, they had put them in a cardboard box and put them away in a cupboard. For all he knew, they were still there.

The thought of someone else having to do this for him made him determined to sort out his affairs. After all, he did have time. He pulled open a kitchen drawer and rifled through the contents. What a hoarder he had become. The thought of his mother clearing out all his clutter made his blood run cold.

He went to bed with a resolve to start in the morning. He was aware that it had actually given him a feeling of being back in control for which he was truly thankful.

He woke in the middle of the night from a muddled dream where he was banging 'For Sale' boards beside all of the roses and staking them to the posts.

He switched on his bedside lamp and sat up. He felt a bit breathless and sipped at a glass of water by his bed. The dream would not leave him. He got up and wandered over to the window, where he could see down to the far meadow and watched a dark shape flitting across the grass, probably a fox.

How he loved this house and garden and he wondered suddenly what would happen to it. Although his mother stood to inherit it, she would never be persuaded to leave her own cottage, not at her age. What a burden he was going to be to her.

He sighed and went back to bed, feeling chilled. He had no sooner switched out the light when he sat up again and put it back on. What if he were to sell the house before he died? That would really tie up all the loose ends. He mulled over the idea and by the time dawn had arrived, he had made his decision. He would spend his last few months sorting out all his affairs, down to the last crossed 't' and dotted 'i'. He had never been a burden to anyone in his life and he did not intend to start now.

CHAPTER THREE

His resolve weakened by the time he was up and dressed. He had spent an hour working in the garden and he was not sure if he could bear to see anyone else in it. The early morning air had been sweet with the scent of the old roses he so favoured and despair had overcome him. It wasn't bloody fair!

He had procrastinated for the rest of the day, arguing first one way and then another. In the end, his pride won. He would go through with it. If he had to die, then he was jolly well going to make it a good death.

He rang an estate agent the next morning, having scoured the Yellow Pages for names. The agent was eager to get the ball rolling and arranged with Gordon to call around that afternoon. Gordon had nearly telephoned twice to cancel, but something stopped him at the last moment.

The agent arrived and used to the mixed emotions of potential sellers, tried to put Gordon at his ease. 'The garden's beautiful. You must be sorry to have to leave it?'

'Yes, I will be, but the time's right. I'm not getting any younger.'

That, at least, was true.

'And are you looking to buy a smaller property, then, Mr. Sinclair?'

'No, no, I'm going to live with my mother in the West Country. She could do with the extra help around the house.'

'Nice part of the country. Very elderly, is she?'

'75 exactly.'

Gordon turned away, unwilling to prolong the agent's visit. The thought of living with his mother had come to him on the spur of the moment. It would do, as a reason. He smiled to himself. He visited his mother about four times a year and she was always pleased to see him, but got very irritated when she could not 'get on'. She longed to pack her son off again after about a day!

The agent was talking business, fees and selling prices. Gordon agreed to a ridiculously large sum, but stressed that the sale needed to go through quickly.

To his horror, the agent phoned him in the morning to say that there were people wishing to view. He rushed around, tidying up and waiting with a deep dread for the sound of a car pulling into the driveway.

A woman in her forties, bleached blonde hair, precision cut, perfectly made up, her long manicured fingers showing off several huge rings, got out of the agent's car.

'What a darling little place.'

The agent suggested Gordon make some coffee whilst he showed Mrs. Anderson around. He fiddled around in the kitchen, feeling like a stranger in his own house and trying to listen to snatches of conversation.

'Needs knocking into one, I suppose … tiny little bathroom.' Unfortunately, Mrs. Anderson was standing right by the open kitchen window when she stated, 'Don't like these old-fashioned gardens. Too much work. I'm a sitting on a terrace sipping a G & T type of gardener'.

She laughed shrilly. Gordon had stopped spooning coffee into the mugs.

'Still, my husband knows a very good garden designer. He should soon lick this into shape.'

Gordon had crossed the kitchen and flung open the back door before he realised he had moved.

'Mrs. Anderson, I'm really having second thoughts about whether I want to sell Rose Cottage or not. Perhaps Mr. Tomlinson could take your details and then when I do decide, he can get back to you.'

The agent's jaw had dropped. The woman looked crest-fallen and then her face started to redden with anger.

'Marty, I thought you said it was actually on the market.'

Gordon closed the door on them both. He put two of the mugs away and took his own coffee out into his beloved garden, walking round it and talking to his roses, apologising for the awful woman's behaviour. He consequently missed the phone call from the agents, but picked up an answerphone message from them that struggled with politeness. Gordon started laughing at the absurdity of it all. OK, so he was dying, but he could and would do those things with integrity and with his principles intact. He would jolly well only sell to people he considered suitable. He phoned the agent back, who told him off quite soundly and suggested that, in future, Gordon might be out when he showed clients round. Gordon, in turn, suggested that he would find himself another estate agent.

'But you've signed a contract!' Tomlinson spluttered.

'Well sue me over it, then,' blazed Gordon, 'but as far as I'm concerned, you are no longer acting for me, Marty!' and he hung up.

Whatever had come over him? He usually bent over backwards to keep the peace and here he was, suggesting somebody sue him. Only they had better get a move on! This dying business did have its benefits, he thought wryly. Enough was enough today. Tomorrow, he would trawl around the town's other estate agents and see if he could find one he liked.

CHAPTER FOUR

It took all morning to find an agent he liked. She worked for a small private firm called 'Perfect Homes' which specialised in cottages. The name was so tacky he nearly did not go in, but was glad he had. Penny Young seemed very sharp, but had also sympathised with him.

'I know this is silly,' Gordon faltered, 'but I really care to whom I sell my house. I sort of feel a responsibility towards it to find it a suitable keeper.'

'What a wonderful thought,' Penny chuckled. 'It will make my job a bit different. Perhaps you need to set them a questionnaire on old roses. All suitable candidates must score 8 out of a possible 10.'

'Well, it's an idea,' mused Gordon and then bellowed with laughter. 'Maybe I'd settle for a 5 out of 10. But no alice bands and they must loathe G & T.'

He was quite high-spirited when he left the agents. He pulled up outside the local garage and the owner, Sandy Thomas, waved a hand in acknowledgement. His son, Toby, strolled over to him.

'How's the Mark 1 going, Mr. Sinclair?'

Car-mad Toby often accompanied him to club nights run by the local branch of the Jaguar Enthusiasts' Club. On Toby's 21st, he had even let him drive the Mark 1 and had been impressed by the way he had handled the car.

'Oh, she's fine. That mysterious knocking sound seems to have disappeared. Coming with me again on Monday?'

'Love to.' Toby answered. It would have to be a like-minded woman who would put up with his car passion, that was for sure. As he drove home in his other Jag, another idea came into his head. What if he were to give his Mark 1 to Toby? But how to go about it?

He was still mulling this one over the next morning when Alice arrived, complete with boxes, newspapers and black rubbish sacks. In one of the boxes was a large fruit-cake.

'Thought we might need something to sustain us.'

'Looks wonderful, Alice. You do spoil me. Now, where shall we start? How about a cuppa first?'

'We'll never get on if we keep having tea breaks before we're ever started. Nope. We'll do the dresser first, then we'll have tea.'

All the china was taken off, washed and put onto the kitchen table to sort. Gordon filled a box of good blue and white to go to auction. The rest he packed into the Scout box. He thoroughly enjoyed the morning, forgetting why he was actually doing the task.

'But you've left nothing on the dresser, Gordon. You're not parting with that as well, are you?'

'Well, it would solve the dusting problem wouldn't it?'

'Well I think you're in a right funny mood, that I do.'

Alice stomped away to start on the open shelves, passing Gordon two decades of accumulated rubbish. He started to put some in a box.

'Now what are you doing that for?'

'Well, it's just stuff I might want to look at properly.'

'Well, I can't see why. You've not wanted to look at it in 20 years.'

Suitably admonished, Gordon threw most of the clutter in the second black sack. He found an old picture of his mother, caught on camera and actually playing her saxophone. His mother, having to curb her rather Bohemian lifestyle when she had met his father, insisted on pursuing her love of music. Right from when Gordon was born, she had played in a local jazz band. His father, anxious to keep up appearances, pretended not to notice these small digressions of hers, as he put it. Gordon passed the photo to Alice.

'Does she still play, do you think?'

'Not that she would ever admit, although the sax is always well polished.'

'Shame how our dreams fade. I wonder if she ever thought she'd become famous?'

'No, she chose the life of a country vet's wife rather than fame and fortune, I'm afraid. She knuckled down to it well enough, but there was always a wistful air about her.'

'Bout time you went and saw her,' Alice chided.

'Yes,' Gordon admitted, 'it's high time.'

He did not relish the visit. His mother was extremely perceptive and she was bound to notice that all was not well. But was it fair not to tell her? After all, she was his only relative. Maybe he would ring her later.

Alice had just left when the estate agent from Perfect Homes arrived. Gordon had forgotten all about it, but was glad Alice had gone. He wanted to keep the sale quiet for a day or two longer. Penny Young looked around the kitchen, at the full boxes and bags of rubbish.

'My, you have been busy. Still, an uncluttered house is always easier to sell. Allows the potential purchaser to visualise their own possessions in the house.'

She openly admired the cottage and exclaimed in pleasure when Gordon showed her the garden.

'This is wonderful. How on earth can you bear to leave it?'

He almost told her the truth. It was only because he suddenly felt too overcome with emotion that he failed to speak. Instead, he beckoned her through an archway and into his wild part of the garden. Mown paths led through a wild flower meadow, bees hovered drowsily over the delicate plants. An old swing in a tree ended one of the walkways.

'May I?'

Gordon nodded and Penny sat on the warm wooden seat and rocked to and fro, closing her eyes at the delight of it all. She opened her eyes and saw Gordon watching her.

'I'm so sorry, it's like an enchanted place - I just love it.'

She jumped off the swing.

'Sorry, I mustn't keep you.'

Gordon made a dismissive gesture with his hand and silently led her back to the house. On the way, he fetched his clippers out of his pocket and cut one of the old roses.

'For you. Thank you for appreciating my garden.'

Penny took the rose. Emotion choked her. She felt the air thick with it. She buried her nose in the deep velvet petals and inhaled the strong, clove-like perfume. The petals were warm and she suddenly wanted to cry. She took a deep breath, 'We'd better talk figures, Mr. Sinclair and then I can begin to measure up.'

The mood changed, the spell was broken.

Lydia Page was in the office on her return. She watched her boss carefully put the rose in water.

'Roserie de l'Hay. Whoever gave you that?'

She went and smelt the rose, sensing a change in Penny. Penny caught her enquiring glance. 'New cottage just came on the market. Rose Cottage in Watery Lane, a Mr. Gordon Sinclair…'

'Bachelor of the parish,' teased Lydia.

'Oh please! He's just put the cottage on with us, but wants us to find a suitable buyer. Someone who will appreciate his roses.'

'How on earth can we find a suitable buyer?' Lydia asked incredulously. 'I thought we were in the business of selling houses, not matchmaking. Anyway, you know how I hate roses.'

'You haven't seen his garden. It's exquisite.'

'But roses! I expect they're in regimented beds with no ground cover.'

Penny smiled. 'You are opinionated! OK, so you're a landscape gardener, but I tell you, this garden is gorgeous. It even has an old swing…'

Her voice trailed off. She busied herself and then handed Lydia the details on Rose Cottage for typing up. Lydia, forthright, passionate, self-opinionated, was also hard working with a large supply of energy. She worked for 'Perfect Homes' two days a week to supplement the income she received from her work as a gardener.

'How's Lord P?' Penny asked.

'A pain in the neck. He wants the water feature in the formal garden moved. Can you imagine!'

Penny grinned. Lydia worked up at the Manor for three days a week and consequently was able to rent a small two-up-two-down in the grounds. But Lord P, as everyone called him, was a very exacting boss and he drove Lydia to distraction. Penny handed Lydia a list.

'When you've done that, give these people a ring about

Rose Cottage. They're all on our waiting list. I'm off out to another viewing.'

As she drove past Rose Cottage on her way out of the village, she noticed the doctor's car parked outside and hoped nothing was wrong. She resisted an absurd impulse to stop and find out. Gordon Sinclair had intrigued her. She shook her head in exasperation with her thoughts and accelerated away.

Tom Lander was not sure of his reception at Rose Cottage, but felt professionally bound to visit. Personally, he was not sure how he felt. Gordon Sinclair had caused him a lot of deep thoughts. It was his duty to save lives, to give patients his best shot, but he could see Gordon's point of view too. The kitchen, he noticed, had changed dramatically since his last visit. Gordon caught his enquiring glances.

'Sorting it all out now. Don't want other people to have to do it. Also means I can give things away to where I want them to go.'

'Do people know, then?'

'No,' Gordon rounded on him, 'and neither do I want them to, not until it's unavoidable. So don't you go saying anything.'

'That really goes without saying. I'm your doctor - everything we discuss is in the strictest confidence. Now what I'm really here for is to just check you over, see if you're coping, if we can give you any support.'

Gordon sighed. This really was not going to go away and maybe he would need the doctor later on.

'I feel OK, really I do. I get tired more quickly and I get breathless.'

Tom nodded, 'To be expected. Any persistent cough

33

yet?'

'No, not really. I just want to keep well enough to see all this through.' He gesticulated around the room. 'I've put it on the market. Want to sell it before I die.'

'Is that wise? Where will you go?'

'Timing.' was all Gordon replied. 'I've got to get it right.' But a fresh wave of fear went through him. If he sold the house quickly, where would he go?

Tom insisted on a physical examination before leaving Gordon alone.

Gordon realised that he still had not phoned his mother. 'Tomorrow, I'll do it tomorrow,' he promised himself.

CHAPTER FIVE

The weekend passed and he still put the task off. Penny had apparently showed one couple round the cottage whilst he was out, but they had wanted a much smaller garden.

Monday came and Gordon picked Toby Thomas up in the evening to go to the Jaguar club night. He got out and handed Toby the keys. 'You drive it tonight.'

Toby's face lit up and he quickly settled into the car. It was a 15-mile trip to the pub where the Jag Enthusiasts' Club met each month, but Toby handled the car expertly and Gordon made up his mind.

For a while that evening, as he chatted and admired various cars, he forgot himself. It was only when the Treasurer appeared at his elbow and asked him to help marshal for the London to Brighton run that the nightmare came washing back. That was in four months' time and he did not know if he would be there then. He felt physically sick. John Green, the Treasurer, put his hand on his arm.

'Gordon, are you OK?'

'Yes, just felt a bit strange, that's all. Look, I'll let you know whether I can help as soon as I can.'

His despondency lasted until he got home. He had let Toby drive back again.

'I've not done anything wrong, have I, Gordon?' Toby

asked anxiously, 'Only you seem a little perturbed.'

Gordon looked at the young man's worried expression. 'Have you got time for a coffee?'

'Well yes, of course.'

He looked even more anxious, but Gordon could not tell him. Not here, in the car. He motioned for Toby to sit in the old rocking chair by the range. He found mugs and started to make coffee.

'Toby, I have to have your absolute word that what I'm about to tell you won't go any further at the moment.'

Toby nodded nervously, fumbling with the button on his cuff.

'Well, there's no easy way to say this and this is particularly hard because I've not told anyone else.'

Oh get on with it man, the boy looks like a petrified rabbit.

'It's just that I only have a few months to live. I'm dying of lung cancer.'

He saw the look of horror on the young man's face.

'But surely…'

'No, there are no 'but surelys''. Now I expect you're wondering why I've decided to tell you?'

He looked at the boy and saw the shock and confusion in his eyes. He turned away, not wanting to witness it.

'I want you to have the Mark 1.'

There, it was out.

There was complete silence, which made him look round. Toby's face had reddened and he had stood up and was fumbling with his coat. One sleeve was inside out and he angrily yanked it the right way round.

'Toby, whatever's wrong?'

Toby looked at him. 'I don't want your car.'

He had pulled on his coat and was heading for the

door.

'But why? I don't understand.'

But Toby had gone, had vanished into the night, leaving Gordon staring after him open-mouthed. Whatever had got into him? Gordon suddenly felt very tired. He had planned this, it was supposed to be a 'feel good' moment. What a mess. Totally dispirited, he went quietly up to bed, but lay awake for hours, just staring into the darkness.

Toby had driven home quickly, his shock fading into despair. He could not get Gordon's face out of his head. He pulled up in the drive behind a Ford Cosworth, which meant that his stepbrother, Robin, was already home. He groaned and went slowly round to the back door.

Robin was in the kitchen, thickly covering slices of bread with butter. He turned when he heard Toby.

'Had a good evening with the old poofter, then?'

He grinned maliciously. Toby could smell the drink on his breath from where he was standing. He knew there was no point answering and walked straight through the kitchen to go to his room. His stomach rumbled. He would have liked a sandwich, but there was not any way he was going to make one when Robin was around.

He closed his bedroom door, threw off his clothes and got into bed. His eyes wandered to the model Jaguars he collected and displayed on a pine unit. He focused on the Mark 1 and then turned over and closed his eyes. He hated his stepbrother right now. His bedroom was over the kitchen and he could hear Robin moving around.

Then he heard him call, 'Dreaming of your pansy, are you, little bruv?'

Toby made a fist and hit the pillow as hard as he could,

wishing it was Robin's head. Because he was shy, he found it difficult to get a girlfriend, which gave Robin ample ammunition to taunt him.

When he had started going to the Jaguar events with Gordon Sinclair, Robin and his friends had become even more malicious. He knew instinctively that Gordon was not homosexual, but he also knew that if he inherited the Mark 1, Robin would make his life unbearable. To him it would be proof, and he would not hesitate in sharing his thoughts in their local. No, he would have to keep away from Sinclair. It was the only option open to him, even if he would hate himself for it.

Tuesday dawned. Rain was hammering on the uncurtained windows. Gordon looked out and saw his roses bowing in the strength of the wind. What a day! He had a call from the agents wanting to show people round, so he disappeared 10 minutes before they were due, walking down to the village to buy a paper. As he passed the garage, he saw Toby and waved, but the boy blushed and scuttled inside. Gordon simply could not face pursuing it, so he went home as dispirited as when he left.

There was a message from the agents to say that the cottage had once again been unsuitable. For the first time in his life, he got undressed and went back to bed. He just wanted a bit of comfort. He slept and woke again at 4:00 feeling feverish. He spent the night either shivering or feeling so hot that he threw the blankets back to get cool.

He still felt pretty unwell the next day, but decided he had to get out or he would go mad. On an impulse, he phoned his mother.

'Gordon, is that you?'

'Mum, how are you?'

'Oh, I'm well. Busy in the garden, actually. Sown a lot of veg this year. Damn carrot flies get through the barricades. Trying to sort it out'

His mother had always talked in clipped sentences, as though she only had a certain number of words to use up.

'I thought I'd come down to see you for a couple of days.'

'That would be nice. I could do with a hand with the digging.'

This was a first, his mother admitting to needing help.

'Are you really OK, Mum?'

'Yes, perfectly,' she snapped. 'Just getting old.'

'Well, I'll come tomorrow, it that's OK. Shall I bring anything?'

'Could do with a bottle of gin, as it happens.'

'Fine, I'll bring you a crate.'

His mother laughed. 'See you tomorrow, dear boy. I'll do lunch.'

Gordon decided he would take the Mark 1 down. He did not usually do that much mileage in it, but what the hell. He would have one last fling in it. He went out and cleaned and polished until it shone. Suppose he would have to advertise it. It struck him that giving things away was going to be harder than he had anticipated. Why were people so suspicious? He even had trouble giving Alice a teapot. It was absurd.

The next day, he thankfully felt a lot better and the drive down was completed in blazing sunshine. Gordon felt more relaxed than he had since 'the news'. He hugged his mother, marvelling at how well she looked. Grey hair swept back in a bun, straight backed and tanned from long hours in the garden. She accepted the two bottles of gin.

'One would have done.'

'I know how you get through it. You even named me after it!'

'Don't be so absurd.'

She went off into a peal of laughter. 'Want one?'

'What, now?'

'Why not? Not often I see you. Too old to wait for the sun to go over the yard arm.'

She poured them both a generous measure and topped it up with tonic, added ice, lemon and a sprig of mint from a pot on the table. Gordon looked round the kitchen - scarlet geraniums were wedged into blue and white Spode serving dishes. A cat slumbered on an old patchwork cushion on the rocking chair, its colours faded by time. It was the most tranquil place he had ever set eyes on. It was as if his mother insisted on quiet and calm. Another cat appeared in the doorway.

'And who's this?'

'That's Billy boy. He found me a few months' ago.'

His mother made it sound as though the cat had looked her up in the Good Guide to B & B.

'I advertised him in the Post Office, but nobody came to claim him so I kept him. Really thin and scrawny he was.'

Gordon looked at the sleek black and white cat and knew it had really landed on its feet. It jumped onto the table with ease of movement and rubbed its head around the geraniums. This released their pungent smell and the cat sneezed and stalked off.

'Silly boy, you never learn.' His mother opened a tin

and filled two dishes. Bumble, the sleeping grey cat, was instantly alert and leapt down and yowled.

'Never any peace,' his mother grumbled.

'You love it.'

She smiled at him and picked up her gin glass.

'Come and see the garden.' She fetched a battered old hat, yanked it onto her head and disappeared out of the stable door with Gordon following. Her garden was an art form. A true cottage garden, with wild flowers mixing effortlessly with perennials and vegetables growing at the front of some of the borders.

'Do you know I rather fancy some running water here.' She gestured to an area at the side of a paved seating area. 'Wondered if you could do a bit of spade work for me.'

'But of course I will. I'll start after lunch.'

And so the day passed. Gordon noticed how much slower he was at physical work and was dismayed at how much he sweated.

'I think you're getting a bit soft.'

Gordon stopped digging and looked up at his mother. Now. Now was the time. But he could not. Instead, he heard himself offer some plausible excuse for his obvious weakness.

'Well stop now, anyway. By the time you've bathed, it will be suppertime.'

Gordon nodded and put the spade down wearily. Luckily, she had only planned a small pebble fountain, otherwise he would never have managed it. He went indoors and ran himself a bath. His mother still would not have a shower.

'New-fangled thing - no relaxation about them at all.' She liked to disappear into the bathroom with a book and her glass of gin.

After supper, he went and picked up her saxophone and took it from its box. It shone as it always did.

'Play something.'

'No, not now. I haven't played for an age. Forgotten how to, probably.'

'But why? You were so good.'

'Didn't get me anywhere though, did it? Only cross words from your father and strange looks from the villagers.'

'But what about playing it just because you love doing it?'

His mother's face shut down. She changed the subject and nothing more was said about the saxophone for the rest of his visit. Neither did he tell her about himself. He caught her watching him a couple of times when he had to sit down and rest, but nothing was said.

He returned home with a box of homemade goodies she had unearthed from the freezer. He had hugged her tightly, but had been unable to tell her he loved her. He had really wanted to, but it was something they never said. It was just accepted, but sometimes he wanted to hear the words between them.

CHAPTER SIX

Gordon drove into the driveway of Rose Cottage, got out of the Jag and was promptly cannoned into by a dog, running at speed, in turn followed by a young woman running at full pelt and yelling. She stopped short when she saw Gordon and then went forward and grabbed the excited dog.

'Who the hell are you and what on earth is that dog doing in my garden?'

'Look, I'm sorry. I can explain. Let me just put Pounce back into the car.'

'What a ridiculous name for a dog.'

The woman shot him a look of pure venom and holding tightly onto the dog's collar, led it to a small red Fiat parked outside the cottage. Then she returned to where Gordon was waiting, arms folded.

'My name's Lydia Page and I work for 'Perfect Homes'. I'd just shown a client round Rose Cottage when Pounce appeared in the drive. He'd managed to wriggle out of one of the car windows. He is a bit of an escapologist.' She looked at Gordon, a touch of defiance in her expression. Gordon, feeling riled from the journey, was not about to let it drop.

'I though Penny was acting for Rose Cottage.'

'She is - well, we both are. We share the viewings on the days I work.'

'And do you always bring your dog to viewings with you?'

Lydia was starting to find the interrogation wearisome.

'No, I don't. I was called in at short notice as Penny was busy and someone wanted to see round Rose Cottage this afternoon. Look, I'm sorry it happened, but he hasn't damaged anything.'

She turned on her heel and strode to her car, a small, purposeful woman with an angry air about her. She drove back to 'Perfect Homes'.

'Met that Mr. Sinclair from Rose Cottage. What an abrasive character,' she complained.

Penny thought back to the gentle man, passionate about his garden who had given her a rose.

'I hope you haven't upset him.'

'No, not as much as he riled me,' Lydia complained.

Penny sighed and got back to the pile of paperwork on her desk. So far, no one had shown any serious interest in Rose Cottage and she could not see why. It was such an enchanting place, but she knew that a serious offer could come along at any moment. That was the name of the game.

She made sure that she did the viewings over the next fortnight and Gordon, for his part, kept out of her way. She could see his anxiety growing over the lack of any firm offer, even though he tried to hide it.

She was showing a middle-aged couple around at the end of the second week, when Gordon appeared. She hoped he would disappear again, because the viewers seemed to be showing encouraging signs. She still had the garden left and Gordon seemed determined to accompany them. Mrs. Bradshaw went into raptures over the roses and soon she and Gordon were deep in conversation.

'Wife's mad about roses,' her husband stated unnecessarily. So it was with little surprise that they offered the asking price when they got back to the office. Their offer was soon accepted and the Bradshaws went away delighted.

Gordon felt a mixture of elation and despair. He felt sure Rose Cottage would be in safe hands with the Bradshaws, but the acceptance of the offer scared him to bits. He sometimes could not believe that he was really doing this. Why not just die in the cottage and let someone else sort it all out? But to him, doing what he was doing made him feel he was taking control.

Although he had done a lot of sorting in the last fortnight, there was still a lot to do. There was no doubt that he got tired far more quickly and he rather suspected this would get progressively worse. He needed to get on and do all this whilst he still could.

He loaded bags of clothes into the Jaguar and headed on to Delaby, which was a town some 30 miles away. Having looked in the Yellow Pages, he had found the town was full of charity shops. He needed to get rid of the first of his clothes in anonymity. He would put the rest of the unwanted kitchen items in the boot, too. The scout jumble had gone well and the auctioned lots had all sold. He enjoyed the drive to Delaby, putting his foot down in the powerful car whenever it was safe to do so - did not really matter if he got a speeding fine now. With that in mind, he parked on double-yellow lines and humped all the bags into 'Help the Aged'.   He was thanked profusely.

He pulled the car into a newly vacant space and pottered in a few shops, buying a card for his mother's birth-

45

day and treating himself to a pot of tea and a scone in a teashop. He could feel his spirits sinking the longer he spent in town. What was the point of looking in shops? Apart from food, it was a sheer waste of money to buy anything else. He used to enjoy browsing in the antique shops, but he felt now he was wasting time. Time which should be spent wisely. But how? And on what? Memories could not be taken with you. He could go on a last holiday, see somewhere he had not seen before. But he would have this heavy sense of finality with him all the time.

He was sure the thousands of other people who were in his situation did not waste their last moments on earth, but they probably had families and did lots of last activities so that the families could carry the memories with them.

He felt as though lead was running through his veins, making him slow and cumbersome. He snapped at a lad who bumped into him on the pavement.

'Look where you're going!'

The boy uttered an obscenity and went on. What did his life really add up to? Extra pounds at a Boy Scout jumble, an opportunity for people to talk about him, briefly, in the village shop, 'Did you hear Sinclair died yesterday?' 'Yes, you remember. Used to run that pine shop in Waresbury. Bought a desk from him once.'

Was that his lifetime's achievement to sell a desk or two? He reached the Jaguar and got in it, resting his head on the steering wheel. And there was no damn time to do anything about it, to make recompense. What if he were to have treatment? What if he was given another six months? What would he do? Write a novel? Join Amnesty International and go out to war-torn areas? At the thought of that, he could feel his insides churning. That was the trouble with him - he was such a bloody coward. He gripped the wheel in despair. What a mess. He suddenly realised he was lonely, he wanted someone to share his life with. He had lived with someone briefly, but it did not work out. He was a solitary man, who liked his own space. He had friends and acquaintances, but none that he could really burden.

'Sid, by the way, I'm dying of lung cancer and I'm falling apart. Will you help me? Be there for me?'

He let out a howl of sheer self-pity and thumped the steering wheel. The horn resounded around the multi-storey car park, making him and two women leap out of their skins. If he did not move soon, he never would as the heaviness in his limbs was getting worse. He wondered if he was dying now and if God was cheating him out of these last few months. There were things he still had to do and he was surprised to find that he minded.

He turned over the engine. It purred as always and he rubbed the burnished walnut board affectionately. If he could take one thing with him it would be this car. Toby's horrified face came into his mind and he gunned the accelerator down to blank it out and sped out of the car park.

Eleanor Sinclair was planting out by the pond when her son's face came into her head with such clarity that she stopped and put down her spade, trying to focus on the image which had suddenly come to her. She felt chilled and restless. She anchored the spade in the soft earth, pulled her jacket around her shoulders and went and sat on the bench. The sun was warm, but her hands felt icy. Billy jumped onto her lap and she leant down

47

and rubbed her face in his fur, smelling his distinctive cat smell, comforting and familiar. An image of Gordon came into her mind, Gordon digging in the pond and struggling. Oh he had thought he had not showed it, but she had seen. She had just chosen to ignore it. She needed to talk with him. She lifted Billy off and stood up, but then sat down again. What the hell would she say? He would think she was mad if she rang him up out of the blue and asked what was wrong. Billy jumped back up onto her lap, treading her with his paws and purring loudly.

'Bloody nuisance,' she told him and fondled his ears absent-mindedly.

Gordon approached the turn off to his road when an animal shot out in front of him. He braked, swerved and then swerved again as a person leapt into his path. He fought to control the car and eventually stopped some way down the lane. He jumped out of the car, adrena-line racing. The woman, as now he saw it was, had hold of a large dog. With a bolt of pure anger, he realised it was the woman who worked at the estate agent and her wretched animal.

'What the hell did you think you were doing. I could have killed you!'

'I'm sorry. He was chasing a rabbit and he wouldn't listen.' She straightened up. 'Oh, it's you.'

'I could wring your neck, you little fool.'

'Well, there's no harm done, is there,' she retorted, her tone sharpening. 'We're all OK - your car's OK. Might have shortened your life a bit, but that's all.'

He was silent, staring at her. Did she know? Had Toby talked to anyone? She glanced up at him and bit back the next retort as she saw the naked fear in his eyes. Instantly she softened.

'Hey, I'm sorry I gave you a shock. I am trying to train Pounce, but he just gets the better of me.'

She saw him shake his head and sigh before turning away as if to go back to his car. Then he turned back towards her. 'Can I give you a lift anywhere?'

Lydia looked at the Jag and then at the dog. 'He's a bit muddy.'

'I've got an old rug in the back.'

He looked at her. He suddenly wanted some company. 'Come and have a coffee if you want.'

She looked surprised and blushed slightly. 'Well, OK, then. Thanks.'

He spread the rug out along the back seat of the Jag and the dog jumped in. He tried to get through to the front, but Lydia scolded him and he sat up erectly, pretending to ignore them. Lydia slid into the passenger seat and Gordon started the engine.

'Quiet, isn't it?'

He could tell that she had been searching for a compliment, that she felt uneasy about the car. He acknowledged it with a nod. She touched the walnut veneer with her finger and then looked out of the window. The dog panted in the back. Gordon thought of things to break the silence. He was never very good at small talk. He was startled when she spoke.

'Why do you drive a car like this?'

He glanced at her clear green eyes. He saw the challenge in them and rose to it.

'Why shouldn't I? Why does it trouble you so much?'

He pulled into his driveway, switched off the engine and turned to face her. The dog yawned restlessly, anxious to be outside. She met his gaze fiercely.

'Because I'm always interested in why people buy ostentatious cars when they serve no more purpose than one a quarter of their price. But what really puzzles me is that you don't seem to fit the mould of the big car driver.'

Gordon laughed, thinking of the cross-section of people who were members of the Enthusiasts' Club. It wasn't the response Lydia expected and she frowned.

'Come and have some coffee.'

Lydia looked doubtful.

'We can sit in the shade in the garden.'

She sighed. She longed to look around the garden Penny had told her so much about, especially as she did not get the chance when showing the last couple around. They had decided the house was too small for them and had not bothered with the garden. She knew he grew roses, but that was all. Curiosity got the better of her and she got out of the car. Pounce scrambled over from the back seat and followed her out the door. Gordon grimaced as he saw a claw scratch in the leather. He licked his finger and smoothed the mark. Mentally shaking himself, he got out of the car and led Lydia and the dog into the kitchen.

'Wow, you've had a clear-out.' She motioned at the empty dresser and uncluttered shelves.

'I need to make a start. I've managed to collect so much clutter over the years.'

'Have you lived here for long?'

'20 years. Long enough.'

'So why the move?' She turned to face him and saw again that flicker of fear in his eyes.

'I … I…,' he could not think what to say.

'Are you having regrets?'

He shook his head. 'I can't afford to.'

'Should sell one of those ridiculous cars, then.'

He thought how presumptuous she was.

'Can I go into the garden?'

He nodded and followed her with the coffee. She was looking at his climbing rose, its coral coloured flowers glowing against the flint wall. Climbing through it was a clematis, its white flowers peeping through the rose's foliage.

'I wouldn't have put those together, but it works, doesn't it?'

'It's what I call my peaches and cream.'

'And I love the geranium underplanting.' She moved on, touching and smelling as she went. He followed her slowly, not talking, until she saw the swing.

'Oh my God, it's perfect.' She walked down the mown path, through the wild flower meadow, until she reached it. Then she sat down and watched him approach. She took the coffee from him and he sat down on the grass, suddenly feeling very tired. The dog tried to lick his face and he pushed him away.

'So, you're interested in gardening?'

She threw back her head and laughed. She always surprised him, never quite responding as he thought she would. She was like quicksilver.

'I only work for 'Perfect Homes' part time. I'm a trained landscape gardener. I work for Lord P. at the Manor and I live in one of the estate cottages.' She looked away, reddening slightly. Gordon had the idea he'd been told a lot more information that she would normally divulge.

'Do you enjoy working there?'

'No. It's not what I want to do, but it's good experience. The gardens are too formal. Also it gives me a roof over my head.'

He could not imagine this woman compromising.

'Do you have a portfolio?'

'Of course.'

'I'd really like to see it.'

'Why? You don't need a gardener.'

'Just curiosity.'

She wriggled uncomfortably, finished her coffee and stood up. 'I must go. Thanks for the coffee.'

He was about to delay her, wanting to know more about her, but he heard a voice calling him. Damn it, it was Alice and she was heading in their direction. Without another word, Lydia handed him her cup, called the dog and strode off. She raised a hand to Alice and disappeared through the gap in the beech hedge.

'Been entertaining, then?' Alice nodded at the cups, a frown on her face. 'Shouldn't mix with her sort, Mr. Sinclair, it'll get you a bad name.'

'Whatever do you mean, Alice, *her sort*.'

'Strange ways, that girl. Works like a man, roams the countryside with that dog of hers.'

'But doesn't she work for Lord P. at the Manor?'

'And what sort of job's that for a woman, eh? Spending the day working the land.' Alice shook her head and Gordon smiled at her broadly, loving her for her prejudices.

'What can I do for you, Alice?'

'Oh …' She had been quite put off her stroke at the sight of Lydia Page striding up the path towards her and had momentarily forgotten her mission.

'Well I'm doing next year's Diary of Events for the W.I. and we've got a slot to fill in July. Wondered if you'd come and talk about roses.'

For just one moment, he forgot and then it hit him like a blow in the stomach.

'Mr. Sinclair, you look quite pale. Are you OK?'

He fought the demons inside himself, taking several deep breaths. 'Alice, I'd love to.'

She nodded, but didn't take her eyes off his face. That girl was to blame for this, she felt sure. Hanging around here, upsetting him.

Gordon smiled rather wanly. 'Just let me have the details and I'll put it in my diary.'

'OK then.' She took the empty coffee cups from where he was still holding them and took her leave. Something not right with him, that was for sure. Still, must try and get to Reg Watts' before she went home, to see if he would bring his bees in August.

She would not have left so quickly if she had seen Lydia approaching the house from the opposite direction. She had left her door keys on the floor of the Jag. She passed though the beech hedge and stopped dead in her tracks. Gordon was sitting on the swing, his arms clasped around him, bent over double and crying. Harsh, racking sobs coming deep from within him. She froze, horror-filled. She was turning to go away when Pounce pushed past her and made for the swing. She had forgotten the dog and now it was too late. Gordon had seen the movement and had looked up. He saw the girl, half turned by the hedge, her hand to her mouth. The dog lay down on its haunches in front of him.

'What do you want?' he heard himself ask.

Lydia moved slowly towards him. He felt exhausted and was trembling, despite the warmth of the evening. He wished it was all over now as it all seemed too much. And now this.

She stopped a distance away. 'I've dropped my door keys in your car.'

She was direct, even now, he thought. He reached into his pocket and threw her the car keys.

'Help yourself, leave my keys in the kitchen.'

She nodded and turned, calling the dog over her shoulder. She reached the car, unlocked it, retrieved her keys and went into the kitchen. She sank into the chair by the Aga, torn and troubled. She had never seen a man cry, let alone sob. Lydia, whose instinct was never to get involved, felt herself doing just that. She saw the brandy bottle on the side, hunted for a couple of glasses, poured two large shots, drank hers straight down and began to walk back down the garden. Gordon was standing by the Roserie de l'Hay, bending over it and inhaling its deep scent. He turned at her approach and she was immediately aware of his greyness, his extreme tiredness. Without a word, she handed him the brandy. He looked at her, at the huge measure of spirit in his best wineglass and felt a flicker of hope in his gut. He downed the alcohol and coughed as it hit the back of his throat. He half-heartedly jested with her.

'You keep your wings very well hidden for an angel of mercy.'

She smiled, aware that she could, at that moment, make a quip and leave. But she did not. She stood her ground, feeling her own anxiety swirl around her.

'What is it?' she asked quietly.

After a moment's silence, he answered, 'I'm dying.'

As he released the words, more tears came. Embarrassed, he wiped them away with his sleeve and automatically deadheaded a rose in front of him. She was still there, biting her bottom lip. The dog was nosing in one of the borders and trod on a plant. Automatically she yelled at him. He slunk along the path towards her and flopped at her feet, rolling over onto his side and lifting a paw, inviting his belly to be tickled and scratched. She absentmindedly rubbed it with her foot.

'What of?'

Her directness startled him again. Did nothing throw her assurance? But he knew that he had, knew from the chewed lip and the lack of eye contact.

'Lung cancer.'

'Do you smoke?'

He suddenly wanted to laugh, imagining for one absurd moment that she was about to lecture him. 'I did. I gave up 5 years' ago.'

She nodded.

'Look, shall we go inside? I can tell you about it.'

She looked up sharply. 'No. Not inside. Here. In the garden.'

She could cope with this whilst her eyes could look at leaf shape and form, but not inside.

Exhausted, he walked to a paved area and sat on a bench. She remained standing, on one leg, her other toe digging into the ground moving stones around.

'Have you had chemo?'

'No.'

It hung in the air between them. A challenge. She was silent, but looked at him. Then she moved closer and sat on the edge of the york stones.

'I couldn't see the point. It meant it would give me another 6 months. I didn't want to feel ill, I didn't want to lose my hair, be sick, have to spend hours in hospital with other sick people, I guess I didn't want to admit to it. Thought that by ignoring it, it might go away. But of course it hasn't and it won't. I know that, I always knew it.'

'Do you regret not having treatment?'

He searched inside and spoke with an honesty he did not know he felt. 'No.'

'I'm glad.'

She slapped at a mosquito on her bare arm and realised it was getting late. She stood suddenly.

'I have to go. I'll be back, probably tomorrow.'

He wanted to keep her here, to let out more words, more thoughts, but he accepted her departure with a wave of his hand. She turned once, at the corner of the house and looked at him. He raised his hand again. She wriggled her fingers at him and disappeared.

CHAPTER SEVEN

The next day, he was cooking eggs and bacon for breakfast when a voice made him jump violently.

'Is this why you're selling Rose Cottage?'

He swore, turned and saw her leaning on the stable door. Then he laughed as, beside her, Pounce was also peering over the door, paws hanging onto the top, scruffy head surveying the scene, his nose twitching at the delicious smells.

'Breakfast?'

She hesitated. 'OK.'

But she stayed where she was, leaning on top of the half door.

Gordon, busy with putting more bacon in the pan and brewing coffee, took no notice of her. He dished out steaming mounds of food, then looked at her quizzically, indicating the plate. She unlocked the door and Pounce exploded into the kitchen with her following. The dog seemed delighted to see Gordon again. It was only when their plates were empty and she was sitting back, coffee mug in hand, that she asked the question again about the house.

'Yes, it is,' he answered flatly.

'But why?'

Gordon sighed. He felt reluctant to share his reasonings with this woman, but he had an idea that she would not give up.

'I want everything tidy. Everything sorted out. An end to all of my affairs before I die. I don't want people clearing up after me. I sort of feel it's my responsibility. I want to give things away and see where they're going.' He stopped, hoping this would be enough. 'And it feels like the right thing to do in here.' He motioned to his gut and she nodded.

'What will you do with the money? Do you have family?'

He looked at her blankly. He felt irritated by her questions. He started to clear up, clattering plates and cutlery.

'Thanks for breakfast.'

He turned round. She was half out of the door, the dog at her heels.

'I … I…'

But she was gone. He stood open-mouthed, never having met anyone like her before.

Throughout the whole morning, her words echoed through his head. He went to see his GP, Tom Lander, in the afternoon for a check up. He felt quite happy going to the village surgery, but still fought shy of setting foot in the hospital.

Tom asked him lots of questions, examined him and sat back down in his chair.

'How's it all going, Gordon?'

'It's OK,' he replied and found himself telling the doctor about his plans. 'Giving possessions away is proving a lot harder than I imagined.' He briefly told Tom about Toby and his reactions to the Jaguar.

'Have you been to see him again?'

'No, but I do have a club night next week so I may pop

in and see if he wants to go.'

'And when are you going to start telling people that you're dying?'

Gordon looked at him sharply. 'Not for as long as possible.'

'But why? You're going to need their support. You probably already do need it. You don't have to do this on your own.'

Tom could see that Gordon's eyes were filling with tears. He brushed at them angrily.

'Is this happening a lot?'

'I have my moments.'

'Do you want some anti-depressants?'

'No, absolutely not. I'm not depressed, just unbearably sad at times. Perhaps it's all the tears I've not let myself shed in this life-time.'

Tom nodded, marvelling at the honesty he always found in this man. 'You know where I am if you need me. Don't hesitate to call. And do think about telling people, it might help.'

On his return to Rose Cottage, he found an answerphone message from Penny Young of 'Perfect Homes' asking him to call back. He made himself a coffee and went out into the garden. Sid passed the drive and on seeing Gordon, ambled up the driveway.

'Any more water in the kettle?'

'Help yourself.'

By the time Sid had drunk coffee and passed the time of day, the estate agents were closed. He simply had not wanted to know about any problems with his house sale and thought he would put his head in the sand for 24 hours. Because why was he selling? What was he going to do with the money? His mother did not need it. At the thought of Eleanor, he had a desperate urge to call her. Instead, he busied himself with making supper, a real favourite, sausages, garlic mash, fresh greens from the garden and thick onion gravy.

He woke the next morning with an idea. He wanted to go and see Lydia. He decided he would go and seek her out at the Manor. With this resolve he breakfasted and decided to walk there. He had visited it many times, as the village held their summer fete in the grounds, but he was interested to see how the formal rose garden was taking shape. Lord P. had consulted him several times during the planning stages, but he had not yet seen it in the flesh. He noticed Lord P.'s Bentley was not in the drive and put aside his thoughts that he had better go and ask if it was OK for him to have a nose around. He was glad. He wanted more than anything to be able to have a chat with Lydia. He walked down the terraced area, past the tennis court and through the arched entrance in the yew hedge. It looked a little like a bombsite with earth and debris scattered around. Working at the far end was a small mechanical digger. As he cautiously approached it, he could see that Lydia was actually driving it. He stood still until she saw him and she cut the engine and jumped out. She was wearing old, torn and dirty jeans and a T-shirt of an indiscriminate colour.

'Hi.' She stood and looked at him, wondering why he had come.

'Sorry to stop you working. Just thought I'd have a look and see what you'd done so far.'

'Well, as you can see - not a lot. Lord P. suddenly decided that the ornamental pond would have to be moved. He wants a window through the yew hedging, each side, so that it frames the fountains. But it needs to be sited centrally to keep the symmetry. So the original plans have been changed. However, I think the planting is pretty much the same. You had a lot of input into that, didn't you?'

Gordon nodded. He had never heard her utter so many words before. 'How many of you are there working on it?'

'Only three of us. Mike and Jim have gone to look at some topiary shapes with Lord P. He wouldn't take me as he knows I hate topiary.'

'So you don't even take orders from a Lord?'

Lydia looked uncomfortable and Gordon laughed, wondering at the dynamics between the two of them. He had always seen Lord P. as a man who got his own way.

'I thought about what you said.'

'About the money?'

'Yes. I'd not thought it all through, I know that. There is so much to come to terms with, but I want to do the right thing though, and I'd hoped you'd help me.'

Lydia looked directly at him. She seemed to be making her mind up.

'If you need me to.'

'The truth is, I don't know what to do with the money. My mother doesn't need it and I have no other relatives. I can't give friends huge sums of cash. So I feel a bit lost.'

Lydia started walking. 'I need to nip into the village. I'll walk back with you and we can talk.'

They crunched down the gravel drive.

'So what causes are close to your heart?'

Gordon looked blank.

'You must have charities you subscribe to.'

'Must I? I'm afraid I don't.'

'Do you never give anything for Children in Need or to Oxfam or something?'

Gordon thought of the bags of clothes he had taken over to Delaby.

'I give if it's unavoidable. Look, it's not that I'm mean - I just never think about it.'

His mother came into his head. She had always given monthly sums to worthwhile causes, usually involving animals or children. So why hadn't he? Didn't he have a social conscience?

They reached the Manor gates.

'Look, I'll come round and give you some ideas.'

'Thanks, I'd really appreciate it.'

'Well I guess the path you've chosen to go on can get a bit lonely at times.'

He smiled at her. She may be abrasive, but she always seemed to know what he was feeling. They parted and he walked home with a lighter step.

Penny Young had driven past the Manor entrance at the same time. She had seen Gordon smiling at Lydia and frowned. How on earth did those two know each other? She thought back to how cross Lydia had been when she had encountered Gordon at the cottage. Something had changed. She put her foot down on the accelerator and her small car shot forward. She would have to call in to Rose Cottage on her way back as Gordon had not returned her phone call and she needed to speak with him about the Bradshaws. She had found his lack of response rather strange. Or was it just that she had wanted an excuse to talk with him? He intrigued her, and not many men did that nowadays, Penny thought. She seemed to lurch from one disastrous relationship to another. But there was a gentleness about Gordon Sinclair that drew her like a magnet.

It was late that afternoon when she drew up outside Rose Cottage. To her annoyance, there was a strange car in the drive. Still, she did have a legitimate reason for stopping. She parked behind the ageing Citroen and went round to the open kitchen door. Gordon was sitting inside with an elderly woman. Penny took in her faded English rose beauty, the grey hair deftly swept into a bun and the piercing blue eyes.

Gordon saw her and leapt to his feet. She noticed he had reddened. 'He doesn't want me here,' she thought. This was made more obvious when Gordon ushered her into the garden and closed the door behind her. Flustered, she looked around, noticing the dozens of bees that were humming lazily from plant to plant.

'I needed to talk to you about the sale.'

'I would have rung you.'

That admonishment was clear in his voice. She wondered why he was so tetchy.

'Well, as I was passing, I thought I'd stop and tell you that the Bradshaw's buyers have pulled out.'

Gordon simply stood and looked at her. Penny started to feel annoyed.

'So we need to know whether to re-advertise, or whether you want to give the Bradshaws time to find another buyer.'

She began to go through the pros and cons of each, not certain that Gordon was even listening.

'I'll give the Bradshaws two weeks to find another buyer. That's all I can afford.'

The abruptness of his answer silenced her.

'OK, that's fine. I'll ring them when I get back to the office. Sorry to have disturbed you.'

She walked down the drive and Gordon knew he had offended her, knew she did not deserve it.

'Penny?'

She turned.

'I've got a Jaguar rally on Tuesday. We're doing a treasure hunt. Would you like to come? It's always been a fun evening.' He had no idea what made him say that. Just a desire to put right his rudeness.

She nodded, her uncomfortableness going, 'I'd love to.'

'I'll pick you up at 7.00, then. Last house on the green, isn't it?'

'Yes, Brandy Cottage. 7.00 will be fine.'

She got into her car and drove off, leaving Gordon staring after her. Then he sighed and walked slowly back to the cottage and his mother. She had simply turned up out of the blue. Had not even rung first. She had never done that before and Gordon wondered if she was all right.

Eleanor had known from the moment she had walked into the kitchen that her deepest fears were right. Gordon had been sitting at the kitchen table, looking through a newspaper.

'Hello son,' she had said and he had jumped, then flushed a deep red. He pushed himself back from the table and rose warily, on the defensive.

'Mum, what a lovely surprise.'

She was not sure why he had said that. It was obviously a surprise, but she doubted whether she was welcome. She took in the kitchen at a glance, at the cleared shelves, at the very transitional nature of it and knew. Knew that her gut reaction of it was right; the gut reaction that had made her get in the car and drive all this way. It had taken all her courage as she had only been

64

used to short local journeys - disliking being in the car for longer than she had to. She looked around now and saw the space where the dresser had been and wondered what had happened to all the blue and white he had collected for years. She felt a pain deep inside her gut and folded her arms across in front of her as if to ward it off. When he had gone outside with his visitor, she had moved her chair closer to the Aga, even though the temperature outside was in the 70s. She suddenly wanted to be back in her own garden, pottering about in the sunshine and not here, waiting for an explanation she was not sure she was strong enough to cope with.

Gordon appeared in the doorway. 'Do you want to come outside - it's lovely in the sun.'

She thought how thin he looked. Thin and drawn. As if he needed a good meal.

'I could do with a drink, if the truth be told.'

'Tea? Coffee? I'll top you up.'

'Something stronger would be nice.'

'Mother, I swear you're turning into an alcoholic.'

'It's allowed at my time of life. I'll have a gin and tonic, if you've got any.'

She wandered into the garden and sat on a bench whilst he prepared the drinks. She had no doubt he would join her and she smiled as she watched him carry two glasses out of the kitchen.

'So, why the sudden visit, Mum?' He sat down next to her and leant back in the sun.

'To see if I was right.'

'About what?'

'You.'

He looked up. She was looking intently at a salvia in the border. Heavy with flowers, it attracted a constant swarm of bees.

'And are you?'

She looked at him then. 'I rather think I am, don't you? Are you going to tell me about it?'

He stood up so abruptly that he spilt his drink. A wasp settled on the colourless liquid, its antennae weaving backwards and forwards.

'I find it almost impossible to say.'

'Well, I think you need to try.' She did not add 'after all, I am your mother', but it was tangible in the air between them. He moved a few paces away and rubbed some greenfly off a rose stem.

'Have you had much aphid damage this year?'

Eleanor sighed. This was not going to be easy for either of them.

'Darling, I really need to know. All of it.'

He looked round at her endearment. She was not one for sentimentality and it brought the ready tears to his eyes. He hung his head as he was suddenly overcome with grief. He felt her arms go round him and hold him.

'My poor, poor boy.'

It was some time before the storm of grief subsided. At some point she silently handed him a tissue and he took it from her and blew his nose. Then the words came and once started, he could not stop. She left him once to fill their glasses, but otherwise they sat, side by side, she listening, he talking. When he stopped, she put her arms around him, again simply holding him. She felt as though she had been punched in the stomach and found it was actually painful to breathe. She wanted to ask him so much, but now was not the time.

Dusk was settling, along with the mosquitoes. Eleanor swatted one that had drawn blood on her arm. 'Come on, or we'll be bitten to pieces.'

They went inside, both listless. It felt like it was the lull after the storm.

'What is there for supper?'

Gordon went into the freezer and rummaged around and the two of them, united in their grief, went about the task of preparing something to eat.

CHAPTER EIGHT

Lydia saw that the car was still in the drive the next morning. She had stopped outside the previous evening, but had not liked to go in. She saw the car as a threat, but she did not know why. She pulled away and drove to the 'Perfect Homes' office. She waved a 'hello' to Penny, who was with a client and went to make them both a cup of coffee. She checked her diary and saw that she was booked to do two viewings that morning. It was not until after the second one that she got to speak with Penny.

'Popped into Rose Cottage last night to tell Gordon Sinclair that the Bradshaw's buyer has pulled out.'

'So, what's going to happen?'

'He's given them two weeks to come up with another purchaser.'

'Are they likely to do that?'

'Well, from what I can find out, their house is in a desirable area, has four bedrooms and a good-sized garden. If it's sensibly priced, they should have another offer within a week.'

'So are we putting Rose Cottage back on the market?'

'Not yet, Lydia. But just make a note of anybody who would be suitable to view. Funny thing is, he asked me out.'

'Who?'

'Gordon Sinclair. Wants me to go to a car rally with him. Should be fun, don't you think?'

She was interrupted by the telephone ringing. Lydia sat and made a pretence of working. Why did she mind so much? But for some reason, she did. She felt almost disappointed in him. She had worked long enough in the office to know all about Penny's many disastrous relationships. Somehow, Gordon did not fit in with the normal type. Well at least the Gordon she knew. She felt strangely proprietorial about him. She desperately wanted to ask Penny about the strange car in the drive, but could not bring herself to. Penny spent the afternoon wanting to ask why she had spotted Lydia and Gordon at the end of the Manor drive, but could not. So it was an uneasy atmosphere in the office and both were glad to leave at the end of the day.

Lydia went straight to her cottage and let out Pounce, who bounded off, sniffing at the perimeters of the garden. He would suddenly look up at Lydia and race over to her, stopping just short of her, feet planted firmly, tail wagging. He wanted a game and Lydia finding his ball under a shrub threw it to him, her mind elsewhere.

Eleanor had left Rose Cottage at about that time, figuring that she had just enough daylight hours to drive home in. It had been a difficult day. After Gordon's initial outburst, he had seemed reluctant to open up any further. It seemed to trouble him that he had let her know. It was only after lunch that he told her about selling Rose Cottage. She looked at her son.

'But is it really what you want to do? Or what you think you ought to do?'

He had gazed at the ground for so long that she thought he was not going to answer her. Then he looked up.

'What I really want is for someone to inherit it. I want to know that my wife and children can wander out into the garden and see me there. I want to know that I've provided a secure future for those I've loved. But as I don't have a wife and children, then yes, I want to see that the money I have does some good. That I can make a difference to someone, somewhere. I don't want to do it through a Will. I want to actually give it myself.'

Eleanor closed her eyes to trap the tears that filled them. Right at that moment, she was not sure how she was going to stand this. Stand seeing her son fade away and then die. It was something every parent hoped they would never have to do. She forced her voice to be normal.

'Do you want me to come and live here with you?'

'Don't be ridiculous, of course I don't.'

Part of her was relieved, part of her hurt.

'But I may come down to you if I sell quickly - if that's OK?'

She reached out for her son's hand and held it. 'Of course it is.'

'But I don't want to be a burden. I don't want nursing. I shall leave that to the professionals when the time comes.'

To her shame, the tears started to fall. 'Gordon, are you really so brave?' He was breaking her heart.

He removed his hand. 'I'm as scared as hell, Mum.'

He stood up and went inside leaving her alone. The tears flowed, but they did not touch the tight knot of anguish under her rib cage. He returned with brandies and she gulped hers back. He started to talk about someone at the Jaguar Enthusiasts' Club and their new car and she was glad to listen, to focus on his words.

When she left, Gordon had gone straight to bed, seeking oblivion in sleep.

Two days later, he picked Penny Young up in the Mark 1. She had dressed carefully in a light, floral summer dress and pretty sandals. A cardigan was draped around her shoulders and her shoulder-length blonde hair was held back by an alice band. Gordon thought she looked good enough to eat. He felt quite chirpy as they drove along the lanes.

'I'm sorry I called around last week. I should have phoned you.'

'It's OK. I had my mother staying and I don't like her to know all my business. You know what they're like!'

He wondered at his ability to lie with such ease. But his companion seemed satisfied by his response. He was met by a lot of enquiring glances when he introduced Penny to a few people around the bar. It had been a long time since he had brought a female with him. Penny's easy manner and good looks meant that she was soon chatting to various people, but it wasn't long before they were handed their sheets and it was their time to leave to work out the clues.

Penny was good, lively company and Gordon found he felt quite relaxed by the time they had all met up at the pub again. Penny accepted a glass of wine and he, feeling quite happy to prolong the evening, had a mineral water.

He drew up outside Penny's cottage just as the church clock chimed midnight.

'Just in time. Wouldn't want your precious Jaguar to turn into a pumpkin!'

Penny laughed at her own joke and he laughed with her.

'Why don't you come in for a coffee?'

His first instinct was to refuse, but suddenly her offer

71

seemed very inviting. He parked up and followed her into the house. The front door opened straight into the sitting area. It was painted in bright, warm colours and with chintzy soft furnishings. There was a vase of flowers on the coffee table and one on the mantelpiece. The whole effect was warm and inviting. Penny motioned for Gordon to sit down on one of the pale sofas and he sank down into the feather cushions. He heard her clattering away in the kitchen and then return with the coffees and two large brandies.

'I shouldn't, really. I'm driving.'

'Yes, but you didn't have anything at the pub and you can always leave your car in my drive and walk back.'

He accepted the brandy, enjoying the feeling of warmth that spread through his body.

'Saw you with Lydia Page the other day at the end of the Manor drive - didn't know you were acquainted.'

Gordon took another sip of his brandy, 'Oh, I'd gone up to the Manor to see Lord P. about some roses and he introduced me to her.' He did not know why he had lied, but the truth was too difficult. He was impressed at how off-hand he sounded.

'How's the garden going?'

'It's a mess. Earth and rubble. But the plans are good. I shall go up and give some technical advice when needed.'

'How do you know so much about roses?'

'It started as a hobby that grew into a passion. Then I did some freelance work for a rose grower and it just went on from there.'

'And now you're an expert?'

'Some seem to think so. It makes me an additional income at times. Helps pay the maintenance bills on the Jags.'

Chatting with Penny was easy and an hour passed quickly. He got up to help her take the cups through to the kitchen. He was putting them on the side when he noticed the rose. Faded, with its petals browned, it sat on the window ledge in a little vase.

'What the…'

He turned suddenly and she was close behind him, her eyes on the rose, blushing slightly.

'It was so beautiful, I couldn't bear…'

He stepped forward, put his arms around her and kissed her with a passion he had not felt in years. She responded eagerly. It felt wonderful to be this close to another person again. As their embrace continued, he felt the loneliness deep inside him ebb away, taking with it that small warning voice, which he was determined to ignore.

He must have dozed off because when he woke, for a second, he did not know where he was. Then he saw the chintz curtains and knew. He turned and saw Penny lying beside him. She slept quietly, breathing regularly, very still, one arm thrown over the coverlet.

He swore under his breath. What had he done? He had got caught up in the heat of the moment. That first kiss had unleashed so much passion that they had not made it beyond the lounge before they had pulled off each other's clothes. He had entered her immediately and their lovemaking had an urgency and an intensity that he had forgotten it could have.

She had eventually led him upstairs to her bed. She had fallen asleep almost immediately and he had dozed off shortly afterwards.

He felt a rising panic and pushed back the cover carefully. Penny stirred and he panicked, not moving a muscle for fear of waking her. This should not have happened. It was a mistake and he needed to escape. He dressed and crept down the stairs, letting himself out of the front door. He gulped in the cold night air and held his head in his hands.

After a monent, he got into the car. He must get away. Right away. He could not understand how he could have added this complication to his life. It was totally out of character.

It was only later when he had loaded the Jaguar with his bags, including his passport, that he thought of how Penny would feel at his disappearance. But his overriding need was to put space between them. And as much as he could. He drove to Gatwick and checked ticket availability. He went to the booking clerk and bought a ticket to Prague.

CHAPTER NINE

Penny woke up and stretched. She tried to think whether it was a workday or not. Then she remembered. She turned over quickly, but already knew inside that he would be gone. She got up and showered, wincing at her unexpected soreness. For a quiet man, he had been extraordinarily passionate. It had been quite a night. She hoped he would pop in to the agents, but if not, she could always ring him on some pretext.

The day dragged. She was on her own, as it was one of Lydia's days at the Manor. She had jumped every time the door opened, but it was never Gordon. She had rung his number twice, but there had only been his answerphone. She had driven out to Rose Cottage when she had locked up the office. She stopped, noticing that the Jaguar was not there. The next door neighbour was watering Gordon's front garden. He was saying something to Penny. She wound down her window.

'No good waiting. He's gone away.'

Penny got out of the car.

'Oh, Mrs. Young. Now what do you want with Gordon. Not thinking of selling is he?'

'Did you say he'd gone away?'

'Yes. Left a note through our door. I was up at 6.00, so it was before that. Said to keep an eye on things until he returned.'

'Did it say where he'd gone?'

'Nope, not a word, Just took off into the blue.'

Penny felt her stomach churning with mixed emotions. 'Oh well, it wasn't important. 'Bye Sid.'

''Bye, Mrs.Young.'

Penny went back to her car. She just wanted to sit and take in the implications of this moonlight flit, but Sid was still looking at her over the hedge. She smiled wanly, waved and drove off.

What the bloody hell was going on? Surely he would have mentioned if he was going away? Of course he would have. A sense of betrayal began to creep over her. She had been treated badly in the past, but this took the biscuit.

Her anger lasted all evening as thoughts went round and round in her head. She re-ran the entire evening like a broken down record. Had she said something? Certainly nothing to warrant this sort of reaction. Perhaps his mother had been taken ill. On an impulse, she 'phoned directory enquiries. There were twelve Sinclairs listed in that area. No, she did not have an address. They would only give her two numbers at a time. She would have to ring back for an extra two each time. Did she want any of the listed Sinclair numbers? No she did not. Angrily she slammed down the phone. Then she felt guilty, the woman had only been doing her job. She should know that, working with the public. She snatched up the phone again and re-dialled their number. She wanted to apologise for her rudeness.

'Hello, BT. Shaun speaking, which name please?'

She slammed the phone down again and burst into tears. After a few minutes, she mentally pulled herself together. Whatever was the matter with her, letting a man get the better of her like this? She really must pull herself together.

The man in question was sitting in a pavement café in the centre of Prague, watching the world go by. He felt nicely distanced from his problems. He had booked into one of the city's best hotels as he had decided to spare no expense. After all, this would be his last holiday. With that sobering thought, he gesticulated to the waiter to bring him another glass of wine. He needed to let his hair down a bit, have some fun. The trouble was, he did not really know how to!

If letting his hair down had brought him into Penny Young's arms, then it was a complication he could well do without. No, he would sightsee with a vengeance. And eat and drink well, too.

On an impulse when he returned to his room he phoned his mother. She answered after the first ring, almost as though she had been expecting him to call.

'Is everything all right?'

He wondered if he would ever have a normal conversation with her again, or whether they would all be peppered with anxiety.

'I'm fine, I just wanted to make contact.'

And he told her about his impulse drive to the airport. She surprised him. 'Well if you do it again, call me and we'll go together.'

'What, you'd give up your space and privacy for a few days? I'd drive you nuts.'

Eleanor thought that if she could just keep him, not let him die, that she could do with 'nuts'.

'It'd be fun. As for Prague. Well I went there with your father on one of our wedding anniversaries. I actually pried him away from the practice for a long weekend.'

At the end of the call, she sat down and mused over her memories of that weekend.

The next morning, she went into the attic to find all her diaries. It suddenly seemed important to her to know which anniversary it had been. It was hours later when she went back down the steep, wooden stairs. It had been their fifth. She had felt that having survived five years as a vet's wife, that she deserved a reward. It had been she that had booked the weekend. At first, Giles had refused to contemplate the idea, but Eleanor had refused to budge. She had even threatened to go on her own, and if he had not given in, she would have. She wanted a taste of something different, wanted to stretch her boundaries. Her lifestyle did not really suit her 'need to know' and her need to be just slightly non-conformist. But on this one, Giles had acquiesced. What is more, he had given in with good grace and they had had a wonderful four days, wandering the streets, looking at the sights, eating and making love. It was as if they had got to know each other all over again and this harmony between them had lasted for some weeks after they had returned. Eleanor had bought her saxophone in Prague during that visit. She already had an old one, which had belonged to her father, but she had fallen instantly in love with this one, when she had seen it in the window of a shop in one of the little back streets. She always remembered that this shop had red shutters and a balcony with red geraniums trailing through the railings. She had known that it had been difficult for Giles - he had disliked her playing, but the mood of Prague had infected him and he agreed readily enough in the end.

So many photos. So many memories. Eleanor closed

an album, realising she was ravenous. She grabbed a hunk of bread, a large piece of cheese and some tomatoes from the garden. Then she took her diary and food outside and sat by the new water feature. This would always remind her of Gordon. She would always picture him digging the small pond. She sighed and on impulse, went back into the kitchen and poured herself a glass of wine. Lovely. She dozed and read for the rest of the afternoon, often dreaming of Prague where her son was now.

CHAPTER TEN

Gordon returned after two weeks. By then, he knew the city intimately, and had grown to love it. Unbeknown to him, he had traced the footsteps of his parents many times. He had even walked past the shop where his mother had bought the saxophone. He had reached a place of calm within himself. Apart from occasional breathlessness, he had refused to let himself even notice his illness. He had even bought a cheap camera and taken two films. He had twice asked a passer-by to take shots of himself, once on the Charles Bridge and once in Wenceslas square in front of the clock.

He drove back from the airport in teeming rain, the Jaguar's windscreen wipers going at full belt. He turned into his drive at about midnight and sat for a moment in the car, suddenly exhausted. He did not want to be back here. He did not want to open his front door and face two weeks of post, of answerphone messages, did not want to have to go shopping for provisions or resume watering his plants and all the other paraphernalia of daily life. He yearned for the simplicity of his hotel room. No belongings, no responsibilities, not even making the bed. All he had to do was arrive at the dining room for meals. He had revelled in his anonymity.

He sighed, got out of the car and walked slowly up to the front door. Inserting the key in the lock, he turned it and re-entered his old life.

It was mid afternoon the next day before he had begun to get everything in order. He had driven to West Stoke, some six miles away to buy food so that he could do so without bumping into anyone. He had answered all his messages, except the one from 'Perfect Homes'.

He was preparing his supper, intent on chopping vegetables.

'So you're back, then.'

He jumped out of his skin and looked round to see Lydia. 'You'll give me a heart attack.'

'Well that would prove the doctors wrong, then wouldn't it.'

She still stood, looking over the half door.

'Aren't you going to come in?'

She pushed open the door and the dog launched itself at Gordon in a frenzy of welcome. When it had calmed down, he saw Lydia had sat down at the table, watching him.

'Bloody uncontrollable animal.'

'Nice to be welcomed so passionately though, isn't it?'

Gordon grinned at her. 'Shame I can't expect the same from you.'

He could have bitten his tongue off as she blushed to the roots of her hair and gazed at her feet.

'Lydia, I'm sorry. I was only joking.'

She looked up with an effort. 'Don't think you're going to work your way through all the 'Perfect Homes' employees.'

Oh God. So she knew. Gordon had passionately hoped she would not. He felt deeply ashamed of what had happened with Penny Young.

'Anyway, I brought you these.'

81

She pulled a bundle of envelopes out of her rucksack. He took them from her and saw various charity logos on the envelopes.

'For you to read. Discuss. Decide. Anyway, I must be off.'

He was anxious to keep her here, in his kitchen for just a little longer. 'No Lydia. Please stay and have a drink of something.'

She heard the note of plea in his voice, but she didn't want to stay. He disturbed her and she did not want that. However, she did not get up. He took this for consent.

'Tea? Coffee? Something stronger?'

'Could I have a mint tea?'

'I don't have any.'

She got out of her chair and was gone. Pounce scrambled to his feet, paws slipping on the flagstone floor in his haste to follow his mistress.

'What the…'

She reappeared seconds later with a handful of mint. He marvelled at the way she 'just did' and never asked. He found this refreshingly open and direct. He also felt he could talk to her about anything, as long as it was not about herself. He had learnt that this just made her clam up.

He took the proffered herb.

'Put it into the teapot with some boiling water.'

He did as he was told, inhaling the pungent steam.

'Mind if I join you?'

'It's your mint.'

They both laughed, the earlier tension dissolving. As always, she headed to the garden and they sat, savouring the last of the sunshine, supping their brew. He had brought the envelopes out with him and together they began opening them and reading the contents. Sometimes they would share thoughts on a particular one.

'Certainly not giving to that one.'

Gordon chucked one aside, asking him to support their local hunt. She smiled at him in delight. It was incredible what she was learning about him from this exercise. Eventually, in front of Gordon were three piles, outright rejects, possibles and definites.

'There's still some more to arrive. I've sent off to a cross section of as many charities as I could find.'

'It must have taken you hours.'

'While you were sunning yourself somewhere.' It was the nearest she had come to questioning him.

'Sorry.'

'Don't be. I imagine it's done you the world of good.'

She was going to let it drop at that, he could tell. But he needed to know. 'How's Penny?'

She looked at him directly, her gaze unreadable. So it was true. There was something between them. She could feel a slow rage burning in her chest, but she forced her attention away from it. She had thought him different, impervious to women like her boss. And then she thought of how he had just left and the rage began to subside.

'She's fine.'

She blanked out the thoughts of Penny's frequent calls to Rose Cottage, of the atmosphere in the office when she had asked Lydia outright why she had been talking to Gordon in the Manor's drive. As if she owned him. She had wanted to reply that it was none of Penny's business, but had made up a story, unknowingly very similar to Gordon's. She wondered if Gordon had opened up to Penny, but knew instinctively that he had not.

It was almost dark by the time they went in.

'Stay and have some supper?'

'No, I need to go back and feed Pounce.'

She was adamant. She put the three piles on the kitchen table.

'Thanks, Lydia.'

She acknowledged him with a nod and a wave of her hand and was gone. She always left as abruptly as she arrived. Before retiring, he phoned his mother and promised to drive down and see her as soon as the photographs were developed.

CHAPTER ELEVEN

This he did in a few days' time. Eleanor looked frailer than when he had last seen her. He guessed it was taking its toll on her, too. She was eager to see the photos. With a jolt, he realised that her eyes were overflowing with tears.

'Mum?'

She waved her hand at him and left the room, returning in a moment with an old photograph, an old black and white image that showed his parents on the bridge - right where he had had his photo taken.

'We asked a tourist to take it. I remember her clearly, even now.'

'And when did you go? I had no idea until you suddenly mentioned it on the phone.' He realised how little he knew about his parents' life.

'It was for our fifth wedding anniversary. We spent four days there. Oh Gordon…' She stopped, the tears overcoming her again.

'What is it, Mum?'

She had stopped at a photo of a small shop with faded red shutters. Spilling over the balcony were a profusion of scarlet geraniums. It was why he had taken the photo.

His mother stood up and bustled around the kitchen, doing nothing in particular.

'That's the shop I bought my saxophone from.'

'I never knew…' he trailed off, amazed at the coincidence. 'Are you sure? It sells chocolates now, I think.'

'Oh yes, I'm sure.'

She reached up to a shelf and brought down a book, inside of which were two or three black and white photographs. She put them onto the table. Gordon picked them up. A picture of his parents in Wenceslas Square, one of his father outside the Cathedral and one of her, standing smiling outside a shop. A shop with shutters. She was holding her saxophone, its case by her feet.

'I played a few notes. It embarrassed him terribly. He was never comfortable with my music.'

Gordon looked across at her. 'Why do you never play now?'

She was fiddling in a drawer, 'Oh, I'm much too old for all that sort of thing.'

It was obvious she did not want to talk about it and he wondered why.

Later, when they were in the sitting room, he went over to the saxophone in its case.

'May I?'

She glanced at him, struggling with her emotions. 'Yes, of course.'

He opened the case and took the instrument out. It gleamed in the light. 'You still clean it, then?'

'Oh yes. I still clean it.'

He held it out to her. 'Play just a few notes.'

'No.'

She got up so rapidly she upset the tea tray. Her empty cup and saucer fell onto the carpet and the saucer broke into several pieces. Eleanor let out a howl of anguish and fled from the room. Gordon, his heart racing, carefully put the saxophone back into its box. Then he collected up the broken pieces of china, put everything onto the tray and took it through to the kitchen. His mother was nowhere to be seen. He had never seen her so disturbed and it shocked him.

It was much later when she appeared in the doorway of the sitting room. She was fiddling with her rings, something she always did when she was nervous.

'Mum… I…'

She had started to speak at the same time as him, coming across and perching on the chair arm, before standing up and crossing to the window. Looking out, she began to talk.

'Your father had gone out for the night - to discuss a new vaccination with a colleague. Shortly after he'd gone, I had a call from Mike Jeffers, whose band I had played in. Their saxophonist was ill - couldn't make a gig that night. He wondered if I might fill in. I still played regularly at that stage, although not publicly. Your father had finally put a stop to that - said it wasn't seemly for the wife of a well-to-do country vet. I tried to remember where your father said he was going, but I don't think he'd told me. But he was usually late in after one of those meetings as there were always so many issues to discuss.'

'Mum, you don't have to tell me all this.'

He saw how difficult it was for her, but equally he desperately wanted to hear what she was imparting.

'No, I do have to tell you. I have to make you see. Anyway, to cut a long story short, I agreed to play. I remember going and getting ready. Dressing up in the clothes I never thought I'd wear again. I was so excited and yet nervous in case he found out.'

'Was he really that much of a tyrant?'

'Oh, he didn't like people to go against him, particularly if that person happened to be his wife.'

Gordon thought back to the images he had of his father. He was a big, hands-on man with a hearty laugh. For his size, he always moved quickly. He was always busy, always dashing off somewhere.

'So I arrived at our venue. We were tuning up on the small stage when I saw your father. He was sitting at one of the tables in an alcove. The sort of place you would sit for a romantic night out. He was on his own. My first thought was to bolt so that he wouldn't see me. Then the devil got the better of me and I thought, no, I'll stay. Let him and his colleague see a different side of me.'

She paused, clutching her arms around her. She had pressed her head against the cool of the window. Gordon wanted to go across and put his arms around her, but he also did not want her to stop. He saw her take a deep breath.

'He still hadn't seen me and I watched as his colleague came and sat back down. He was a tall man, with fair hair and a small, neat moustache. As he settled, he reached across the table and took your father's hand. Oh, they thought they were unobserved, sitting in their dark, private corner. But I could see them. Their body language was obvious. They acted like two lovers.'

Gordon stood up so abruptly that his mother turned round.

'Are you saying what I think you're saying?' He could hardly believe his ears.

She looked at him then. Directly. 'Oh yes. Your father was gay. Only, of course, we didn't use that expression then.'

Gordon could feel the heat inside him, heard his cries of denial, knew that he had to escape from this room and these words that his mother was uttering.

She found him in the garden, sitting in the dark on the bench. She had left him for over an hour, feeling the shock in him that she had felt at the time. She came and sat near him, but he did not look at her, just spoke into the darkness.

'Did you confront him with it? Did he deny it? What happened to you that night? Why, if this is true, did you stay with him? How come I didn't know? Why haven't you told me before?'

She gently put a hand on his to stop him. He removed his own hand from hers, but was silenced. She felt exhausted.

'Of course I confronted him. He never denied it. Seemed secretly relieved that I had found out. Promised he'd always be discreet. We'd always slept in separate rooms so why would you have known? Why should we tell you? He was still your father.'

'But how come he married you, if he was a homosexual?'

'I actually think he was bisexual, Gordon, but he preferred men in the end. In those days it was all so different. I guess I provided a smokescreen for his activities.'

'But how could you live like that? Live a lie.'

'Isn't that exactly what you're doing now?'

He looked at his mother in fury and stood up. 'That is not the same at all.'

'Isn't it?'

He paced up and down, trying to get his thoughts in order and failing hopelessly. Eleanor simply sat and watched him. He was aware of a pain in his chest and had to stop to catch his breath. His mother was suddenly at his side.

'Enough of this. You need some rest. What I've told you has been a huge shock. Now come on.'

She led her son back into the house and upstairs into his room. She was suddenly the strong one. She left him, went back downstairs and made two large mugs of cocoa, liberally sweetened. When she went back into his room, he was lying on the bed, fully clothed. He did not acknowledge her so she just left the mug on the bedside table and went to her own room.

Gordon knew he was not well when he woke the next morning. The sheets were soaked with his sweat and he felt as though he had been mown over by a large vehicle. When he did not appear for breakfast, his mother came up with a cup of tea. She took one look at him and came and put her hand on his forehead. It was burning hot. She made him get up and sit on the chair whilst she changed the linen. He felt ashamed that his elderly mother had to look after him, but he had no energy to argue. He sank with relief back into the soft bed.

'Have you been like this all night?'

'I woke up with it. I'll be OK.'

His mother ignored him and left the room. He knew she was ringing her surgery. What a mess everything was. He dozed feverishly for most of the morning, jerking awake each time he coughed. A GP came to see him at lunchtime. His mother had obviously briefed him because he asked Gordon only the minimum of questions whilst he examined him, listening to his chest, checking his blood pressure and taking his pulse.

'You need complete rest until your temperature's gone down. You've caught a chill. Not alarming in itself, but in your condition, far more serious. I need to give you some antibiotics. I take it you would rather stay here?'

Gordon looked at him.

'As opposed to going into hospital.'

'I'll stay here.'

'It's what I thought.'

He gathered up his things and left the room, a taciturn, overworked man. Gordon heard him talking to his mother in the kitchen before a car door slammed and an engine started.

Eleanor appeared and sat on his bed. 'I feel responsible. I should never have told you. The shock was too much.'

'And I feel a burden on you. So I guess that makes us quits.'

'It's nice to have burdens sometimes. We have so few at our age because people think we're too old and senile to look after others,' his mother said wryly.

He stayed in bed for three days, gradually beginning to pick up strength. They talked very little about what had gone on. Eleanor would sit and read the papers with him in the mornings, her chair in the sunshine, which poured through the bedroom windows. She was never far away, but never intrusive. When he got up, he felt shaky and very quickly out of breath.

'I want you to see someone,' Eleanor announced.

'Who?'

'My reflexologist. She works from her home in the village.'

'Why on earth would I want to see her?'

'Because she'll make you feel stronger. I wanted to suggest it before, but I thought you'd just turn me down.'

'And now?'

'And now I think you probably don't have the strength.'

They both laughed.

'Bloody impossible woman!'

He went to see Heidi Clarke that afternoon. Eleanor could sense his scepticism.

'Just try it. It won't do you any harm.'

The session was extraordinary. Heidi worked his feet with enormous skill and at times, he could feel tingling in his spine or in his head. When she had finished, he was so relaxed he could barely stand. She warned him he would probable feel much worse over the next 24 hours and instructed him to drink lots of water.

'With Scotch in it or without?' he jested.

But it was true. For the rest of that day, his body felt as though it was in battle, but he woke the next morning with more energy and sense of well being.

'It's quite remarkable,' he told his mother later.

'Yes, it is. Perhaps you ought to find yourself a reflexologist when you go home.'

'I could do.'

It was something he had never imagined himself ever doing. But then neither had he imagined himself dying. He knew he had to, but it was always something that would happen in the future - something that he always promised to look at, but never quite did. The nearest he ever got was when he had to attend a funeral. There Death stared you in the face for a while, but like everyone else, he was only too eager to return to normality.

'I need to go back home pretty soon. I should think the estate agents are growing demented.'

His mother gave him a quick hug. 'Are you feeling better about it all?'

He knew she wasn't talking about his illness, or the house sale. Images of his father, larger than life, ran through his mind. He had never known, so he supposed his father had been a good one to him. He sighed. 'It's hard to come to terms with.'

'I know. I'm not sure I ever did. I just learnt to live with it.'

'But why did you give up your music, Mum? Why that? That's what I still don't understand.'

'Because it always reminded me of that night. The feel of the saxophone against my lips as I saw my husband kiss his lover's hand. The shock of it was too great. I guess the heart went out of me. You need passion to play well.'

'What a waste.'

The words hung heavily between them, until Eleanor started chatting about a plant she wanted to find for her garden. Gordon thought of his. Thought how it would have overgrown, knew that he did not have the strength for it any more. Another reason to off-load the cottage quickly before twenty years of love and toil were spoilt.

It was the garden that finally spurred him to return. It was time, also, that he faced up to Penny Young.

CHAPTER TWELVE

He drove back early the next morning. He had wept when he had said goodbye to his mother. She, in turn, had thought her heart would break as he drove off. She had never thought she would have to face up to losing her son before she died and it made her feel very alone. She needed the activity and stimulation of friends, but the last few days had exhausted her. For the first time in her life, she went back to bed and slept until lunchtime.

While she slept, Gordon rang 'Perfect Homes'. Lydia answered the phone. She was her usual forthright self and told him that the Bradshaws had not yet found a new buyer and that Rose Cottage had gone back onto the market. She ran through the people who had viewed it, but none had shown any interest.

'Might help if you give the grass a cut,' she said.

Gordon laughed aloud at her effrontery. 'I have been away.'

'I gathered that. Can't you get someone else to tidy it up for you?'

'When are you free?'

'Me?'

'Well, you're a gardener, aren't you?'

He could imagine her small face, screwed up into its usual frown as she assessed the question. He realised that he suddenly very much wanted her to say yes.

'I could do a Tuesday, but I couldn't say whether it

would be morning or the afternoon.'

'That's settled, then. Can you start tomorrow?'

She arrived promptly, dressed in old jeans and a T-shirt. He noticed how brown she was, and how strong she looked, despite her slightness.

She was pretty businesslike and started work as soon as he had shown her where the equipment was kept. She handled the mower expertly and he left her to it. He thought he would feel odd letting someone else work in his garden. His space. But it was OK. She was OK.

It was dusk when she had finished her time. He poured them both a drink, taking a guess that she would drink a dry martini.

'Oh thanks. I mustn't be long as I've got to let Pounce out.'

'Why don't you bring him?'

'I didn't think you'd want him crashing around amongst your plants.'

He thought back to the first time that he had seen the dog, when he had escaped from Lydia's car. His whole being seemed to have mellowed since then.

'It'll be fine. I'd like to have him around.'

'Thanks.'

She almost gulped her drink and was gone. He realised it was just her way. She didn't like fuss and good-byes came into that category. He also realised that each time he saw her, he was more intrigued by her. He really knew nothing about her at all, and there was no reason why he should. He was only employing her as a gardener, after all.

A car pulling into the drive interrupted his reverie. He glanced round the side of the house and to his dismay, saw it was Penny Young. She spotted him and walked over. She flushed slightly and he could tell she was nervous.

'Hello Gordon. I thought I ought to let you know the situation about your sale.'

'Didn't Lydia tell you I phoned in yesterday?'

He realised he sounded sharp.

'No, she didn't.'

Penny did not know why she lied. She had seen his call logged in the book, but she wanted to actually see him face to face. She wanted to have it out with him, but did not have the nerve. And yet she could feel her anger rising as he stood there, so collected. He looked thinner, though, she thought, and drawn. His tan could not hide the tightness of the skin over his cheekbones. She immediately started to feel an irrational fear - what if he was ill, what if he had AIDS?

She had to get him talking. 'Have you been away?'

'Yes, twice. Didn't I tell you?'

He knew he had not, but he did not feel strong enough for a confrontation. He just wanted to get rid of her as quickly as possible.

'Anywhere nice? Only you didn't mention it last time I saw you.' There, it was out. The words fell between them like a gauntlet, waiting to be picked up. Gordon flushed.

'Look, Penny, I'm sorry about that night. I never wanted it to happen. I guess we just got carried away, because I don't make a habit of doing things like that.'

'Was it that bad?' She had to know. Had to torture herself.

'Of course it wasn't. You mustn't think that.'

'Well what the hell else am I supposed to think?'

He took her arm and led her round to the seat. 'Gin and tonic?'

She nodded, not looking at him and he realised how much he had hurt her and was immediately terribly sorry. He returned with the drinks and she sipped hers. He was appalled to find that Lydia kept coming into his thoughts. Finally she faced him.

'So why, Gordon? You're free, I'm free. We seemed to enjoy each other's company. We were good together, I thought.'

Gordon had an image of Penny's naked body beneath his. He felt a stir of longing. This was worse than he thought it would be. What a fool he had been. He sighed.

'Yes, we were good together. It's just not a good time for me. I couldn't possibly give a relationship the time and energy it deserves. I'm so sorry.'

She put her hand on his knee. 'I'm pretty low maintenance, you know. Why don't we see how it goes?'

She knew she was playing with fire, but did not care. She wanted him but she knew he did not really want her. But she also knew she could be very persuasive.

'Lydia… I…'

She snatched her hand away. 'What did you call me?'

In an instant, she was on her feet and facing him, her face bright red.

'So that's how the land lies, is it? You've been sleeping with that little slut. Well how could you! She's young enough to be your daughter!'

Gordon recoiled in the face of her venom. 'It's not like that at all. For goodness sake…'

But she suddenly reached out, slapped his face and then ran off, her high heels clattering on the flagstones. He just sat, too stunned to move. His face stung from the blow and his head had started a dull ache. God, the woman was mad!

He felt his face, felt the heat in it. He fished an ice cube out of the glass and rubbing it over his cheek, suddenly laughed at how absurd he must look. It was the first time he had ever been deliberately hit. Firsts were quite a feat at his age. She must see him as a complete swine. He fantasised for a few minutes about his new role of cad and bounder and thought of all the poor, unsuspecting women in the village he could ruin! He hardly thought so. He had always been very shy as far as the opposite sex were concerned, which was why this thing with Penny was so out of character for him. He recognised that Penny must have had some pretty bad experiences to have reacted as she did and he felt genuinely sorry that he had added to them. But what was done was done and he did not intend to make it any worse by getting involved with her. He decided that he would have to re-market Rose Cottage. He would contact another agent in the morning. It was getting to be quite a habit!

He spent the rest of the week seeking out another agent. He also telephoned the Bradshaws to tell them what he had done, in case they suddenly came back into the market.

The letter he wrote to 'Perfect Homes' was one of the most difficult he had ever done. He decided to be business-like and he got an equally business-like letter back reminding him that on the sale of the cottage, he would also owe them a fee.

He had advertised the newer Jag in the local paper and he was lucky enough to sell it to the first viewer. He had not felt right since the episode at his mother's and he realised that he had better get a move on if he wanted to sort out all his affairs.

He was troubled with a persistent cough and had

popped in to see Tom Lander for another examination. He was offered medication, but declined. Only if he was in pain, he insisted. He had been Tom's last patient of the day and they had popped into the Rose and Crown for a quick drink. To Gordon's consternation, he had spotted Penny at one of the tables chatting to a man, but if she had seen him she did not acknowledge it, to his enormous relief.

He liked Tom. Respected him as a GP and found him hugely entertaining as a person. Their one pint turned into several and Gordon had been glad he had walked to the surgery. He was using the Mark 1 now, which had caused a few comments amongst the locals who liked to tease him about his Jaguar obsession.

Tuesday arrived and no Lydia. Gordon realised he did not have her home phone number, in fact, was not even sure where she lived. But on Wednesday, he got the car out and decided to go and see if she was OK. He had done quite a lot of work deciding which of the charities to leave money to, and he wanted to discuss this with her. She seemed to have become his sounding board.

He drove to the Manor, parked and went over to the formal garden. A lone figure was mapping out a border with wooden pegs. He wandered over and the man stood up as he approached.

'Can I help you?'

'Yes, I'm looking for Lydia Page.'

'Lydia Page?'

Gordon wondered how many Lydias there were working on the estate, but nodded. The man seemed to be summing him up.

'She's not here.'

Gordon stifled a howl of frustration. This could take

forever. 'Any idea where she is?'

' 'Appens I do.'

He waited, trying not to sigh out loud. 'I'd be rather grateful if you could point me in the right direction. I really do need to contact her.'

'She's at home.'

'Well the trouble is, I don't know where she lives.'

At this moment, two spaniels hurtled towards them. A man appeared bellowing at them, but they were already rolling onto their backs with ecstasy as Gordon fussed them.

'Bella! Barby! Heel!'

Lord P. approached, yelling furiously and the dogs slunk off.

'Sinclair! My dear man! What can I do for you?'

He shook Gordon's hand, a big, hearty, no-nonsense man with a grip like a vice. 'Bloody dogs. Never do what they're told. Sarah spoils them rotten. Never make a gun dog. Useless! Now, to what do we owe this honour?'

Gordon explained why he had come. Lord P. directed him to her cottage in the grounds.

'Not going to filch her away from under my nose, are you Sinclair? Bloody good worker. Cold as an iceberg though. Eh?'

Gordon assured His Lordship that he was not going to steal his prize worker and walked over to the three small terraced cottages. Lydia's was the one on the end. He opened the picket gate and walked up the brick pathway to the green front door. The knocker was an old horse-shoe. He announced his arrival and waited and he could hear Pounce scrabbling at the door. Eventually, just when he thought she must be out, the door opened. It was Lydia and she looked terrible.

100

'What the hell do you want?'

She started coughing violently, bending over nearly double. He realised she was sick. The unfriendliness of her greeting startled him, but he could not leave her - not like this. Pounce forced his way past her, desperate to be out.

'Now look what you've done,' she wailed. She went to go after him, but a fresh paroxysm of coughing overtook her.

'Lydia! You need to be in bed. I'll get the dog. Now go on inside!' he was surprised when she turned and went indoors. He let the dog have a five-minute race round and then called him over. He came willingly enough and he led Gordon into the cottage.

'Lydia?'

A voice answered. 'Shut the dog in and go away.'

He traced her to a small sitting room. It was sparsely furnished, the walls needing a fresh coat of paint. He shivered. It was colder inside than it was out. She was sitting, curled up in a chair, which had seen better days. She scowled at him, her face white and pinched.

'I don't want you here.'

'Lydia, I don't know what's happened to you, but you're ill. I'm going to call a doctor.'

Her denial brought a fresh bout of coughing. He went back into the hall where he had spotted a telephone and called the surgery. A quick search found the kitchen. Days of dirty dishes were stacked haphazardly on the sink and surrounding work surfaces.

'God, what a mess.'

He located the kettle and found a half-opened packet of teabags. Lydia appeared in the doorway, but not before he noticed that her fridge and cupboards were probably empty.

'How dare you barge into my house…'

He stared at her, meeting the hostility in her eyes until she looked away.

'Lydia, I want to help you.'

'What, like you've already done.'

'Whatever do you mean?'

He took a step towards her, but she backed off.

'Telling Penny Young all those lies about us.'

'What lies? I don't know what you're talking about.'

'That we'd slept together.'

His mouth dropped open in astonishment and his words trailed away. So this was it. He suddenly saw Penny's angry face as she had attacked him in the garden. He knew he had to get this right. Lydia was watching him closely. She had seen the look on his face, and suddenly thought she was wrong. Very wrong. The realisation made her cough until she thought she'd never get her breath. He was leading her back into the sitting room, his arm around her shoulders.

She wanted to push him away, but suddenly didn't have the strength.

'I'm going to go and get some food and then I'll be back to light a fire. The doctor will be here soon.'

She said nothing.

'If you don't let me in when I come back, I shall break the door down.'

He left and bought all the necessary provisions, plus some extra ones. As a last minute thought, he purchased some flowers from the greengrocer. That front room needed all the help it could get.

On his return, he found the door ajar. Tom Lander's car was outside and he heard voices upstairs. He busied himself in the kitchen, lighting the old boiler, heating water to wash up the dishes and making a steaming mug of Ovaltine. This he took upstairs whilst he was waiting for the kettle to boil. He knocked on her door and Tom opened it.

'Gordon! Whatever are you doing here?'

Gordon explained briefly that he had come to see Lydia after she had failed to turn up to do his garden.

'She's got bronchitis and is very run down. I'm not happy for her to stay here, if I'm honest. It's too damp and she needs looking after.'

Gordon thought of his own guest bedroom. Warm and comfortable and he knew what he had to do.

'She can come home with me.'

'Well, that should get the village talking,' his GP said with a grin.

'I think they're already doing that well enough.'

'Well, it would be a good solution.'

'Stop talking about me as if I wasn't here!'

Gordon looked round the door. The room was small with the minimum of furniture. A large, much loved bear sat incongruously by Lydia's pillow. She looked like a child, with the covers pulled up to her chin.

'Are you going to pack some things, or am I?'

Lydia scowled. 'I'm not going anywhere.'

Tom Lander spoke with authority. 'You either go to Gordon's or I call an ambulance and you'll go to hospital. Your choice. I'm not going until you're out of here, one way or another.' He winked at Gordon and motioned him to go downstairs, following on his heels. They went into the kitchen and Gordon busied himself with the washing up.

It was not long before Lydia appeared, clutching a holdall and coughing violently. Gordon had just finished the last plate. He took Lydia's case, the perishable food and flowers he had bought and put them in the car. He grimaced as Pounce leapt onto his leather seats. Tom appeared with Lydia and deposited her into the passenger seat. He secured the front door, handed Lydia her keys and departed. Gordon followed his Alfa Romeo down the grand driveway. Lydia shivered next to him and he turned the heating up. She had not said a word all the way to the cottage. He took her bag, let Pounce into the garden and led her straight upstairs.

'Oh, it's lovely!' She was looking round the guestroom, charmed by its eaved ceiling, white walls and soft pink furnishings. The old pine furniture gleamed in the afternoon light.

'Put yourself straight to bed. I've got to go and get your prescription. I shall let Pounce in. He'll find you soon enough.'

Without another word, he left her and went back down to the village. On his return, he arranged the flowers, took up a large bottle of mineral water and her pills. She was fast asleep, her face flushed. The dog was lying on the bottom of the bed. He looked at Gordon warily, his tail wagging hesitantly. Gordon pulled an ear and the dog rolled over in ecstasy, his tail now thumping on the bedcovers.

'Shhh... you'll wake her.'

He deposited everything and scouted around for some gardening magazines, which he left on the bedside cabinet. He then went downstairs and carefully prepared a light supper. He enjoyed cooking and liked it even more when he had someone to cook for. When he put his head round the door with the food tray, she was awake.

'Grub up.' He waited until she had sat up, the movement causing her to cough and then handed her the tray.

'I feel awful.'

'You look awful.'

She pulled a face, but began to eat and he left her. When he went to fetch the tray, she was fast asleep again. He pulled the curtains, left her a note pinned to her teddy, which she had packed with her other things. *Wake me if you need anything, I've let Pounce out.*

Then he went to bed, too exhausted even to read.

CHAPTER THIRTEEN

The next morning he was woken by the dog. He had left the door ajar in case Lydia had called him and Pounce, restless, had decided to explore. This included the contents of beds and Gordon felt a sudden weight on the duvet, followed by a cold, wet nose sniffing his face. He pushed the dog away and lay there for a moment, listening to his own body. He still felt incredibly tired and heavy limbed. He sighed. How wonderful it would be just to stay here with a good book.

Instead, he rose and went and tackled the usual morning chores, which now included seeing to a dog. He banged on the window as he saw Pounce scrabbling at something of interest in the herbaceous border. Probably would not have a garden left if she stayed very long, he thought. He returned upstairs with the tea and toast for Lydia to find her awake. She looked at him from under the covers. The shutters were up again.

'I shouldn't be here. You need someone looking after you, not the other way round.'

'I'm fine. I just need my gardener better again.'

'Sorry. I'll get up today. Maybe I could do some weeding.'

'You'll do no such thing. You're ill.'

'I'm never ill.'

'Well, you are now. And until you're completely better,

you're staying here. It does me good to have someone to think about other than myself.' He saw her eyes fill with tears and pretended not to notice, turning away to open the curtains.

'Bloody dog's digging in the herbaceous border again. Whatever's he found?' He turned to look at her and saw the moment had passed.

'He probably just thinks he's helping,' Lydia replied.

'How do you feel today?'

'Not so desperate. I actually slept last night without the coughing waking me every five minutes.'

'Good. Now do you want me to ring 'Perfect Homes' and tell them you won't be in?' He saw the guarded look come across her face again. She was wrestling with something.

'They sacked me.' She wouldn't meet his eyes.

'What the hell for?' But he knew already. He just wanted to hear Lydia confirm it.

'Because they said I'd acted unprofessionally.'

'In what way, Lydia? Did you steal money, send files to other companies? What?'

She was pulling at her bear's ears. 'I told you before, Penny Young thinks we're sleeping together and told Head Office.'

There, it was out. She had blushed a deep red. He fleetingly thought how naïve she was about certain things, and how up front about others. It made him like her even more. He felt protective towards her.

'I shall go and see them. Sort it out.'

'No!'

The vehemence of her reply made him stop. She was half out of bed and the sudden move made her cough violently.

'But it's not true. You can't let people get away with that?'

He thought of Penny Young in the pub with her male companion. He wondered if she had told him and everyone else in the village. *That dirty old man in Rose Cottage. Did you hear? Half his age. Had a bit of a thing with the other agent, too. Who'd have thought it!*

Oh well, let them think it. But he would have to do something about Lydia's dismissal because he felt responsible. It was clear to him that if he had not rejected Penny's obvious advances the other night in the garden, none of this would have happened. But that was tantamount to blackmail.

Lydia was still watching him warily.

'Get back into bed. We'll talk about it later.'

'But you won't go there, will you?'

'Do you think I've got time, with a poorly patient and a naughty dog? I shan't leave the house. Promise!'

She relaxed a little, but her eyes were still anxious. She reminded him of a wild animal. Real trust would be very hard to gain. He walked Pounce down to the meadow and played ball with him before sitting on the swing and letting his thoughts drift past. It was so pleasant here in the early morning sun. He closed his eyes and rocked gently. What bliss.

He was not sure how long he had been there, when he heard his name being called. The dog, sensing a stranger, had gone on ahead up the grassy path. He followed and saw Alice Stamp coming towards him, fielding off the excited dog.

'Alice!'

'You'd forgotten, haven't you?'

'No, I mean yes.' In a sudden impulse, he put his arm

through Alice's and squeezed it. 'Sorry.'

She blushed and pulled away. She had always had a soft spot for him, not that she would allow her practical no-nonsense mind to admit it for a second. But this spring-cleaning gave her an opportunity to be with him and to be of use. This seemed to be her main mission in life, at the expense of her own personal happiness. Sharp-tongued and to the point, she had a heart of gold and would help anyone.

'What's he doing here?' She was looking at the dog, sniffing amongst the rose bushes. For a second, Gordon felt reluctant to explain. He sighed. He knew she would find out sooner or later.

'Lydia Page is staying here at the moment as she's not well.'

Alice looked up at the bedroom windows as if she expected to see the woman looking out. He knew he would not get away with as little information and he was right.

'Well what on earth is that to do with you?'

He wondered how to explain. Even he was not sure why.

'She's been doing some work for me in the garden and…'

'Doing some work in your garden?' She was looking at him in askance. 'Something wrong with you? Why should you need help?'

This was going to be worse than he thought. Sudden and unbidden, he heard his mother accusing him of living a lie. She was right. He was.

'Alice, there's something I need to tell you.'

She had wept openly in the end, clutching at a lace handkerchief. He poured her a large brandy despite her protests, but she drank it down immediately. She ques-

tioned him inexhaustibly, trying to make some sense out
of what she had been told. Now that she knew, it was as
if the scales had dropped from her eyes and she could
see the physical changes in him, could see his thinness
and his slight lack of breath, could sense the lowering of
energy. The brandy worked.

'Well I suppose we'd better get to work on that study,
then, hadn't we.'

He laughed. 'I'm not going just yet!'

She waved her hands at him and bustled out. He could
hear her muttering to herself. He fed Pounce and went
up to see Lydia, but found her still sleeping, oblivious to
the drama. She woke when Gordon brought up a lunch
tray as he had insisted on cooking for all three of them.
Lydia smiled wanly at him.

'I've not slept so much for years.'

'Do you good. Probably what you needed more than
anything.'

'Don't want to be a bother.'

'You're not. Now eat! I've got Alice Stamp here, helping me sort out the study.'

The wariness returned. 'Does she know I'm here?'

'Yes. She knows everything.' He nodded at her unspo-
ken question.

'Well, so much for wanting to keep it a secret. The whole
village will know by teatime.'

'I'll have to lock her in the study then, won't I!'

But despite the lightness of his answer, it did trouble
him. He spoke with Alice late in the afternoon when they
had nearly completed the task.

'Only I don't want everyone to know. Can't bear the
tea and sympathy routine.'

'Well, you're going to have to tell them something. I'm

110

surprised word hasn't got out about you putting the house on the market.'

Gordon shrugged, looking around the study, which had been cleared of all its clutter. They had carried out boxes and boxes of books to the car, which were going, partly to charity and partly to the specialist bookshop in Delaby. This would be tomorrow's task, as he suddenly felt too tired to do any more today. He said as much to Alice and she made him go and sit in the garden while she made some tea. She had brought her usual cake and she reluctantly cut three pieces and made three cups of tea.

She had always thought of Lydia Page as being rather odd and she was secretly dismayed that she was here. She put a mug on a tray, went upstairs and knocked on the door of the guestroom. As there was no answer, she went in and to her relief, the girl was asleep. She plonked the tray on the side table and was about to leave when she saw the bear clutched in Lydia's arm. There was something incongruous about this sharp-faced female cuddling a teddy. Just for a second, something shifted in Alice's heart. Then she tutted and went downstairs. *Getting daft in her old age, she was.*

On Friday morning, Lydia appeared in the kitchen as Gordon was preparing breakfast.

'What on earth are you doing down here?'

Lydia flopped in the rocking chair, Pounce at her feet.

'I feel much better. I can't lie up there forever, not if I want to keep my job at the Manor.'

'I've phoned Lord P. Explained how unwell you are.'

Lydia thought how simple it was for him. How he just did tasks she would have dreaded and would have put off.

'So you can go back to bed.'

111

'Is it OK if I go and sit in the garden?' She suddenly felt shy.

'Yes, of course it is. But no gardening!'

She smiled at him and he marvelled again at how different she looked when she did. She took her breakfast and disappeared, sitting herself on a sheltered bench in the sunshine. The dog vanished into the meadow and she could hear him giving the occasional excited *woof* as he found something to chase. She ate her breakfast and dozed, thinking how easy it was here. How peaceful and how calm. She had begun to like it, and that simply wouldn't do.

He left her that day to go into Delaby. As well as distributing the books, he also had an appointment to see his solicitor, as he needed to set wheels in motion.

He returned home late that afternoon, having phoned Lydia at lunchtime to make sure she was OK. The meeting with Simon Cayser had been difficult and had exhausted him. He was perturbed at how he was less and less able to do things. His stamina was declining far quicker than he had thought. On impulse, he called in to see Tom Lander and waited in the surgery.

Tom checked him over and confirmed his fears that yes, in his opinion, the disease was causing the fatigue and that it was perhaps progressing more quickly than they had thought. But he refused to give Gordon any indication of time, saying it was not his field of expertise. He offered to make Gordon an appointment to see the consultant again, but he declined.

A great wave of self-pity overcame him on the way back to Rose Cottage. He had distanced himself from his death, as though it was something that was happening to someone else. But he was no longer able to do that. It was creeping up on him and suddenly he did not think he could bear it.

He arrived home, glad that Lydia was not around, although he could hear her whistling tunelessly somewhere in the garden. He went in and poured himself a large scotch. He though how dependent he was becoming on alcohol, which was not good at all.

By the time Lydia appeared in the doorway, he had composed himself. She had a bit of colour and had obviously been outside for most of the day, he thought. He settled Pounce who seemed ridiculously pleased to see him. Lydia stretched sleepily.

'I found your lounger in the shed. I've been snoozing on and off all day.'

'You're looking much better.'

'I feel much better. I shall go home tomorrow. I'm perfectly well enough to look after myself now.'

He was amazed at how much this dismayed him. He suddenly did not want to be on his own.

'There's no hurry for you to go back. Why don't you stay here until you're a lot stronger?'

She was looking at him in her intense way. 'Are you having a bad day?'

He nodded and to his horror, felt the tears surge up. He could do nothing about them. Embarrassed, he turned away, fumbling for a tissue. He knew she was just behind him and then felt her small hand on his arm. He blew his nose loudly.

'It's OK.'

'I'm sorry, it just comes over me sometimes. What a fool you must think me!'

She had let go of his arm and he heard the chair scrape on the flagstone floor as she sat down. He wiped his eyes vigorously and took a few deep breaths. Still she had not spoken and eventually he turned to look at her. She was playing with the sugar spoon, digging it into the sugar bowl and running the sugar up the handle. She looked up and was obviously troubled.

'I didn't mean to upset you...' he began, but she silenced him.

'I'm just trying to feel what you must be feeling and I can't. No matter how hard I try, I can't. To know for sure that you only have a limited time left must be almost unbearable to live with. I just can't imagine. But you always seem so positive about it. I've never been with anyone who's dying before and it scares me. I don't know what to say or what to do.' She held her hands out in a gesture of defeat.

'Lydia, you're doing just fine. You can have no idea how wonderful it is to be able to talk about it all, without that person collapsing in a heap. You've been brilliant.'

'But I'm scared I won't cope. How will I know what to do? I can't stay here, I need to be able to go home.' Her eyes were pleading with him. 'I know you've looked after me and I feel I owe you...'

'No! You don't owe me anything. Never think that. I wanted to help you and I don't expect anything in return.'

'Well, you're not like most people then.'

'No, I'm not. And neither are you. Which is why I told you about me dying. Now we'll say no more about it. Just give me the no-nonsense, practical help you've given me all along.' He reached up onto the shelf and picked up some papers. 'These, by the way, are the charities I've decided upon.'

He handed them to her and she started to browse

through them. She was actually quite interested as people's choice of charities gave a lot of clues away as to who they really were. She had always been accused of giving to animal charities to the exclusion of all others. And thinking about it, she supposed it was probably true.

'What are you smiling at?'

She looked up, unaware that she had been. 'I was just thinking that if it'd been my pile, it would have had 'Save the Whale', endangered species, animal rescues, wildlife funds and dolphin aid to name a few. Your choices seem pretty balanced.' She pulled one out. 'Water Aid. This looks interesting'.

'I thought so. Such small amounts can give a whole village clean drinking water. I probably use a week's supply on my roses each night!'

'Are you giving equally to them all?'

'I don't think so. I feel more passionate about some than others.'

Lydia counted the charities represented in the literature. Fourteen. All varied, all obviously carefully thought out. Three local ones, including a hand-written slip with 'Village Church Appeal' on it.

'What's this?'

'They're trying to get sponsors to replace the church's plain glass windows with stained glass ones. They've already completed behind the altar on the west side. I thought I'd pay for the three on the east side. I wanted to give some money back to the village.'

'Can't you make a list of worthy villagers and leave a wadge of notes on their doorstep?'

She said it as a joke, but she could see by the look on his face that he liked the idea. She groaned. He really was impossible at times!

'I was only joking.'

'But why couldn't I? I was standing behind Mrs. Delaney in the Post Office yesterday and Evelyn asked her if she was going away. She'd said she couldn't afford a holiday this year as she'd had to have her old boiler replaced.'

'But you can't go round leaving £5 notes on people's doorsteps like a modern-day Robin Hood.'

'Why not? It's not illegal. It's my money.'

She was alarmed at his enthusiasm, but secretly her mind was beginning to whirr with the possibilities. He was getting more excited.

'I've got all my shares to sell yet, quite apart from the house. I could use that money.'

He noticed her frown and grabbed her hand. 'Lydia, this would be such fun. Surely I deserve that at least. And it wouldn't harm anyone, would it?'

She sighed. 'Can't you have fun going off on holiday?'

'I've done that, haven't I? I need something to concentrate on. Something which will stop me thinking about myself and getting more and more miserable.'

She realised it was useless. 'How much can you realise with your shares?'

'About £35,000.'

Lydia, who had never had any sort of savings, choked on her drink. 'Well, that would buy Mrs. Delaney a hell of a holiday. Fly her round the world on Concorde.'

'But there's other Mrs. Delaneys. You must be able to think of some deserving causes.'

'Well, there's Pounce. He could do with a new collar.'

Gordon laughed, looking at the dog lying prostrate in front of the range, one of its back paws against the warm door. He got up, uncorked a bottle of wine, poured it into two glasses and got some paper and a pencil.

'I'm going to make a list. And Pounce's collar shall be right at the top of it. Any particular colour?'

'I think I'd like a blue one. With a silver buckle and fancy name tag.'

Gordon wrote it down with Mrs. Delaney and 'holiday' beside her name.

'How much are you going to give her?'

They debated this, backwards and forwards before allocating her £750, because Lydia insisted that she wouldn't go abroad anyway.

'£750 would probably get you a month in Margate,' she added wickedly, warming to this new game. He was right, it would be fun.

'So that's one holiday and one dog collar. A total of £850.'

'£100 for a new collar. That's obscene!' she exclaimed.

'Nonsense. Posh collars don't come cheap you know.'

She laughed. 'Shame it's not going on a posh dog.'

Pounce suddenly sat up and scratched vigorously and then wagged his tail as they roared with mirth.

'So come on, who else? We still have £34,150 to spend!'

'I do know that Peggy Wright's lost her husband and can't do her garden herself. She can't afford anyone in and her garden's already getting out of hand.'

Gordon rummaged around in the kitchen drawer and produced a calculator. He started tapping numbers in. 'How many hours a week would it take to do her garden?'

'Oh I'd have thought three - to do it properly.'

'Right then… So three hours a week for the next five years is… £6,240.' He wrote a figure onto the list beside her name.

'How are you going to guarantee that the money you give them will be spent on what you've given it for?'

Gordon thought for a minute, filling up their glasses. 'Put yourself in their shoes. If you found money and a specific note saying what the money was to be spent on, wouldn't you do so?'

'So would I spend £100 on a dog collar?' Lydia thought for a moment. 'No, I'd probably buy myself some new tools.'

He laughed. 'Well, I shall have to come back and haunt you, then!'

She sighed, suddenly sad. He sensed her change of mood.

'Come on, one more person before we put this away for the night.'

They mulled over possible recipients. Gordon came up with someone, but Lydia wouldn't hear of it because she kept her dog chained up all day. Someone Lydia suggested Gordon knew had a drink problem and thought spare cash might fuel his habit. They decided to sleep on it.

Lydia went to bed soon after supper, still not feeling very strong. She snuggled down between the covers, the dog lying at her feet. She could get used to this room. Used to being here. She had never felt so comfortable with a human being before and it scared her. She needed to go back to her cottage and distance herself from him. Trust her to become close to someone who was not going to be here for much longer. But perhaps that was why she had allowed it to happen. She dozed off, more exhausted by her day than she would like to admit, even to herself.

CHAPTER FOURTEEN

She had her old nightmare again and she woke with a start, soaked in sweat, her heart racing, and her mouth dry with fear. She put the light on and sat up, not daring to go back to sleep. She heard a tap on her door and pulled the covers up over her nightshirt.

'Who is it?'

'It's Gordon. Are you OK?'

He did not appear.

'Yes. Fine.'

'Only I thought I heard you scream out.'

God, she had started that again. She used to wake to the sound of her own screaming. 'Just a bad dream. I'm fine, really.'

'OK then. Just thought I'd check.'

She sighed with relief and reached for her book. She would read for a while, just to make sure she did not revisit the nightmare.

Gordon went back to bed feeling troubled. He had only just turned in, having stayed up to watch some of the Grand Prix. The noise had made him jump out of his skin and had left him with goosebumps. The cottage was silent afterwards, but he heard the click as she switched on her bedside light.

He slept restlessly for the remainder of the night, troubled himself by snatches of dreams. He woke to the sound of heavy rain, the water lashing against his bedroom window. He would have liked to have just lain in bed and dozed, but he remembered he had people coming to view the cottage. He dressed and went down into the kitchen. It seemed to be the only room he used any more. He tidied up and loaded the dishwasher. A quick wipe round and it looked presentable. Lydia appeared just as the agent was arriving. She disappeared into the study with the dog.

Before the day was out, Matt Gower had shown another three couples round the cottage. One couple came back with an offer later in the day. By then, Lydia had insisted on returning home and Gordon had dropped both her and the dog off. He had gone down to the village and had got her in some food, as he sensed she still needed rest. She looked embarrassed at accepting it, but he insisted. He had also lit the fire in the grate, as the house seemed damp and unwelcoming, particularly as the rain had not relented all day.

Now, much later, he sat at the kitchen table, having just put the phone down to the agent. He felt disturbed and restless, but he was not sure why.

The reason came to him that evening. The rain had finally stopped and he had wandered down the garden, dead heading as he went, enjoying the freshness of the twilight and the smells the rain had released from the earth. He looked back at the house, and suddenly he knew. He wanted Lydia to have Rose Cottage, not some stranger. He felt as if he had known her forever and yet he realised that he hardly knew anything about her at all. He seemed to know the essence of her and that was enough. He thought about how she had disliked taking the food from him earlier and knew she would never accept this. He would just have to tell little white lies to her and by the time she found out, it would be too late for her to do anything about it.

The feeling of heaviness left him and in its place he felt a rising excitement. He stopped by a rose and inhaled the strong scent. He gazed at the frilled, pale pink petals of Rosa Céleste. It was one of his absolute favourites. The thought of Lydia smelling the same sweet scent, digging in the herbaceous border and sitting on his swing gave him a thrill of pleasure. All he had worked for, all the roses he had collected over the years, fed, watered and loved, would be looked after now. It gave him great comfort. She would have to keep that wretched dog under control, of course! It was too late to ring the estate agents. They would think he was crazy, but he suddenly did not care. And he would still have enough money to play at being god within the village.

He walked back into the house. The charity information seemed to glare at him from the shelf. Perhaps he could still contribute to 'Water Aid'. He still had a few more assets to dispose of. Perhaps they could go to that. He thought of his remaining Jaguar and then of Toby. He would still really like the boy to have the car, but had been secretly hurt at his reaction to Gordon's news. Maybe he would go and have a chat with Sandy Thomas, his father. One thing was for sure, Toby had definitely not told anyone in the village, because he was being treated the same as he always was. No suddenly ended conversations when he went into the village shop, no whisperings in the village street. Which meant that Alice Stamp must have also kept quiet. Alice! He wondered how she would take to Lydia living in the cottage. Well really, what he did with his property was nobody's business but his own. He would tell his solicitor and that was all.

He wandered up into the guestroom where Lydia had slept. It was such a pretty room and he decided, suddenly, that he would keep it just as it was. The rest of the furniture he would slowly sell. She needed to feel that the house really was hers and not his. With this in mind, he went round each room, making a list of things he would leave and those he would sell or give away. He decided to empty his bedroom and the other bedroom. He would leave the old bookcase on the landing and the kitchen table and chairs. For a moment, he regretted selling the dresser. He would empty the study, except for the desk, and in the dining room he would leave the dining room table and chairs. He reached the lounge and into his head came an image of Lydia's tatty old sofa and mismatched chair. He had to leave the suite. At least then she would have the bare bones of furniture, but without it seeming as though he had not moved out. He would have to spend the next month doing all the odd jobs that needed doing, such as mending the toilet flush. He would also get a double delivery of logs so that it would see her through the winter. Apart from a few minor repairs, he had kept the cottage in excellent condition. He was anxious that he was not going to give her a liability she could not afford to keep up.

With these thoughts churning in his mind, he was surprised he slept at all. He woke late the next morning to the sound of hammering on the front door. He pulled on a robe and still bleary-eyed, went down to see who it was. He had no sooner opened the door when Alice Stamp pushed past him.

'Good gracious, man! It's nearly 10 o'clock!' She looked

at his dishevelled appearance crossly. 'Can't let yourself go, you know.' She bustled into the kitchen and filled the kettle with water.

'Er… I'll… um… just go and get dressed.'

'I should think so too. Got lots to do, if you remember.'

He showered and dressed hurriedly and went down to the kitchen, which was smelling deliciously of bacon and eggs. He saw mounds of bacon, mushrooms, eggs and toast being kept warm on the range.

'Alice, this is wonderful. What a treasure.'

She blushed furiously and started dishing up. She plonked a heaped plate in front of him.

'There, that'll fatten you up.'

She picked at a meagre plateful while he ate ravenously. He pushed back his chair, drank a mouthful of tea and grimaced. Alice always put sugar in tea. He had stopped this years' ago, but could not break her of the habit - 'Hot and sweet,' she'd say, 'that's how tea should be.'

'So, have you made a start, then?'

He vainly tried to remember what he should have started on, and failed. He spread his hand in a gesture of helplessness.

'On the attic. We agreed that the last time I was here.'

It came back to him in a rush. It was the area he had least wanted to do and Alice, being Alice, had insisted that for that very reason, it must be where they started. There was no deflecting her. She untied her floral pinny and put on a dull grey one. She meant business and he had better look sharp! He stacked the plates and then headed into the attic.

After an hour of sorting, when it still did not look as

though they had even made a start, he cursed the architect who had invented attic spaces. They really were just a refuge for unwanted clutter, which should have been ditched years ago. Some of the stuff in his own attic had been there since he had moved into the house. He had never looked at it, never needed it, so those boxes he did not even sort, just labelled them 'Charity shop'. Alice had filled two boxes with items she thought were suitable for the next church bazaar. By mid-afternoon, he had had enough and insisted that they down tools. He had filled his car with boxes, which meant another trip to Delaby. Alice produced a cake, as if by magic, and they sat and ate it with huge mugs of tea.

'So how are you, then?' She was fiddling with the cake knife, avoiding his eyes. He knew she did not really want to hear the answer.

'I'm fine. A bit tired after all that hard labour.'

'Mmm. Good, good. What's next, then? I mean once we finish the attic?'

Gordon thought of all the boxes remaining there still. 'Oh give me a break, Alice. Let's get one area done first.'

She looked at him, not used to the sharpness in his voice. 'Yes, well. No use hanging around, is there?'

He thought that never was there a truer word spoken.

That evening, after Alice had gone, he took the Jag out again. Just drove, aimlessly round, savouring the leather steering wheel beneath his hands, enjoying the glances the car always got wherever it went. On an impulse, he pulled into a pub on a quiet country road in a village about five miles from Delaby. He was dismayed when he heard music coming from inside. He halted, not sure whether to go in or not, when the urge for a pint got the better of him. He opened the door to a round of applause. He looked round and saw that there was a karaoke evening in progress, but before he could back out, the landlord spoke to him.

'What can I get you, sir? Hope you hadn't expected a quiet pint?'

Gordon grinned at the man. 'Not going to get it, am I?'

The landlord smiled back. 'Not our usual scene, live music, but we're doing a charity night for one of our locals. Not from round here, are you?'

Gordon shook his head, surveying the real ale pumps in front of him. There was certainly a good selection of beer.

'I'll have a pint of Fiddlers, please.'

'Straight or handled glass, sir?'

'Straight, please.'

'Going to have a go, then?'

The landlord nodded in the direction of the makeshift stage where a young blonde woman was crooning into the microphone, trying to keep up with the lyrics on the monitor. She was actually rather good.

'Not really my thing.'

'Well, if you change your mind, it's for a good cause. Sarah, one of our young lasses, lost her leg in an accident. Drunken driver ploughed into her as she was walking home from work. Awful it was.' He shook his head at the memory. 'National Health gave her a leg of sorts, but it doesn't fit and it looks awful. We're trying to raise enough money to buy her a proper one, one which looks right as well.'

Gordon took an instant liking to this big, honest man. He sat on a barstool and watched the next act who did a passable impersonation of Tom Jones. He began to relax. It was actually quite good fun and the atmosphere in the pub was very convivial. The bar was busy as people drank more to give them Dutch courage. He fancied another pint, but knew he had to drive. Oh, what the heck...

He called the landlord over. 'Can you call me a taxi later - is that possible?'

'Of course, no problem at all. Another pint, then?'

Gordon supped it readily. He was really enjoying himself. It was a mixed age group of people, but several locals had stood and chatted to him, including him in their midst. He had a further pint.

'Going to have a go, then?'

He realised he was being spoken to by a young woman. She was rattling a tin.

'You wouldn't want to put up with my singing.'

'That's what they all say. Go on, it's only a fiver.'

'What! I have to *pay* a fiver?'

'Yeah. At the end of the evening, we all vote on the best act and the winner gets to go home with a magnum of champagne which Mick's provided. All the entry money goes towards buying Sarah a proper leg.'

'Can't I just pay a fiver and not sing?'

'Only if you want to be a party pooper.'

The singer on stage now was awful and still she was getting cheers from the audience. He could not be any worse.

'OK then. Although I must be mad.'

The girl beamed at him, collected his £5 note and gave him a list of songs to choose from. He picked a Nat King Cole.

'You're on third from now. Good luck!'

The landlord gave him a thumbs up sign. He moved in closer to the stage and someone pulled a chair out for him so that he could sit with their group.

'Get you a drink, mate?'

'No, I'm fine, thanks.' He gestured to his half-full glass.

'Got room for a top-up in there.'

The man rose and got everyone a refill. Gordon smiled at the pretty, dark-haired girl sitting across the table. She leant towards him.

'Thanks for joining in.'

'You're welcome. You probably won't thank me when you hear my voice.'

She laughed. The man returned with the drinks.

'Have you met Sarah, my daughter?'

Gordon shook his head, and held out his hand to the girl. She shook it, giggling. In his intoxicated state, he loved her on sight. He loved all these people. He felt at home, at one with them.

He realised it was his turn to go on. He stepped up onto the stage and took the microphone to huge applause. He doubted that they would be as enthusiastic after the song, but he was wrong. They seemed to be with him when he mumbled a word or could not hit a note. He made his way back to the table and Stewart, Sarah's father, thumped him on the back.

'Well done mate, well done.'

The young blonde woman had won the champagne and when she had to do an encore of her winning song, they all joined in. He did not remember much after that.

Gordon woke in the morning with a ferocious headache. He got up slowly, the room still spinning and his head pounding. But my God, it had been a good night. He would have to see if Sid would run him down to the pub to pick his car up.

It was not until the afternoon that he felt well enough

to attempt the rescue. Sid was out with the car, Maisie informed him. He'd gone bowling as the team was a player short. She asked him in for a cup of tea and he unwillingly agreed. An hour of Maisie's non-stop chatter was all his head needed. But the large piece of homemade cake and two cups of tea helped to settle his stomach. He now knew all the village gossip. He smiled to himself as he stepped into the lane through their gate. Maisie could run a village newspaper, as nothing seemed to escape her eagle eye.

A car was approaching and he saw it was Lydia. She slowed and turned into his drive. She eyed him speculatively.

'You look as if you've been 'Maisied''.

He laughed. 'I have.' He told her why he had gone in there and she offered to take him to pick up his car. He pushed Pounce into the back seat and got into her car, having wiped the worst of the mud off the front seat.

On the way he started to tell Lydia about his night, about Sarah, and about his plan. She listened closely. She pulled into the car park and parked alongside the Jag before turning to face him.

'You can't give her all that money.'

He looked at her. 'Why ever not? She needs a new leg. I have the wherewithal to buy her one. Why can't she be one of our charity causes?'

Because you'll destroy all this.' She waved her hand in the direction of the pub. He looked puzzled. 'You've talked the whole time about what a wonderful evening you had last night, about what wonderful people they were, how they were all pulling together as a community.' He nodded, about to speak, but she stopped him. 'So to suddenly give the family a cheque for the whole

128

amount would end all that.'

'But she's young and pretty and she needs this leg.'

'And she'll get it. How much have they raised already?'

'Three and a half thousand.'

'And how much do they need?'

He groaned, searching his muddled brain for the information. 'Ten thousand.'

'Well, give them £1,500 then, but no more. Let them continue to fund raise, because to suddenly take away that need will do more harm than good.'

He was silent, sifting through what she was saying. She prodded him.

'Go on! Car! I've got work to do.'

'My, but you're bossy today.'

'You just know I'm right, but don't want to admit it.'

He scowled at her and got out of the car. 'Thanks.'

'For the lift or the wisdom?'

'Both, you wicked woman.'

On his return, he saw the answerphone flashing at him. There were three calls from the estate agent and one from his mother. In the excitement, he had forgotten about the offer on the cottage. It was 5:30 and he doubted that there would be anyone in the office, but he had better try. He was relieved when their answerphone clicked in as he had not been looking forward to making the call. He sat at the table and made a list:

Estate Agent

Solicitor

Bank/stockbroker

Charity Shop

Tomorrow, he thought, he would do all the things he had been putting off. He rewarded his good intentions with a night slumped in front of the television.

CHAPTER FIFTEEN

He woke late, feeling peculiar. He got up slowly and was alarmed at how breathless he was, so much so that he was still lying on his bed when someone knocked on the front door. Aware that it was past 10 o'clock, he pulled on a dressing gown and went down to open it. The visitor knocked again as he was halfway down the stairs.

'OK, OK, I'm coming.' He unlocked the door and opened it. Tom Lander stood looking at him.

'Morning, Gordon.'

Gordon stood aside and indicated for him to enter. He could do without this today. He wearily made Tom a coffee. He felt exhausted as though he had lead running through his veins.

'You OK?' Tom looked at his patient, noting his pallor, his seeming lack of energy.

'Yes, just got a bit of a chill, I think.'

Tom silently thought it looked a bit more than that. He took a sip of his coffee. 'Thought it was about time you came down to the surgery.'

'What for? What's the point?' To his horror, the despair sounded in his voice. He sat down and took a long draught of his coffee in order to recover his composure. He saw Tom undo his case and take out a stethoscope. 'Oh please…'

Tom waved aside his objections and spent some time listening to his chest. Eventually he put down his stethoscope. 'How do you *really* feel? Is the breathlessness getting worse?'

Gordon nodded.

'Fatigue?'

Gordon nodded again.

'Coughing up blood?'

'Yes.'

'And you still don't want any treatment?'

'No.' He was amazed his voice did not falter. Inside he wanted to yell - *yes, I want to be cured. I want you to save me. I don't want to die!* But all that came out was the curt *no*.

Tom nodded. 'I understand that but I want to give you some tablets to ease your breathing. I'll also give you some painkillers.' He wrote out a prescription. 'I really need to see you each week to monitor how you're doing.'

He handed Gordon the prescription. 'If I were you, I'd take a day off and stay in bed. You're doing really well, but there are going to be days when you just have to give in.' He put his hand briefly on Gordon's arm. 'Call me if you need me. Any time. Don't hesitate.'

Gordon nodded and saw him out. To his horror, Matt Gower was walking towards them down the path. It was getting worse and worse! Gower's face had a fixed smile fastened to it, which was only just hiding a great deal of annoyance. He passed the doctor and nodded an acknowledgement. Gordon saw the peeved look begin to disappear as he reached him.

'Morning, Mr. Sinclair. Not feeling too good?' He took in Gordon's attire and the presence of the local GP. He had played rugby with Tom Lander - a good, no-nonsense man. Sinclair must be quite sick to have requested a home visit.

Gordon sighed and let his visitor in. He had a mental image of Gower leaving and Alice or Maisie arriving. All he wanted was to go back to bed and seek oblivion.

He did not offer the agent a drink, as he did not think he would be staying long. Not when he heard what he was about to tell him.

He was right. He imagined that if he had not been in his dressing gown looking out of sorts, that Gower may have been sharper with him still. As it was, he left without being seen out and the front door had been closed barely short of a bang.

He locked the door behind his visitor and went slowly back upstairs, feeling as though he had been out of his bed for days. He slept for most of that day and rose at suppertime by which time he felt rested and much stronger. He heated up some soup and opened his post, a letter from his mother, two unsolicited mailings and a letter from his stockbroker confirming that all his shares had now been sold. He added a visit to the vicar to his list of tasks and deleted the estate agent. He needed to start distributing his income and the first stop would be to see about the stained glass window in the church.

He telephoned the vicarage first thing in the morning and caught the vicar having a late breakfast. When he indicated why he wanted a meeting, he was fitted in that morning. Gordon dressed and decided to drive to the church and then on to the chemist. He was aware of the need to conserve his energy and that he still had rather a lot to do. The wrapping up business was taking a lot longer than he would have thought possible.

He had asked to meet the Reverend Turnball at the church, as he wanted to see exactly what it was he was pledging. He arrived a few minutes early and sat on a bench to wait. He watched a man in his early forties dismounting from a racing bike and come towards him and it was not until then that he saw the man was wearing a dog collar. It looked incongruous with his corduroy trousers, but also practical. He took in the curly hair and the steady gaze and liked him immediately.

'Lawrence Turnball. You must be Gordon.' He held out his hand and Gordon shook it. 'Now I wish all my mornings could start with such positive news. Come and see the church.'

He led Gordon through the churchyard, chatting freely about repairs he was having done in the vicarage.

'Nightmarish old place, really. Would probably be cheaper to knock it down and rebuild, instead of trying to patch it up. Still, I think we're supposed to welcome draughts, it's a vicar's penance, I believe. Far be it for us to enjoy double-glazing and central heating!' He unlocked the church door.

'Is it always open?'

'Oh yes, we only lock it at night.'

'Isn't that unusual?'

'Around here it seems to be, unfortunately. It's a bit of an issue with me, I'm afraid. I believe a church is here as a place of refuge, of worship, of quiet contemplation and not as a museum.'

He beckoned Gordon through and gave him a whistle-stop tour of the church finally stopping in front of three, plain glass windows. 'And these are why we're here, I believe.'

He looked at Gordon and Gordon looked up at the arched windows and then around him at the old building, wrapped in a centuries old stillness. He found it hard to believe that he had never visited it before, never pushed open the old oak door and inhaled the mingled scents of this sacred place. He realised that Reverend Turnball was still awaiting an answer. He nodded. 'Tell me a little about what we need to do.' He saw Lawrence look at his watch.

'Oh look, if I'm keeping you.'

Reverend Turnball grinned. 'Not at all. I was just looking to see if the Jugs Head was open. Come on, let's do this over a pint.'

Gordon agreed readily, warming to the man totally. They walked to the nearest of the village pubs and sat outside. The Reverend Turnball sipped his beer, leaned back on his chair and sighed contentedly. 'This is the life. What I call a brief lull in the storm. No births, deaths, marriages or illnesses. So time for a beer.' They chatted idly for a while before getting back to the windows.

'We've done the groundwork. The Diocesan Advisory Committee and the Archdeacon have approved the replacement of the three lancet windows. We are now in the process of fund raising. I have ideas about a design, but nothing concrete, as this will need to be discussed with the congregation. Obviously, we need to get the final design approved.'

'So how much money are you looking for?'

The vicar leaned back in his chair and began to talk about the various costs. Gordon did some sums in his head and made up his mind. 'I'll give you a cheque for all three windows.'

The vicar grinned in delight. 'Well, that's marvellous. But why? I have to ask you out of sheer curiosity. You're not a churchgoer. In fact, I would hazard a guess that you've never ever been in the church until today. So why this generosity?'

For a moment, Gordon thought he would come clean with him and then in the same instant, changed his mind. 'I just feel I want to make a financial contribution to the village I've lived in for the last two decades and this seems like a good way to make it.'

Even to his ears, it sounded a bit lame, but the vicar just nodded. He watched Gordon write out a cheque for the amount specified and handed it over to him. Lawrence was still finding it difficult to come to terms with this gift out of the blue. He knew his Lord worked in wondrous ways, but this certainly was one of the most unexpected. He detected an underlying anxiety in the man opposite him, but could not put his finger on what it was about.

'Well I think this calls for another pint,' he heard Gordon say.

'Only a half for me. It wouldn't do for me to be tipsy in front of my parishioners. And I'll get them. It's the least I can do.'

He went to the bar and Gordon saw him chatting to a man on the way in. He wondered what it must be like to be in the role of father figure to the village, always having to be there at all times, to listen. Exhausting, he thought. He also thought how good this morning had felt. It had been the right decision. He was reflecting on this when Lawrence returned with the drinks.

'It makes me so mad. Just been talking to Ian Langley who used to work at the farm before he retired. You heard he was burgled?'

Gordon nodded as Maisie had told him when he had bumped into her that morning.

'He'd lost his wife, you know. He was actually at the funeral when it happened. He'd taken his savings out to

135

pay for the costs and of course, they've gone too.'

'Well surely he's insured?'

Lawrence shook his head. 'No, unfortunately not. Couldn't afford the premiums any more. Every penny went on Eva. Makes me mad. Anyway, let me not burden you with village issues. Now, we'll set up an open meeting with the congregation to discuss designs for the windows, probably after the service next week. Hope you'll be able to make that?'

Gordon shook his head. 'I must keep my part in this a secret. I don't want people to know that I donated the money.'

The vicar looked surprised. 'So I'm to talk about our mystery benefactor?'

'Well... Yes. My anonymity has to be the condition I give you the money.'

The Reverend Turnball nodded. 'OK, I'll get on to 'Light Designs' today to check that their artist can be available on that day and we'll get cracking. At least I can tell you how grateful we all are to you.' A woman was hovering near their table. 'Looks like my time's up.'

Gordon excused himself and left the vicar with the villager. He still had all the boxes to shift and so he went straight on to Delaby. Having off-loaded them, he called in to his solicitors and was surprised when Simon Cayser was able to see him. He had decided that the only safe way to distribute the money to the villagers was through his solicitor. He would be bound to secrecy and nobody would connect him with a solicitor thirty miles away. He gave Simon a list, which he read down with his eyebrows raised.

'There'll be more,' Gordon uttered, 'but I'd like to get those sorted out.'

'Well, this is all very unorthodox. Are you sure you want to do this?'

'Quite, quite sure.'

'But why don't you just give them the money yourself?'

Gordon thought of Alice and the teapot, Toby and the car. 'Because people are not very good at accepting things. Besides which, I hardly know some of these people. I just know that they need help and I'm in a position to do it.'

'And have you told people you're... umm...'

'Dying? No. Only one or two and I want it to stay that way.'

'May I ask why?' He had recovered from his earlier reticence.

'Because I don't want their pity, I don't want them to look at me differently or treat me differently. People don't know what to say or how to act around death. It embarrasses them. They struggle to find the right things to say. I'd hate it. Now there's something else as well.'

Gordon told him his plans for Rose Cottage and they discussed ways of making sure that Lydia did not have any taxes to pay. Gordon left, with the solicitor promising to draw up a Will as soon as possible.

He got back to Lowesdon to find Alice hard at work in the attic. She stood up from beside a box of kitchen equipment when she saw him in the attic doorway.

'Thought I'd press on a bit.'

'That's fine. I'll go and make us some tea.'

'What, you're not going to help?'

He turned back to her, his face etched with weariness and pain.

'No, no, I can see you're not. I'm sorry, I shouldn't have

said that.'

He suddenly crossed the space between them and gave her a strong hug. Flustered, she straightened her pinny.

'Well, whatever was that for?'

'Just because, Alice, just because.'

He left her clucking to herself.

He must have dozed off in the garden, because he woke slightly chilled, as the sun had dropped below the trees, giving the evening air an autumnal feel. Alice was no-where to be seen, but evidence of her hard work sat around the kitchen; boxes, their tops sealed with tape and labelled with a thick, black marker pen. Gordon looked at the handwriting and hoped she had not over-done it. The shakiness of the script brought it home to him, how she, too, was getting on. Not that he could ever see her giving up or getting ill. The thought made him smile wryly to himself. She rarely let her defences down and she must hate old age for that reason alone. He cut a thick slice of cake, which had been left on the table, washed it down with a mug of tea and a couple of the pills the doctor had prescribed him. His eating hab-its were getting worse and worse. He was not sure if he could be bothered to cook because he felt so weak or he felt so weak because he was not eating properly. He thought of his mother. She had always believed that you were what you ate. He visualised himself as one of Alice's fruitcakes and laughed.

Alice had worked until six and had then gone outside to find Gordon asleep on a bench, his jumper rolled up under his head as a pillow. She had stood and looked at him, wanting him to wake up, but not liking to disturb him. Now, sitting at home, she could see his face, sof-tened by sleep, but still with a greyish tinge. She was not sure she could cope with seeing him die and the fear of it was eating away at her insides. She wanted to tell someone, to share the burden, but knew that she could not break her promise to him. That, at least, was something she could do for him. She sat until darkness overtook her thoughts and then realising her face was wet reached, with exasperation. for the box of tissues on the side table. She snapped on the light and blew her nose loudly. *Silly old woman. Need to put the kettle on and have a strong brew.* She made her way into the kitchen, her slippers padding across the linoleum and made herself some tea. Then looking over her shoulder, as though someone might be watching her, she opened a cupboard door and surreptitiously poured in a strong slug of whisky.

Elsewhere in Lowesdon, Lydia was curled up on a chair in her living room, her fingers picking at the hole in the arm and widening it. Pounce stirred in his sleep and gave a small yelp. She absentmindedly poked him with a bare toe and continued to stare into space, her thoughts much the same as Alice's.

Eleanor put the last of her things in the car, locked her front door and began her journey.

CHAPTER SIXTEEN

She got to Lowesdon in the early hours of the morning, parked up on the common and slept under a rug for the rest of the night. She had felt an irrational fear last night, so strong, that it had sent her on her journey straight away, rather than waiting until morning. She had driven past her son's house last night and it had been in darkness. She had begun to feel a little foolish at her hasty flight, so she had a cup of tea from her thermos and then drove slowly to Rose Cottage.

Gordon was frying bacon and eggs whilst trying to read the paper at the same time. He sensed someone looking at him, turned and saw his mother looking over the stable door.

'Mum!'

'Better put some more bacon on.' She opened the lower half of the door and came into the kitchen, taking in every nuance of her son. 'Don't I get a hug, then.'

He had put down the spatula he was holding and held his arms out. They talked little over breakfast. It was only when Gordon went to help her bring her bags in that he knew.

'How long are you planning on staying?' He indicated the paraphernalia on the back seat. His mother looked uncomfortable and shrugged, not meeting his eyes.

'Oh, you know…'

'No, I don't know.' He could feel something inside him,

something uncontrollable and ugly. 'What you mean is, that you've come down to watch me die, haven't you.'

'No, don't be…'

'Well you can go again. Get in your car and go.'

She had never seen him like this, had never seen him so angry. He had slung the case back into the boot and slammed it, and was now holding open the driver's door of the car. She tried to put her hand on his arm, but he shook her off.

'Don't do this. Don't push me away.'

'Just get in the car and go home. I'm not a circus.'

'Oh Gordon.' She got into the car. He slammed the door and hurried round the corner of the cottage, out of sight. Eleanor sat, too stunned to move, her hands shaking on the wheel. She had never known him to be cruel before. She started the engine and pulling out of the drive, drove slowly down the lane until she came to the village green where she stopped. Facing her was a small hotel, sitting in its pretty grounds. She thought for a moment and then resolutely drove into their small car park.

Gordon dug until his vision blurred and his breathing was harsh and rapid, his spade hitting the patch of soil with a metallic thud. Finally, he had to stop. He hurled the spade across the lawn in frustration and anger, went in, poured himself a huge slug of whisky into a teacup and drank the lot. The effect was to completely take his breath away and he coughed and spluttered, his eyes running. It was at this moment that Lydia appeared. She thought he was choking, ran into the kitchen and thumped him on the back. He swore violently at her and pulled away.

'I told you to bloody go…'

Her features emerged from the blur and Lydia's face

took shape. He witnessed the hurt expression and knowing she would bolt, reached out and grabbed her arm.

'No! I didn't realise it was you. Don't go.'

He held onto her until he was sure his words had sunk in. Then he sank wearily onto the edge of the table. She watched him, taking in the whisky bottle, its top lying beside it. A suspicion crept into her head. Who was he talking about? Who had he thought she was? Surely he wasn't still seeing Penny Young?

He realised she was waiting for an explanation. 'I thought you were my mother.'

'Oh.' She felt absurdly relieved and then curious. 'But...'

'Please don't ask. Just come and walk round the garden with me.'

She did as he asked. He walked, deep in thought, stopping occasionally to deadhead something or smell a rose.

'Look, I really ought to start work.'

He realised it was Tuesday and that she was here to garden. Bitterness rose up in him again and he answered her icily. 'Oh yes, yes. Of course. Please don't let me hold you up.'

She had not come to see him at all. She was here because he paid her to be here. Stupid idiot that he was.

Lydia turned, unable to cope with the emotion she saw etched across his face. 'I'll get on, then.'

She left him standing there and presently he heard the sound of the mower down in the meadow. *Well, that's all right then,* he thought bitterly, *she was happy.* He kicked at a stone on the path and it scudded into the bushes. His anger was leaving him, draining from his body, leaving him feeling shaky and utterly miserable.

He needed to get out. He got his car keys, backed the old car out of the garage and just drove, trying to get away from the thoughts churning in his head. He stopped by a small lake and sat, gloomily, watching a boy and his father sailing a motor-controlled boat.

The boy had the controls and the boat crashed into the bank, to his cries of glee. His father took over the controls, a frown on his face. Gordon knew what it felt like to be like the boat. He felt his life was steaming along, totally out of his control, leading to the headlong smash into oblivion.

He started the car. It did not have to be like that. He could take control. He could end it now. Accelerate into a corner and just not stop. Just keep going until he hit something harder than the car. His foot hovered over the accelerator. He would have to be sure he would not hurt anyone in the process. It was to end his suffering, not cause anyone else any. So where? The beck came into his head. A stone bridge crossed it with quite a drop to the water below. More importantly, you could see the road winding down the hill towards the bend and the bridge. He would be able to see if anyone was coming in the opposite direction and it was only a few minutes' drive away.

He stopped in a field gateway about 200 metres away from the bridge. His hands were sweating on the steering wheel, his breathing shallow and his heart rate rapid as the adrenaline pumped into his system. He focused on the top of the hill, watching the road. There was one point that was out of sight. He would have to wait a few minutes to make sure nobody was coming. The tension in his shoulders was making his head ache. A minute had gone and no car had appeared. The road must be clear. He had not taken his eyes off the top of the hill. One more minute and then it would all be over.

CHAPTER SEVENTEEN

Lydia spent the last ten minutes of her day sorting out the tools. She had found a spade just left in the middle of the lawn and had replaced it on its hook in the tool shed. She had not seen Gordon all day and had alternated between being thankful and being uneasy. He had obviously taken the car out as she had checked the garage, but had left the house unlocked. She dithered about trying to leave it secure, but was not sure he had his keys. In the end, she decided to trust to luck and just pulled the stable door to behind her. She whistled for Pounce, who was nowhere to be seen. He appeared after a few minutes, looking sheepish and smelling appalling. He had obviously found something awful to roll in. She debated whether to hose him down and then decided she could not be bothered. Her car was so filthy anyway, it probably would not make any difference. She still had to drop off at the village store for some supper items and she was already feeling ravenous.

She parked outside the shop, grabbed Pounce's collar just as he was about to escape out of her car door and went inside. The proprietor, Madge Hardwick, was deep in conversation with a customer. She saw Lydia and pointed at her.

'Well I never. We were just talking about you.'

'Me?' Lydia tried, as much as possible, to stay out of village life. She hated tittle-tattle.

'Haven't you heard?'

Lydia shrugged, 'Heard what?'

'Peggy Wright's been left a fortune.'

So he had started. It had begun. 'Well, what's that to do with me?'

Madge beckoned her nearer, her voice dropping to a dramatic whisper although there was no one in earshot and even if there had been, Madge had probably told them.

'It's to be spent on her garden. The letter said so.'

Lydia realised she was expected to inveigle the information out of Madge bit by bit. Her stomach rumbled and she groaned inwardly. 'What letter?'

'It came from a posh solicitor in Delaby, along with a cheque for £6,000. The letter said that it had come from a well-wisher who wanted to remain anonymous, but that the whole sum should be put towards the upkeep of her garden.'

The other woman chipped in, 'Not sure I'd do that. I'd rather have a holiday, me.'

Madge pretended to look aghast, 'Yes, but she'll have to, won't she. I mean, with not knowing who gave it to her or anything. They could be keeping an eye on her to make sure she does as requested.'

'Yeah, but they're hardly likely to ask for the cheque back, are they? I'd spend some on the garden and still have a nice holiday.'

'You've no morals, Ivy.'

The two women had lost interest in Lydia and she filled her basket with a few items before putting it on the counter to pay.

'So looks as though you'll have a job. Peggy wants you to see to it.'

145

Lydia suddenly wanted to laugh. She bet Gordon had not predicted that outcome.

'Well, you don't look very pleased.'

'Oh yes. I am. I'm just tired. I expect she'll give me a ring. But if you see her, just tell her it's fine.' She handed over a note, collected her change and excused herself.

'Well, she's a cool one, that's for sure,' Ivy commented.

'It's the company she keeps,' Madge said darkly.

Despite Lydia's lack of interest in cars, even she could spot Gordon's, parked rather crookedly the other side of the village green. She shook her head. He was spending too long in the pub, in her opinion.

The Reverend Lawrence Turnball sat down opposite Gordon and put a cup of sweet tea with some Rescue Remedy on the table in front of him. He noticed that Gordon's hands were still shaking violently. He felt a little shaky himself, to be honest. He was used to dealing with crises, but the sight of Gordon, sobbing and running wildly across the village green had unnerved him. He had, quite simply, caught him in his arms and held him, shushing him like a child, while all the time Gordon had said, 'I couldn't do it to her', over and over again.

He glanced round the green, but it had been empty. Hopefully, nobody had noticed Gordon's headlong flight. Holding the man's arm, he had led him back to the Jag, had removed the car keys from the ignition, closed the door, which had been left open, and had locked it up. Then, still talking to him as he would a child, he had led him back to the vicarage. He had considered ringing Tom Lander, but had decided that he would deal with this himself. Gordon seemed to be calming down, although tears were still trickling down his face. He opened the bottle of Rescue Remedy.

'Open your mouth. I need to put this on your tongue.'

Gordon looked up.

'It's a herbal shock remedy. Nothing sinister. It will calm you down.'

Gordon meekly opened his mouth and took the remedy.

'Now have some of your tea. Then you can tell me all about it.'

Gordon looked at him directly for the first time. Lawrence breathed a sigh of relief. They would get through this, whatever it was. Gordon took a gulp of his tea and grimaced as the sweetness hit his senses. He realised that the vicar was looking at him. Waiting. He felt calmer, like the lull after a storm. Maybe it was something to do with that concoction he had been given. He took a deep breath and then released it. The Reverend Turnball had risen and had gone over to the window.

'Must get out and start dead heading. There never seems to be any time, though. You have a gardener, now, don't you?' He turned to look at Gordon, who nodded. 'Is she any good?'

The idea that anyone should ask that of Lydia made him want to smile. It occurred to him how he had just left her this morning. His behaviour had been unforgivable. An image of his mother came unbidden into his head and he groaned. This had the effect of the vicar sitting back down and fiddling with his fingernails as though he had dirt under them.

'Why don't you tell me what's happened to make you so unhappy?'

Gordon looked up at the man's face and thought, *Yes, I probably can tell you. You won't judge and you won't preach.* He took a deep breath, 'I'm dying,' he said quietly, 'and this morning I decided I wanted to die when *I* chose and not when fate or the illness chose.'

He looked directly at the Reverend, who looked back at him, his expression clear.

'Only I couldn't do it. I was going to run my car into Halliton Bridge at the bottom of Long Row. I sat in a lay by, waiting to make sure the road was clear, when I suddenly started to listen to the engine. It was so sweet, so perfect, that I simply couldn't do it. I couldn't destroy the car as well, she didn't deserve it.'

'So that was the 'her', Lawrence thought, *'not a woman at all! A car.'* He wanted to smile, but knew he must not. The Lord really did work in mysterious ways. He sat then, quite still, while Gordon told him the whole story, albeit haphazardly. He pieced all the episodes together and understood. Gordon finally sat silently, feeling as though a great weight had been lifted from his shoulders as he opened up and shared his innermost thoughts.

'So are you still going to keep it to yourself?'

'Yes, I am, for as long as I can. I feel as though I've come to terms with it today. I made a choice and I'll stick with it now. What I will do though, is to let my mother share it with me, and Lydia and Alice.'

'Good. I'm glad. And you know that I'm always here if you need another outlet.'

Gordon nodded. He got up. 'I'm going to go and ring my mother and try to make amends. He went to the front door, turning as he went out. 'Thank you from the bottom of my heart. And thank you for not trying to push your faith onto me. You're a very special man.' He gave a small bow, turned and went down the path, through the overgrown garden.

Lawrence watched him go and then quietly closed the door.

CHAPTER EIGHTEEN

Gordon walked slowly across the village green towards his car. He suddenly felt exhausted and getting into the Jag, rested his head for a moment against the seat. Then he started the engine and drove home.

The telephone rang and rang at his mother's. He pictured her sitting in the garden, giving her time to dislodge a cat from her lap and make her way indoors. But still it rang and after five minutes, he hung up. He felt panic rise in him again, but he refused to let it get the better of him. She was probably out at a friend's, discussing how impossible her son had become. He suddenly did not want to be on his own. On an impulse, he walked round to Maisie and Sid's. Sid was, as always, pottering in the garden. Maisie leaned out of the kitchen window as he appeared.

'Hello, stranger. Like a cup of tea?'

'He wants something stronger than tea,' a voice said behind him.

He was welcomed with open arms and he soaked up the company, the easy camaraderie. When Maisie offered him supper, he agreed readily. It struck him that he had never eaten a meal with his neighbours before. They acted as though his turning up on the doorstep and staying for hours was a regular occurrence and nothing to be remarked upon. He loved them both dearly, he thought, as he staggered home as the time approached midnight.

He tripped over a loose flagstone and giggled to himself. The stairs looked pretty difficult to climb, so he negotiated them on his hands and knees. He kicked off his shoes and crawled into bed fully clothed. He was asleep before his head hit the pillow.

Eleanor had spent the evening in the hotel.

Mike Collier, the hotel's owner, was very congenial company and he made her feel very relaxed and welcome. She had enjoyed her supper enormously and had taken her coffee out into the garden. There she had become engrossed in a conversation with a couple who were on holiday in the area. They were avid gardeners and the three of them were soon discussing gardens they had visited. They were arguing over Sissinghurst, when Mike appeared.

'Anything I can get you?'

They decided on a nightcap and Eleanor invited Mike to join them. This he did until he had to go and answer a query at Reception. Eleanor retired to her room. She threw open the windows and leaned out. The nights were still warm and she inhaled the dusty scents. She felt inexplicably content, despite the awful start to her day. She refused to dwell on Gordon, trusting it would sort itself out in due course. She, too, slept deeply.

Lydia lay on an old picnic rug in Crooked Holm Wood. She was trying not to move a muscle as the badger cub she had been watching snuffled closer and closer to her. She realised she was holding her breath and she let it out as slowly and as quietly as she could. Another cub appeared and the first one ambled over to greet it. They moved with surprising speed and agility, their strong snouts grubbing in the undergrowth. They went out of sight and Lydia rolled over onto her back and stretched her aching muscles. She must have been rock still for over fifteen minutes. She breathed a sigh of happiness. The evening had been pure bliss, really spiritual. However, she realised she was feeling chilled and decided to make a move. Besides, she had left Pounce an age ago and he would be anxious to be out, collecting his own night smells. She yawned, stood up and roughly folded the rug. A branch snapped behind her, but she felt quite at ease, although darkness was descending rapidly. She knew the wood like the back of her hand, knew its smells and its noises. She felt quite at home and unafraid. It took her ten minutes to reach the cottage, flanking the lawn in front of the Manor house, hoping that she would not disturb the dogs.

Pounce went into ecstasies when he saw her, spinning round and round and grinning ridiculously. She let him out and he bounded into the garden. She made herself a hot drink and sat on the doorstep, listening to Pounce's scrabblings. She wondered what it must be like to have his acute sense of smell and his hearing skills. When she was little, she always said that she would have rather been a dog. She thought wryly that if she had, she might have been treated better, although when her father went on one of his serious drinking bouts, he was liable to lay into anything. She forced her thoughts away, not wanting to bring up the tide of feelings which usually arose when thinking about her father. Pounce was coming towards her, his nose smelling the ground in front of him. She called him over, put her arms round him and fussed the top of his shaggy head.

'I love you, you daft dog.'

He pulled away from her, anxious to be out of her reach, half-afraid lest she shut him indoors again. She sat out with him until he pushed past her and went and lay down in the kitchen next to his food bowl. She closed the door and opened a tin of dog food, wrinkling her nose at the smell.

'Rather you than me.' She grabbed an apple and a lump of cheese, as it was too late to cook anything and besides, she could not be bothered. She would have a breakfast tomorrow at the Manor. For all his difficult ways, Lord P. believed in feeding his workforce hearty food. She started her day at 6 o'clock by making her way to the old kitchens where Mrs. Jessop dished up monumental plates of bacon, eggs, baked beans, sausages and fried bread, followed by huge white mugs of tea.

She went upstairs, brushed her teeth and collapsed into bed. Pounce settled down on her feet. Gordon's face appeared before hers as she was dropping off to sleep. It looked troubled and she turned restlessly.

CHAPTER NINETEEN

Gordon woke with a cracking headache. He got up and rummaged around in the kitchen for some head tablets. God, he had had a skinful last night. Despite his head, he felt perkier and he greeted Sid warmly when his head appeared over the kitchen door. He looked equally jaded.

'Tea?'

Sid nodded and then groaned. 'She wants me to dig out a couple of shrubs from one of the borders. No sympathy, that woman. I said I needed to check you got home all right.'

Both men roared with laughter at the possibility of Gordon not being able to negotiate his driveway.

'Mind you, I did find the stairs a bit tricky. Easier on all fours, by far.'

'Well you did better than me. I only got as far as the sofa. Then this morning, all loud noises and exasperated sighs. It's not as if I let my hair down very often. But that's women for you!'

They took their tea outside and whiled away an hour of the morning in the sunshine. Gordon's head slowly cleared and when Sid had gone he tried his mother's number again. Still no answer. A frisson of fear went through him. Supposing she had had an accident? He would try again later.

At about this time, Betty Delaney was hurrying to the village store, clutching an envelope. She rushed into the shop and was thankful that only Madge and Evelyn were behind the counter. Without a word, she put the envelope on the counter and indicated that they should open it. Madge did so, read the contents and then inspected the envelope, before handing it to Evelyn.

'Whatever am I to do?' Betty Delaney was wringing her hands.

'Get yourself a travel agent, by the look of it,' Evelyn replied.

'But I can't accept it, can I?'

Madge snorted. 'Why ever not? Don't look a gift horse in the mouth, Betty. Wish someone would give me some money.'

'Yes, but I don't know who it's from. And why me? I've never had this sort of cash before.'

'No, neither had Peggy Wright until this week. It seems as though we have a modern-day Robin Hood in our midst.'

'Yes, I heard from Ivy that she'd had a mystery cheque. What's she doing about it?'

'Spending it, I think. Mind you, she has decided to use it for exactly what it's been given for. She's asked that funny girl from the Manor to come and do her garden'.

'So she's not trying to give it back?'

'Now why on earth would she want to do that? I think she called the solicitor, but he refused to divulge any more information. Just told her it was from a well-wisher and to enjoy it.'

'Oh, I don't know. Where would I go?'

Madge sighed, 'That's half the fun of going away, looking through brochures and trying to decide where to go.'

Evelyn chipped in, 'Why don't you ring Saga? They do a lot of holidays for the over 50s and I understand they look after you.'

'I could go and visit my sister in Bournemouth, I suppose.'

'I hardly think that's in the spirit of things, Betty. It's hardly going to cost you £1,000, is it?'

They coaxed her into catching the next bus into Delaby and going round the travel agents. They watched her walking slowly to the bus stop, looking as if she had the weight of the world on her shoulders.

'Well, if I had that in the post, I'd be skipping all the way to the travel agents,' grumbled Madge. 'Some people are so ungrateful.'

The money was the sole topic of conversation for the rest of the afternoon and everyone had an opinion. When Maisie came in late afternoon, they questioned her on it.

'Well I can add to your story. I've just been doing my stint for Meals on Wheels and old Ian Langley also received a cheque in the post.'

She had their full attention.

'And?' Madge prompted.

'It's for £3,000 and is to cover the funeral expenses, plus 'beer money', it said.'

'Well I'll be damned,' Madge said, and sat down. 'Who'll be next, I wonder?'

Gordon tried his mother's number several times during the day, but each time, the phone rang and rang. He knew he had the number of her next door neighbour, somewhere. She had given it to him in case of an emergency, but he could not remember where he had put it. He spent a good hour searching and eventually found it at the back of one of the unsorted kitchen drawers. 'I *must get on and finish these,*' he chided himself. A woman answered the phone on the third ring. He pictured a tall, aristocratic woman with grey hair cut with a severity, that only someone of her stature could get away with.

'I thought your mother was with you, dear. I'm feeding Bumble and Billy until she gets back. She said she could be some weeks, but I don't mind looking after them. Gives me something to do.'

Gordon could not match up the image he had of her, with the idea of her ever being lonely. He imagined a stalwart of the local Conservative Party, doing a stint in a charity shop and probably being on the church cleaning and flower rota. He made some excuse saying he expected his mother had been held up somewhere, thanked her and hung up. So where on earth was she?

He would never have guessed. Eleanor had actually spent the day with Mike Collier, the hotel proprietor.

She had been breakfasting in the hotel conservatory when Mike struck up a conversation with her, enquiring as to how she had slept. He was dressed in a pair of casual trousers and a shirt. He let on that it was his day off and that he was going to visit his brother in a nearby village. Eleanor knew it was the location of the garden the couple had been raving about the previous evening and without thinking, she asked Mike if she could cadge a lift. He agreed readily, saying he would be glad of the company.

They chatted easily in the car and she discovered that he was a widower of some ten years. He had bought the hotel with his brother, who was a sleeping partner, leaving Mike to do the day-to-day running of the place.

He dropped her off at the entrance to the estate and would not hear of her getting public transport back. He picked her up at 4:00 and then proceeded to give her a tour of the local beauty spots, which included walking up to a deserted priory on the top of a hill.

On the way home, he pulled into a restaurant car park and suggested that they had dinner. Eleanor was enchanted by the location. The restaurant had been converted from an old mill and was situated by the edge of a lake. A terrace overhung the water's edge; containers with a profusion of plants tumbled over the side and were reflected in the surface of the water. Tables were laid in the huge conservatory, each one with several candles flickering on it. It drew her, but she saw dinner as a complication she did not want. He felt her hesitation.

'We can get back if you'd rather. It's just I don't usually have the opportunity of eating here.'

He had said the right thing. He had stepped back and had given her the opportunity to end the day. She realised, suddenly, that she wanted to dine here, to have this experience. It had been a long, long time since a man had taken her out.

'No, I'd like to.'

He held his hand out, indicating that she was to go inside where they were met by a waiter, who saw them to a table by a window.

The surroundings and the meal were faultless. Mike was easy, understanding company, a fine raconteur. She found herself laughing out loud several times.

She visited the ladies and inspected her flushed face in the mirror and knew that she had drunk too much. This was all new territory for her and she suddenly did not feel comfortable. She wanted to be on her own, in her room. She felt very tired and far too old to be bothered with all this. As she walked back to the table, she saw Mike stifle a yawn.

'Sorry.'

'It's OK. I'm feeling absolutely shattered myself. Missed out on my afternoon snooze.'

'We'd better get back, then.'

He got the bill and paid it, not heeding her desire to pay her way. The journey back to Lowesdon was made in near silence, the easy conversation had dried up. Eleanor thought how difficult it was to spend a long time in someone else's company when she was so used to just her own.

Mike pulled into the car park and she got out of the car quickly, ignoring the ache in her back. She looked at him across the car roof.

'Thank you for a lovely time. I hope you don't mind if I retire straight away. I'm rather in need of my beauty sleep.'

'Don't you want a night-cap first?' He looked disappointed.

'No, thank you. I really am all in. I'll see you in the morning.' She turned and made her way across to the hotel entrance, knowing that he was standing watching her. She thought she had probably been horribly rude, but the need to be in her own space was suddenly overwhelming. She reached her room, opened the door and sighed with relief. She threw open the window and went and got ready for bed. She was just brushing her long hair when there was a knock at her door. She felt her heart thud. The knock came again. She pulled her dressing gown around her and opened it a crack.

'Room service.'

'But I haven't ordered anything.'

'Mr. Collier's sent you a brandy with his compliments.'

She felt herself blushing and thought how ridiculously

she was behaving. She opened the door, took the glass from the tray and took the drink back to bed with her.

CHAPTER TWENTY

Twice more Gordon tried his mother's number before his first visitor announced themselves. He opened the front door to find the Reverend Turnball waiting. He invited him in.

'How are you, Gordon?' his visitor enquired.

He looked directly at him and sat himself on a chair and waited. He was not just asking out of politeness, he really wanted to know. Gordon told him about the disappearance of his mother.

'I feel so guilty. I said such awful things to her. I'm scared I might die and not make it up with her. I mean, where can she have gone?'

'I can't answer that, but she'll show up in her own good time. You probably did hurt her, but your relationship seems strong enough to weather a small blip like this. Besides, I would have thought it was highly unlikely you were going to die that quickly.'

Gordon liked the way this man spoke so honestly. 'I don't know how long I've got. Everyone's so vague. I don't know whether I'm going to get worse slowly or just drop dead one day.'

'Why don't you talk to Tom Lander again. It seems as though you could do with asking a few questions. They may not be able to answer them specifically, but they must be able to hypothesise a little.'

'I don't mind going to see him,' Gordon agreed. 'He

seems to respect your wishes. I'm scared stiff that if I set foot in the hospital again, I'll never see the light of day again.'

'A lot of people feel like that, but of course it's not true.'

'I think it's very hard to be heard, to have a say and a choice in what treatment you do or don't want.'

'And you don't want to try anything?'

Gordon shook his head. 'As long as I have time to tie up my affairs, then that's all I want.'

'Well, that's what I've come about. We had the meeting last night with the stained glass artist and we've thrashed out a possible window design.'

He laid three pieces of paper on the kitchen table. Gordon looked at the photocopied drawing while the vicar talked him through the significance of the designs.

'And the roses?' Gordon pointed to the Briar Rose trailing around the edge of the design.

'My idea. I know you wanted to remain anonymous, but I wanted something of our benefactor in the window. I suggested it as it is our national symbol and it fitted in with our countryside theme of 'All Creatures Great and Small.'

Gordon nodded. 'I think they'll look wonderful.'

Lawrence put a colour acetate sheet over one of the photocopies. 'Just to give you an idea of the colours.'

'Looks good. So what happens next?'

'Our artist will do a life-size mock-up on paper and bring it back for us to view and alter if we wish. Then it's on with the actual glasswork.'

Gordon absentmindedly traced the briar rose outline. Then he stood up abruptly and went over to look out of the kitchen window, his hands in his pockets. 'This is when it's bloody hard. I won't see the finished windows and I find I really mind.'

'I guess that's the same for all of us - there will always be something we didn't get to see - or do - or say.'

'But at least most people don't know that. People who die of heart attacks, or in their sleep, or in car accidents.'

'Yes, but neither do they get the chance to tie up all their loose ends like you're being able to do.'

Gordon was silent. Then he turned and smiled. 'Not sure which is best, really.'

He suddenly wanted the vicar to go. He wanted to ring his solicitor about the Will. He needed to get on. Lawrence, as if sensing his mood, gathered up the designs.

'Must dash. Got a wedding this afternoon. Perhaps we can visit the artist as she's working. I'm sure she'd keep a confidence.'

Gordon nodded. 'Yes, I'd like that. A good compromise. Thank you.'

Lawrence smiled and left the room, letting himself out of the house.

Gordon watched him pause as he walked down the garden path to smell a rose. He inhaled deeply and then Gordon saw him sigh. He looked suddenly troubled and knew it was on his account. On an impulse, he called after him, 'Lawrence!'

The vicar looked back. Gordon was suddenly aware that perhaps he should not have called him by his first name. 'I just wanted to say 'thank you' for putting the roses in the window.'

The vicar held his hand up in acknowledgement.

'It means a lot to me.'

He could suddenly feel himself near to tears. He took a deep breath and waited until the vicar had gone from sight, before slowly letting it out. Not now. Not here.

There were things he wanted to do, to get done. He felt a sudden urgency.

He picked up the telephone and called Simon Cayser, his solicitor. He was put through to his secretary who explained that he was with a client. Gordon made an appointment to see him later that day and asked that she made sure he had the Will ready. The woman tutted and said she was not sure it was possible, but he ignored her and disconnected. *'Solicitors! They need a bomb up their backsides!'* he thought.

Next on the agenda was to go over to the Thomas' garage. He wanted to sort out the Jag. He would have a word with Sandy and then if he thought it was OK, he would go ahead with his plan to give the car to Toby. It really mattered to him that it went to a good home. It wasn't just a car, it was a friend and one he had lavished hours and hours on.

He jumped out of his skin as a shaggy head leapt up at his back door.

'Get that bloody dog down, it's scratching my paintwork,' he bawled. Lydia's head appeared next to Pounce's.

'Is it safe to come in or are you in a vile mood again?'

He looked taken aback. 'What do you mean? Vile mood. When have I ever been vile to you?'

She snorted and unlatched the door letting Pounce race round the kitchen, almost bent in half with ecstasy.

'I don't know why he's always so pleased to see you, seeing as you're always so nasty to him.'

Gordon rubbed the delighted dog's scruffy head and braced himself as the dog leapt up and put his paws on Gordon's chest, frantically trying to reach his face to lick it.

'Pounce! Get down!' Lydia pulled his collar, yanking the dog away. Gordon brushed his jumper down.

'I think his enthusiasm's probably got something to do with the meadow and the rabbit warren,' he ventured.

'Well, I only come for the swing,' Lydia retorted and helped herself to a piece of cake from the tin. Gordon watched her. She caught his stare and stopped, hand halfway to her mouth. 'Is it OK?' She had blushed with embarrassment.

'Of course.'

'I just…'

She did not finish her sentence, but bit into the cake. He secretly loved the way she was in his house. Never on ceremony, just herself. He suddenly felt a wave of contentment at the thought of her being here, padding around the kitchen in her bare feet with the dog asleep by the range, his paws twitching as he dreamed. It was so comforting.

'It's not your day, is it?'

'No, no. I just wanted to know how you were.'

He felt ridiculously pleased. Pleased that she had come just to see him. He thought of the last time she was here and the day's events and shivered. As if to echo his thoughts, she added, 'You seemed strange the last time I was here. On edge.' She fiddled with the dog's collar and he realised this was difficult for her. 'You scared me.'

She met his eyes. He leant towards her.

'What do you mean? I don't understand.'

She did not answer, her eyes lowered. She chewed the edge of her thumbnail.

'Lydia?'

She sighed. 'You've made me care about you. Somehow. I guess it's because you seem to care about me. It doesn't matter how I am, you don't change. I don't want to care about you because you're not going to be here for long. I don't want to watch you die, but I also can't turn away. And it scares the hell out of me.'

She glanced at him from under her lashes. He knew he had to handle this right. 'Well, I don't have any options about the dying bit, Lydia.'

She flushed slightly. 'I didn't…'

'But you do. I'm not asking you to stick around. If you don't want to continue to do the garden, then don't. But if you are around, then all you can be is honest. As you already have been. I can't give you any answers, as I don't know them myself. And that scares the hell out of me.'

She got up and walked to the window. 'I must be really selfish to say what I've just said.'

'No, not at all, I value your honesty. I also value you being here. You're…' he searched for a word, '…different. I know where I am with you. I find you far more comforting than someone who dishes out tea and sympathy.'

She had recovered her composure and slid onto the worktop, her legs dangling over the side. The dog had slumped under the table.

'How about Alice? How is she about it?'

Gordon thought for a moment. 'Alice is trying to pretend it's not really happening. Oh she's helping me sort everything out, but we mustn't mention why.'

She nodded, strangely happy with his answer. 'And your mother?'

He fell silent, thoughts and emotions churning inside him. 'I think it would be fair to say that I'm the one not coping there.' He briefly and hesitantly told her of his mother's unexpected arrival.

An image came into Lydia's head of seeing a woman in the hotel grounds while she had been walking to the shop. She had only seen a photo of Mrs. Sinclair, but the resemblance between the photo and the hotel guest had been remarkable.

'I think I know where your mother is,' she offered.

'What do you mean?' Gordon had stood up.

'I'm not sure, but I think she's staying at Thatchers. I'm sure it was her I saw in the garden.'

It suddenly all made sense to him. Her absence from home, her stubbornness. It would be typical of her to do such a thing. He grabbed his car keys, gave Lydia a big hug and drove to the hotel. Lydia sat and shook her head. Then she smiled and gave Pounce a hug.

CHAPTER TWENTY-ONE

Gordon swung into the car park of Thatchers. He immediately spotted his mother's car parked next to a BMW. He turned off the engine, sat for a moment and took several deep breaths. Whatever was he going to say to her? He could feel his heart beat quicker as his adrenaline increased. His hands felt cold and sweaty and he wiped them on his trouser fronts. A movement by the gate to the garden caught his eye. It was his mother, dressed in a summer frock and wearing a straw hat, despite a distinct autumnal chill in the air. She was walking towards her car. He bent his fingernail back in his haste to open his own car door and swore.

'Mum!'

She looked up at her son crossing the car park, his feet crunching on the gravel.

'Hello, Gordon.'

She did not seem surprised to see him, but just stood, her key in her hand and waited. Up close, he noticed how brown she was - weathered he would call it.

'I've been trying to reach you for days. I've been ringing and ringing.' He sounded peeved, even to his own ears.

'I imagine you have.'

He felt a surge of irritation. She did not even look pleased to see him, merely as if he had interrupted her in something.

'Look, I'm sorry about what I said to you.' There, it was out. The apology seemed to hang in the air between them. Still she stood and said nothing.

'I didn't mean to hurt you or push you away.'

'Oh, I think you meant to do precisely that.'

God, this was hard, he thought, *bloody woman is incorrigible.*

'So why have you come now? What do you want?' She slammed the boot down and turned to look at him properly. It was his turn to be silent. 'Yes, it's as I thought. You don't know.' She walked round the side of her car, opened the door and got in.

'What are you doing?' He rounded the car and pulled the door out of her reach.

'Going to Wilbury Gardens. Now please will you shut the door.'

He had never known her so cold. Was she really punishing him? His own mother? Her voice softened.

'Gordon, I'm not going anywhere. If you really need me, you know where I am.'

And with that, she reached out and pulled the car door to. Astounded, he watched her start up, reverse and saw her stiff little wave as she drove out of the car park. This was not how it was meant to be. He had visualised them embracing, his mother shedding tears of relief and her moving in to his spare room.

A man looked over the wall at him. 'Can I help? Are you booking in?'

'Er, no. Sorry,' was all Gordon could mumble before getting in his car and driving back home.

Lydia was weeding the border under the kitchen window, taking out some of the summer bedding, which had gone past its best. She stopped and straightened her back, wiping her forehead and leaving a smear of dirt on it.

'You were quick. Wasn't she there?' She sensed his disquiet, 'What's happened?'

She came towards him and touched his arm. He noticed her dirt-encrusted fingernails and had this absurd thought that he hoped she never made pastry. He started to smile in spite of himself.

'Gordon!' she was waiting. He went into the kitchen, calling to her.

'I need a drink. Do you want one?'

'No, I never drink in the day. Too much to do.' She had followed him in. She watched him knock back a whisky and then another. 'Should you be?'

'Oh please don't start lecturing me.' He realised he had snapped at her and was instantly sorry. 'I didn't mean that, I'm just a bit wound up.'

'I can see.'

He took a deep breath. 'She was at the hotel. In fact, she was just going out to some garden. She didn't seem in the least bit pleased to see me.' He related the events.

'I think she's just giving you what you wanted. What you asked for.'

'What do you mean?'

'You told her, in no uncertain terms, that you didn't want her here to watch you die. Why would she suddenly think you'd changed your mind?'

'But why is she here in the village. Why didn't she go home?'

Lydia though for a moment. 'I guess in case you do change your mind.'

'Are women always so complicated?' He smiled at her.

'Oh yes, always.' She glanced at the kitchen clock. 'I

170

have to go to Mrs. Wright this afternoon. Did I tell you she gave me the job of gardener?'

Gordon shook his head. 'While we're on the subject of that, I sent cheques to the people on our list, but I also sent one to the school and also one to Tom Hinds. I heard his car packed up last week.'

'Well, it was virtually tied together with bits of string.'

'Exactly. Well he needs it for his old mum, living right out in Lower Beech Cottage.'

'So you've bought him a new car?'

'Well, yes. I was going to actually buy one myself and have it delivered, but I thought I'd take away half the fun if I did that.'

Lydia went out of the back door. 'For a grumpy old sod, you're very thoughtful.'

The ringing of the telephone stopped him replying and he went to answer it. It was his solicitor. He had forgotten all about his appointment.

'The Will's ready to be signed. I suggest as soon as you can.'

Gordon arranged to go over in the morning and hung up, having given his apologies.

Alice was due again later in the afternoon and between them they finally cleared the attic. Gordon carried the last box down that evening. Once again, his car boot was full. It was slightly obscene, he thought, to have accumulated so much unwanted stuff. After much pressing, Alice had gone home with a few more pieces of blue and white china that they had found in a box.

He sat watching the news, turning the volume down if he heard a car approaching the cottage. By 10 o'clock, he was certain his mother wasn't going to come. He went to bed, knowing he would have to try to make amends.

CHAPTER TWENTY-TWO

Lydia locked Pounce in the house. He had followed her into the hall, his ears pricked when he had seen her pick up her car keys. 'No boy, go and lie down,' she had said and he had slunk back into the kitchen, ears down, tail between his legs. Until she had had him, she had no idea a dog could sulk so much and no idea that he could also make her feel so guilty. However, she was going to put another two hours into Mrs. Wright's garden. It had become so out of control over the summer that for a few weeks it was going to need longer than the allocated three hours a week. Mrs. Wright had thought long and hard as the solicitor's letter had stipulated three hours a week and she had become almost superstitious about deviating from it. But Lydia had convinced her that if the donor really cared about her garden, as he or she obviously did, then they would see the sense in what she was suggesting. Also, Lydia added, they could always reduce the hours in the winter. Balance it up that way.

Twice last time, someone had stopped to look over the garden gate at what Lydia was doing. And twice it had set Mrs. Wright into a session of handwringing. 'Do you think that was him or her?' she would ask. In the end, Lydia had asked if it mattered.

'I just want to be seen to be doing as they wanted, that's all.'

'Yes, but the money was given to you to spend on your

garden as you please. It's still your garden.' She had not realised the money would cause so much anxiety.

These thoughts were pushed aside when she drew up outside Mrs. Wright's house and was met by two people, a man and a woman. Her employer was nowhere to be seen.

'Are you Lydia Page?'

She nodded and closed the car door.

'The gardener?'

She nodded again.

'We'd like to talk to you about the money left to Mrs. Wright. Have you any idea who might have done such a thing?'

She knew now who they were and instantly felt her guard come up. She shook her head. 'No, I'm sorry, I have no idea.' She went to walk past them, but the woman stood in her way, right in front of the gate.

'You realise other villagers have also received cheques and someone has donated a large sum of money to replace the church windows?'

Lydia said nothing, simply stood and waited.

'Do any of these people have anything in common?'

Again, she was silent.

'Lydia, we're prepared to offer quite a substantial reward for any lead on this. We're very anxious to find our Robin Hood.'

She looked up then, straight into the eyes of the woman. 'Why?'

'It's a wonderful story, but people don't just give away large sums of money like that. Not without a reason.'

'Well, I'm sorry, but I was simply asked by Mrs. Wright to come in and tackle her garden. Now if you'll excuse me...'

She physically pushed past the woman and went into the garden, opening up the shed and selected a fork. 'Those people…'

As she left the shed, she heard the whirr of a camera motor and looked up to see the man taking photos of her. She advanced on him with her fork. She must have looked extremely menacing, because he hurriedly closed the gate behind him and they walked off down the road.

When they had gone, she heard the front door open and saw Mrs. Wright coming down the path.

'Thank goodness they've gone!' She looked really pale and flustered.

'Are you OK, Mrs. Wright?'

'Oh yes, dear. They were just a bit persistent. Got to stick their noses in something, haven't they?'

Lydia nodded and carried on with her digging. She had not foreseen this complication and she would hazard a guess that Gordon had not either.

Gordon decided to go to the solicitors before trying to see his mother again. This was something he knew he could achieve. Simon Cayser leant back in his chair when Gordon had sat down, the documents in a tidy pile in front of him. He seemed to want to chat, asking Gordon about the reaction of the people he had given money to. Finally, he got to the Will.

'Are you sure this is what you want to do?'

'Of course. Why wouldn't I?'

'Well, I thought your original idea of selling up and distributing the money was odd, but giving your house to someone you hardly know seems rather rash to me.'

Gordon had a mental image of Pounce in the kitchen, on his back, with his paws against the range. 'Look, I've got rather a lot on, so if we could get on with it.'

Simon sighed and pushing the documents over to Gordon, proceeded to explain them. Within minutes, Gordon had signed and dated them all.

He then chatted with Simon for a few minutes about two other beneficiaries he wanted to include for what he called his 'Robin Hood' game. As he left and walked down the wide concrete steps onto the pavement, he felt he had achieved a lot that morning.

He called in to the Henty Arms for a pint. Without the karaoke, it was a different pub. Dick Loverage, the landlord, greeted him like an old friend. He came round to Gordon's side of the bar with a half and sat down.

'Done any more singing, lately?'

'Only in the bath! 'Bout all my voice's good for.'

Dick nodded out of the window at the Jag. 'Got your lot coming here next Friday. We're your 'Pub of the Month'. Quite an honour.'

'No, it's just that we have to choose pubs with large car parks.'

Dick laughed, 'Oh thanks, and there was me thinking it was for the fine beer and warm atmosphere. Lovely old car, though.' He had walked to the window. 'Looking forward to seeing the car park full of Jaguars. Should be a good night.'

He wandered back over, collecting a couple of glasses on his way. 'Talking of good nights - I don't suppose you know who could have sent Sarah Carter a cheque for £3,000?'

So this was where the conversation was leading. Gordon shrugged, 'No idea, wasn't there a name on the cheque?'

'Only a solicitors from Delaby.'

'What a mystery. Mind, she must have had several anonymous donations.'

'Yes, but none as large as that. It's given them enough now to fly out to the specialist limb unit in America and get the ball rolling.'

'I'm so glad,' Gordon felt quite emotional. 'Send her and her father my best wishes when you see them.'

Dick nodded, 'Will do. And just in case you do hear who gave them the money, pass onto him their huge thanks.'

'Or her,' Gordon said.

Dick shook his head, went back behind the bar and topped Gordon's glass up, waving away his money. He though he had better order a sandwich and ate that before driving to Thatchers, but to his annoyance, his mother's car was not in the car park.

He spent the rest of the day doing minor repairs around the house. He was clearing out a drain when Lydia arrived.

'Ugh.'

He smiled at her and removed his rubber gloves. 'To what do I owe this pleasure?'

She had sat down on his bench. He was starting to feel a little cold and suggested that they went indoors.

Lydia thought he looked pale and she noticed a tremor in his hands. She suddenly felt inexplicably afraid and curling her knees up under her chin, hugged them tight to her chest. He sat down beside her.

'Lydia, what is it?'

She shook her head, 'Nothing. I just came to tell you that the press has been sniffing around today.'

'What?' He sounded alarmed.

She had his full attention and told him about the earlier episode. 'They've been around to everyone, poking and prying. Including the vicarage. They've also got word of the new windows.'

Gordon sighed, 'I suppose we should have expected something like that. I never thought...' he trailed off.

'No, neither did I.'

'Well they won't find out anything. The trail will stop stone dead at Simon Cayser's.'

'You're sure he won't say anything?'

'Simon? No. More than his job's worth. No. We're quite safe.'

He did not feel so sure the next morning when the local paper dropped onto his doormat. Emblazoned across the front page was the headline, *Who is Robin Hood?* He went on to read that the paper was offering a reward for information leading to the identity of the unknown donor. A reward! Whatever next? The story continued on the next page and included a picture of Lydia emerging from a shed, clutching a fork. He smiled, cut it out and stuck it onto one of his kitchen cupboards. He guessed she would be furious and chuckled to himself.

He managed to spend an hour in the garden, dead heading and cutting back. He had to leave anything that required more exertion to Lydia. There was a real autumnal feel to the air this morning. He went and sat on a seat with a mid-morning coffee, feeling exhausted.

It was here that his mother found him. She stood and looked at her son, asleep on the bench, noticing his pallor. She felt a terror she had never experienced before and she had to take several slow breaths or she knew she would become hopelessly emotional. This should not be happening. It should be her dying, not her son. She had read somewhere that losing a child was the worst thing that could happen. She felt it was against the natural order of things, but knew that this was not strictly true, that it happened to people everywhere. But why to her? Her only child.

Gordon opened his eyes and saw her standing there, a look of anguish on her face. 'Mum?'

She could not speak, but sat down beside him and put her arms around him. She rocked him like a baby, noticing that he was cold from sitting. She could not stop her tears anymore, but she felt him weeping too. She sniffed and fumbled for a hanky. She always kept one up her sleeve. It had always amused her husband when she took her jumper off, because a tissue always flew out onto the floor. He had claimed he was forever picking them up after her and why on earth couldn't she use a proper handkerchief. 'Probably,' Eleanor had said, 'because he wouldn't be able to afford to replace them.'

She wiped her eyes and blew her nose. 'Cup of tea?'

This suddenly made her want to laugh. In a crisis, no matter how dire, there was always the offer of a cup of tea. It was the great British comforter. He nodded, trying to compose himself. She patted his hand and went inside, pouring herself a glass of water and drinking it, trying to stop the tears that still threatened to overcome her.

Gordon had not appeared by the time the tea had brewed, so she took it outside. She had suddenly felt the need for something sweet and had helped herself to a piece of cake from the tin. Obviously, Alice was still very much in evidence. But when she came to eat it, it stuck in her throat and she left it on the side. She handed Gordon his cup and he drank it almost immediately, warming his hands on the hot mug.

'You feel cold. Why don't you go inside?'

He shook his head, 'Are you staying?'

'Do you want me to?'

'Yes.'

She felt a wave of relief sweep over her. 'Then I'll go and get my things later on.'

She started to tell him about her stay at Thatchers and her day with Mike Collier. She wanted to lighten the moment, get them away from this heavy sadness. It seemed to work and later, when she went back to the hotel, she had left Gordon chatting to Sid, who had called in to borrow something. She had checked out of the hotel without seeing Mike. She had tended to avoid him as much as was possible after that day and an awkwardness had developed between them. The trouble was, she liked him, but getting to know someone right now was not high on her list of priorities. She breathed a sigh of relief when she drove her car out of the car park and headed for Rose Cottage.

When she arrived, Gordon was cooking lunch and the colour seemed to have returned to his face.

It was after lunch when they were both sitting reading that Lydia appeared. She saw the woman sitting in the chair and grabbed Pounce, who was doing his best to wash Gordon. She felt a darkness within her. Felt the change.

Gordon saw the scowl appear on her face and got up. 'Lydia, what a nice surprise. This is my mother, Eleanor.'

Eleanor looked at the young woman, saw her face and thought, *she doesn't want me here.*

Lydia shook the outstretched hand and then pulled Pounce into the hall and back to the kitchen. Gordon followed her.

'Want a drink?'

She shook her head. She had got to the back door when he stopped her.

'Hey, what's up? What had you come to tell me?'

'It doesn't matter.'

'Oh, yes it does. It does to me.'

He let go of her arm and waited. She was like a sulky child, he thought.

'I just wanted to make sure you'd seen the papers.'

'Oh yes, I've seen them. And I see we have a new superstar in the village.'

She looked up then and followed his eyes where they rested on the photo of her, which he had pinned on the cupboard door.

'Oh you! It's an awful picture.'

'I thought it was rather true to form. Scowling with a fork in her hand.'

Lydia grinned. She hated being teased, but from Gordon, it was different. She went and looked at the photo up close.

'Could be very bad for business - a gardener with such attitude.'

'Actually, it's been very good. I've had two more phone calls already this morning offering me work.'

'You're joking!'

She shook her head, 'Actually, I'm not.'

'Well, I suppose people are desperate these days...'

'Bastard.'

They both laughed.

'Don't you let my mother hear you say that.' He regretted saying it immediately as the mention of his mother caused the frown to appear. 'So are you going to accept the work?'

'Yes, if I can fit it in.'

'Well, I think you should enjoy your moment of fame.'

'I was thinking of going for the reward, actually.'

'Lydia!'

She laughed, called the dog and was gone with a wave of her hand. Gordon went back to his chair and resumed his reading.

'Funny girl.'

He looked up. 'What makes you say that?'

'Got a very unfortunate attitude. Does she always just let herself in like that?'

He did not need this and wanted to get his mother off the subject as quickly as possible. 'Yes. But it's fine by me.'

'Seems a bit strange. Hope she's trustworthy?'

He went back to his paper, leaving her question unanswered.

The word appeared in his head again as he was trying to get to sleep. *Trustworthy.* He knew with a certainty that he trusted Lydia absolutely.

CHAPTER TWENTY-THREE

It was strange having his mother there. Over the next week, he had begun to get used to it, but felt as though she was always watching him. Also, he had not set eyes on Lydia. She had telephoned to say that she would not be able to garden that week as she had a dentist's appointment. The press had run one more story on *Robin Hood*, but the reward was still there. Simon Cayser had sent off two more cheques, but as yet, there was no mention of these. Obviously, the recipients had decided to keep quiet about them.

He had taken Eleanor to the Jaguar BBQ at the Henty Arms and had run into Malcolm Potter, Sarah's father. It had been a good evening, but Gordon knew that he would have to sort out the ownership of the Jaguar soon. He could not keep putting it off. He knew that he could sell it if he needed to. In fact, the landlord had questioned him as to the cost of keeping such a car.

It was now Tuesday again and approaching the time Lydia should appear. His mother had gone to see another garden, but this time it was with Maisie.

Lydia had sat at the end of the road in her car. She had not been sure what she was going to do, until to her relief, she saw Mrs. Sinclair pull out of the drive and head away from the village. She pulled into the drive and Gordon came to meet her. He was absurdly pleased to see her.

'You've just missed mother. She's gone to Crackerly Gardens with Maisie.'

'Oh has she?' Lydia answered with as much innocence as she could muster. 'Gone all day?'

He grinned, 'Oh yes, you're quite safe.'

He impulsively put his arm around Lydia's shoulders and hugged her. She reddened, but did not look displeased.

'What do you want me to do today?'

The morning passed quickly, with Lydia working deftly. He thought how much she knew about plants. He had not a quarter of her knowledge when he was her age. He was glad his beloved garden was going to be left in her capable hands. He pottered while she worked, taking her out a coffee halfway through the morning. He told her about the further two cheques which the solicitors had issued and she nodded her approval.

'And what about the house? Is the sale nearly through?'

It was the question he most dreaded. He hated lying to her, but it was the only way. 'Actually, I've changed my mind about selling.'

'Why? Whatever for?'

He wanted to blurt out the truth, but knew he must not. He knew she would not accept. 'I decided I wanted to carry on living here for as long as possible. I wanted that stability, if nothing else.'

As he spoke the words, he suddenly knew them to be true. She was biting her bottom lip. He could tell she was annoyed and knew he had to intercept her. 'Lydia, I'm not asking you to understand, but just to accept it.'

She said nothing, but stood up and walked off down the garden path

She appeared in the kitchen at the end of the afternoon. 'So all that choosing of charities was for nothing. You've just turned your back on them all?' The accusation was flung at him. He could feel his temper rising.

'I've still got enough money to give to one of the charities. In fact, my solicitor sent a cheque off to 'Water Aid' this morning.'

'I thought you were a man of principle!'

'And just what is that supposed to mean?'

'I thought you were going out on a limb, doing something I thought you cared about.'

'Oh, and giving to the church, the school, various villagers, isn't doing that?' He realised he was shouting at her. She stood facing him, her hands on her hips. 'Anyway, I can damn well do what I like. It's my house, and if I choose to die in it, then I shall do just that.'

'Am I interrupting something?'

They both jumped. Eleanor walked into the kitchen and Lydia took one look at her and fled. Gordon flung open the cupboard door, grabbed the bottle of whisky and poured himself a large glass. He held out the bottle to his mother.

'No thank you. I'd rather have a cup of tea. It is only 5 o'clock.'

With a gesture of fury, he snatched up the bottle, plonked it on the table and walked out of the kitchen.

Well, thought Eleanor, *perhaps I should have stayed here.*

Lydia drove home, hot tears running unchecked down her face. In her agitation, she had forgotten Pounce and had to reverse back down the road to where the dog was anxiously waiting by Gordon's gate, his tail between his legs. This made her even more furious with herself and she drove like a wild thing.

184

Gordon spent the evening in low spirits. His mother chatted on about the garden she and Maisie had been to, but he barely listened. The argument with Lydia had been so unexpected, and it had really upset him. He felt his chest get progressively tighter and by nine o'clock had excused himself and gone to bed.

Sleep eluded him for hours as the thoughts in his head churned round and round. He fell into an exhausted sleep in the early hours of the morning and did not wake until after eleven.

CHAPTER TWENTY-FOUR

Penny Young sat in the Jug's Head, reading the article in the local paper about the person they had dubbed *Robin Hood*. As she read the story, a tall, fair-haired man in his mid forties sat down on the chair opposite her.

'Interesting story?'

She looked up and smiled.

'Sorry I'm late Pen; got caught up in the traffic. Drink?'

She nodded. 'Usual, please.'

She watched Mark go to the bar. Shame he was not more her type physically. She preferred dark to fair. But he would do. And he was loaded. He rejoined her.

'Anything of interest in there?'

He nodded at the paper and she handed it across to him. He read the article intently.

'Funny, that.'

'What?'

'I saw one of your old clients coming out of the solicitors they've mentioned in the paper.'

He had her attention back again.

'Which client?' She took the paper and scanned it for the solicitor's name.

'The chap who mucked you around so much over the cottage and then took off with your assistant.'

'Gordon Sinclair?'

'Is that his name?'

'And you saw him coming out of the same solicitors?'

'Absolutely sure it was him. Got into an old Jag. Anyway, probably a complete coincidence.'

'But why would someone travel so far to a solicitors when there's a perfectly good one in the village?'

Mark shrugged and took a long drink of his beer. He was getting bored with the conversation. 'Come on, Pen, loads of people travel miles to their solicitors. Some keep the same one all their lives, no matter how much they travel around. Now, what about a spot of lunch.' He eyed her cleavage. 'Unless, of course, we go back to your place.'

Penny was re-reading the article again, her mind a whirr. 'No. Lunch here would be good.'

Mark sighed and went and fetched a menu. *Bloody women, always so unpredictable.* He could have done with an afternoon of sex, but obviously her mind was on other things.

Gordon had got up, but had gone back to bed shortly afterwards, his whole body felt lethargic and he did not seem to have the energy to deal with it.

Eleanor sat downstairs, a book in front of her. She had been trying to read the last page for about an hour, but just could not concentrate. She had made them both some vegetable soup for lunch, working easily in Gordon's kitchen, but food had felt as though it would choke her. She felt completely tense and knotted up.

Mid afternoon and she put her book down. There was not a sound from upstairs. On an impulse, she went into the hall and flicked through the Yellow Pages, looking for a reflexologist in the area. She found one who lived about ten miles away, but when she spoke to the woman, she found that she actually worked one day a week at Thatchers. Delighted, she managed to book a session in for the morning. She never liked to drive far after a session, as it made her feel a little lightheaded where she had relaxed so much. It was just what she needed and if she could get Gordon there too at some stage, she would.

She looked in on him later. He smiled wanly at her.

'Fussing around again.'

'Just brought you up a cup of tea, that's all.'

He sat up and she saw how difficult it was for him to breathe. She went back downstairs and after a few moments dithering, picked up the phone and called the surgery.

Tom Lander arrived within the hour. Eleanor showed him upstairs and he examined his patient.

'It's all a lot of fuss over nothing. I just overdid it.'

Tom took off his stethoscope. 'I'm afraid it's a bit more serious than that. You've got some fluid on your left lung. It's what's making it hard for you to breathe and causing your lack of energy.'

'So you can give me something for it?'

Tom Lander shook his head. 'It needs draining. You'll need to go in.'

'No.'

'Look, you really don't have a choice. I'll call an ambulance.'

'No, Tom, please.'

There was such despair in Gordon's voice that the doctor stopped, his mobile phone in his hand.

'Please. Not an ambulance. Please, it's important.'

'It's all due to this secrecy about him being ill.'

Neither of them had heard Eleanor come into the room.

'It would hardly do for an ambulance, complete with sirens, to come charging through the village, would it? It

188

would be all round within minutes.'

'Well then, you'll have to get him there, but it needs to be now. I'd take you myself only I've other calls to make.'

It was early evening before they reached St. Moorcrofts. All the way, Gordon had repeated, *I'm not staying. They can't make me.*

She had glanced at her son sitting beside her, his winter coat wrapped round him, despite the warmth of the car. He looked shrunken. She wanted to get him into hospital, into what she saw as a place of safety, where he would be looked after. She had never liked hospitals, had always done her best to avoid them, hating the smells and the sounds, the polished floors and the closed doors. But this was different. This was her son.

Shortly after he was admitted, a houseman saw him and she realised that she would just be in the way. She waggled her fingers at him, blew him a kiss and left, trying not to see the look of desperation in his eyes. She slept little that night and phoned the ward in the morning, to be told that he had had treatment and was insisting on returning home.

She wondered how she was going to cope, but knew that she had to. She had never had to watch anyone die before. Her husband, Giles, had just dropped dead one morning after surgery. He had left that morning as robust as ever and the next moment, he had been lying in the undertakers. There had been no lengthy in-between. No watching him slowly deteriorate. Friends had said it was a blessing when people died suddenly, but she had not been sure. She did not know what she felt even when her husband's lover had turned up at the funeral. Watching him weeping as they stood by the graveside had sickened her, but also caused her to invite him back to the house afterwards. He had looked startled when she had spoken to him and did not take up the invitation.

She had only seen him once after that, many years later, walking down the High Street, chatting animatedly to a much younger man, his own youthful good looks faded into middle age.

She bustled around, getting herself ready and left for the hospital where Gordon was waiting for her. He looked brighter, but a new weakness seemed to have settled itself in his movements. She felt her eyes fill with tears and turned away so that he would not see them. She had to get a grip on herself. She tried to talk him into having her reflexology appointment, but he would not hear of it, so she left him wandering down to the meadow and the swing. She noticed he still had his coat tightly wrapped around him.

It was after her reflexology that she bumped into Mike Collier.

'Eleanor! What ever are you doing here? I thought you'd long gone.' He was holding her at arms' length, looking at her and she flushed a deep red.

'No. I decided to stay on in the village.'

'Oh?'

'Look, I really must go. I'll...I'll catch up with you later.' Her words sounded hollow, even to her. She hurried past him, got into her car and drove off, not even glancing in his direction. The relaxation she had experienced during her treatment had gone. She felt tired and tense and knew she was close to tears. She suddenly wanted to be in her own home, with her two cats and her familiar things.

When she got back, Gordon was in the office, writing a letter.

'Shouldn't you be in bed?'

He turned round at the sound of her voice. 'I'm fine. I need to get these done.'

'Suit yourself.' She shrugged and went into the kitchen. He appeared after a few minutes.

'What's wrong?'

She busied herself at the sink, washing up her breakfast things.

'There's a perfectly good dishwasher, you know.'

'Oh, there's only a couple of bits and bobs. Won't take me a moment.'

He shook his head. 'Stubborn old woman.'

There was still a sharpness to her voice when they were having supper. He questioned her again.

'Oh, I'm just missing home and the cats. It's all so terribly silly. And selfish.'

'Not at all.' He thought for a moment. 'Why don't you go and get them and bring them down here?'

She just stared at him, mulling over the possibility. 'Well, I could...I suppose it would save my neighbour the chore of looking after them.'

'Good. Go and get them in the morning.' He silenced her, as she was about to interrupt. 'I'll be fine. Just go. No arguments.'

She left early in the morning, promising to be back as soon as she could. Gordon spent the morning writing letters and then drove himself in to see Simon Cayser. He had decided not to tackle Toby about the car, but to leave it to him in his Will. He suddenly felt that his time was running out. His last stop was to a jewellers in one of the back streets of Delaby.

His mother arrived back two days later, complete with the two cats. She had also brought her saxophone.

191

'That's good. Does that mean you're going to start playing again? I'd love to hear you!'

She shook her head and he knew better than to press the point. She propped the instrument up against the bookcase in the sitting room.

'It just makes me feel better, having it around.'

The cats settled in fairly well and by the fourth day, were desperate to get outside and explore. They went out nervously, sniffing out their new territory, ready to run back to the house at the slightest noise. Gordon, who had not heard from Lydia, knew it would be a good excuse to ring her. She sounded defensive when she heard who it was.

'Just wanted to let you know that my mother's brought her two cats to stay and so you may need to keep Pounce on a lead until they all get used to each other.'

He was matter-of-fact, as though they had never quarrelled. He made it sound as though he expected her in as usual in the morning.

Lydia arrived a little earlier than normal. She had left Pounce at home. She walked around the corner of Rose Cottage and bumped into Eleanor Sinclair. The two women eyed each other warily. Lydia broke the silence, scuffing the toes of her sandals in the gravel as she spoke.

'It's my gardening morning. Gordon...Mr. Sinclair is expecting me.'

Eleanor put her hands on her hips. 'You know he was rushed into hospital after your row last week.'

Lydia looked at her then, her face a mass of confusion. 'I...I'm sorry.' She did not know what to say in the face of the older woman's open hostility.

'I don't know what you said to him, but it mustn't happen again. Just make sure you concentrate on the garden. After all, that's the only reason you're here.'

To her horror, Lydia could feel tears welling up inside her and pouring down her face. Gordon's voice, full of concern, made them both start.

'Lydia, whatever's the matter?'

She was sobbing now, wiping her arm across her eyes, sniffing loudly.

'I was just reminding her why she was here and warning her not to upset you again.'

'How could you?'

The coldness in his voice startled her.

'I just thought...'

'Mother, just go away. I'd like to talk to Lydia.' He glared at her and she turned without a word and went into the house.

'I'm...sorry. I didn't mean to make you ill.'

He wanted to put his arms around her and hold her, but could not. Instead, he handed her his handkerchief. She wiped her eyes and blew her nose loudly.

'She had no right to say that to you. You're not to blame for what happened. It's just the illness taking its course.'

'But you shouldn't be under stress. That makes it worse.'

'So stop crying and come and help me decide where to put these new roses. They arrived yesterday and we need to get them in.'

He walked off, hoping she would follow him. He felt her behind him and soon they were involved in a discussion about the new arrivals. Eventually, they decided where to put them.

Gordon touched Lydia's arm. 'I'm going to leave you to it - I'm whacked.'

She immediately looked concerned.

'Please don't look like that. I've enjoyed this morning,

but it's time to let the real expert crack on.'

Lydia snorted.

'Cup of tea or coffee?'

She nodded, 'Coffee'd be great.'

'As good as done.'

He wandered back up the path, stopping to stroke Billy who rolled over onto his back with delight.

His mother was nowhere to be seen. He glanced out the hall window and saw that her car had gone. He refused to worry about it. He took the coffee out to Lydia, cursing as hot liquid spilt over the rim onto his fingers. She accepted it gratefully. Billy had found his way down the garden and was making use of the newly dug soil. Gordon laughed as Lydia cursed the cat. He had turned to go back when Lydia stopped him.

'Gordon. I'm really sorry for the things I said. I was really out of order.'

He knew what the apology had cost her. 'Apology accepted.' He started to move away.

'Gordon?'

He walked back to her. 'What is it?'

'I want to share something with you. Can you meet me at my house at about 7 o'clock?'

'This sounds very mysterious.'

'It's not. It's just something I want you to see.'

'And I'm not allowed to know what it is?'

'That would spoil the surprise.'

He nodded, acquiescing. 'Seven o'clock it is, then.'

His mother came back after Lydia had left and he felt it was no coincidence. She put a bag of shopping on the table.

'I thought I'd cook for us tonight.'

'I'm sorry, but I'm not going to be here.'

'Oh?'

'I'm going to see Lydia.'

'Oh Gordon, do you think it's wise?'

'Mother, I'm only going to be out a short while. It's all completely innocent.'

Her *huh!* was loaded with meaning, but he refused to be drawn, leaving promptly at ten-to-seven. Pounce greeted him with wild enthusiasm, but Lydia shoved him back into the house. She handed Gordon an old jacket.

'What's that for?'

'You'll need to be warm.'

And without another word, she disappeared across the lawns, heading towards the woods. He caught up with her, short of breath.

'You might need to go a bit slower.'

She was immediately contrite. ' I'm so sorry. I didn't think.'

'No, and that's what I like about you. You treat me normally and not as if I was about to break.'

She looked at him, 'Well maybe that's how we should be treating you.' And with that, she headed off again, but moderating her pace. At the entrance to the woods she turned, 'We need to keep as quiet as possible now. No talking at all.'

'*Where on earth is this strange young woman taking me?*' he thought. After about ten minutes she left the path, took a rucksack off her back and laid a rug on the ground.

'What…'

She put her finger to her lips and motioned him to sit down. He did as she requested. It was nearly dark, but his eyes had become accustomed to the lack of light. He felt her hand tap his arm and looked where she was pointing. He watched in utter amazement as a badger appeared from a hole, almost hidden under the tree roots. He was absolutely riveted as two smaller badgers ambled after their parent. One of them clipped the other with a paw and they rolled and tumbled together, making strange play noises. A further badger appeared and headed off in the same direction, snuffling through the undergrowth. A bat swooped just over Gordon's head and he gasped. The badger stiffened, listening. They froze, holding their breath until he relaxed and continued his foraging. Eventually, he went out of sight, although they could still hear his movements.

Lydia put her mouth to his ear, 'Do you want to stay until they return?'

He nodded, raising his thumbs. He would not miss this for the world.

They moved one-and-a-half hours later. Gordon was glad of the old, but warm coat that Lydia had loaned him. She seemed to respect his need for silence on the way back. He was reluctant to break the spell the badgers seem to have created within him. They crossed the grass in front of the manor and reached her gate. She hesitated, seeming to weigh something up. Still he had not spoken. The walk had warmed him up slightly, but he still felt shivery.

'Do you want a coffee?'

He nodded, 'I'd love one.'

Pounce was whining and scrabbling at the front door. She opened it and he shot out, circling them and barking. When he realised they were going indoors, he trotted off round the side of the house.

Gordon held the cup of coffee in his hands, warming them. They sat in her tiny kitchen and talked about the badgers. Pounce had reappeared by now and was lying by Lydia's feet. She absentmindedly scratched his stomach with her toe. His back leg twitched whenever she hit a point of ecstasy.

'Can I ask you something?'

He looked up at her, 'Of course.'

She hesitated.

'Go on, spit it out.'

'Well, have you thought about your funeral?'

He was dumbfounded, a mixture of emotions battling with each other.

'I'm sorry. I shouldn't have asked. It just seems so important.'

'Important?'

She sighed, 'Look, it doesn't matter.'

'Oh no, it does. I want to know why you asked. I must admit, I haven't even considered it. I guess it's fear. If I discuss my own funeral, it means I'm going to die.'

There was a silence.

'Well, aren't you?'

'God, she could be direct!' he thought. He was not sure that he could handle the way the conversation was going. The magic of the evening had gone.

He stood up, 'Lydia, I need to go to my bed as I feel shattered. I can't tell you how privileged I feel at having been able to watch the badgers. I'm really glad you took me there. Thank you.'

She stood up, her eyes showing a mixture of emotions. 'I'm glad you enjoyed it,' was all she said.

He let himself out and stood for a moment in the chill night air, before getting in his car and driving home. He refused to think about the question she had asked. He blocked it out when it threatened to come into his consciousness.

Penny Young rolled as far away from Mark's snoring as she could. Eventually, she shoved him in the back. 'Shut up, for goodness' sake.' He snorted and his breathing quietened. She turned on her side and sighed, mulling over the evening. As usual, he had drunk too much and sex had been quick and unfulfilling. She had also had to pay for the meal as Mark had left his credit cards at home, by mistake. She did not mind, but it was the second time in a week it had happened. Their relationship was a disaster. As all her relationships were. She chose the wrong sort of man every time. Except for Gordon Sinclair. He had been different. She had seen him that evening turning in through the gates of the Manor. He was obviously going to see that little slut. She had no idea what he saw in her. She felt a tug of jealousy. She needed to decide what to do with the information Mark had inadvertently given her the other day. It had baffled her why, if it was him, he should be giving away such large amounts of money. She needed to try and find out a bit more. She could do with the reward as she had a ball coming up and she really needed a new dress. She would do a bit of asking around in the morning, see what she could unearth.

She began in the village shop. It took a while to get Madge to talk, but she guessed it was because she usually kept her distance from her. She found out no more than she could have gleaned from the newspaper. After listening to Madge embellishing all the stories, she wished she had not bothered. No. She would go straight to the horse's mouth. She would make an appointment

198

and go and see the solicitor in Delaby. She was sure she could inveigle some information out of him.

She managed to get an appointment the same afternoon, which suited her as Lydia's replacement was in the office. She would make a pretext about wanting to write her Will. She guessed it would cost her, but thought, on balance, it was probably worth it.

Unbeknown to her, she missed seeing Gordon leaving the solicitors by only a matter of minutes. He treated himself to a pint at the Henty Arms and spent a pleasant half-hour chatting to the landlord about cars. He had signed the codicil to the Will and all was now in place. But no matter how hard he tried, he could not block Lydia's question from his mind. He slowed as he reached the Manor gates and then, with a sigh, turned into them. As he drove up the driveway, he saw Lydia walking across the grounds from the direction of the new rose garden. She saw him and stopped and waved. He pulled up beside her.

'Want to come and have a look? We've got the water feature working.'

'I'll just park up.'

Lydia waited for him and they made their way through one of the arches in the yew hedge where Lord P. was standing, looking at the water feature. He greeted Gordon warmly.

'Isn't this bloody marvellous?'

Gordon had to admit it was. The whole garden was totally transformed, and although all the planting was in its infancy, he could visualise what it would look like when it established and matured.

'And just come and smell this - it's simply divine.'

He led Gordon to a side bed and bent down to smell one of the roses.

'Just like cloves and honey.'

Gordon inhaled the intoxicating scent and then surveyed the rest of the garden. 'You must be delighted with it.'

'Oh I am. I bless the day I employed her.' He smiled at Lydia, who blushed and scraped her boot on the path edging. 'Even if she can be a real vixen and as stubborn as hell. But I guess you must have found that out by now. Eh?' His attention was caught by his wife waving her hand at him from the doorway. 'Got to dash. Must be time for me to get ready to go out. She never trusts me to remember. Treats me like a five-year-old.' He guffawed, gave Gordon a hearty slap on the back, winked at Lydia and left.

Gordon laughed. 'He's right, though.'

'About what?'

'The garden is a real credit to you. Well done.' He sat down on a bench. She sat beside him. 'Not sure about the vixen, though…'

He stopped and laughed as she scowled at him. His expression suddenly became serious. 'What did you mean last night? About the funeral?'

'Look, I'm sorry I said anything. It was none of my business.'

'I disagree. I want to make it your business.'

She looked at him warily.

'You've been here for me through so much of the last few months, that I can't shut you out over this. And you obviously think it's important. I'd like to know why.'

She was silent, picking at the skin round her fingernails. A bee hummed in the background and a blackbird started to sing in one of the trees. Suddenly she stood up.

'It's getting cold. Let's go back to the house.'

Without another word, she got up and walked off, not waiting to see if he was going to follow her. By the time he had caught up, she was in the kitchen, feeding the dog. She pulled two lagers from the fridge and handed him one.

'My grandmother's funeral was awful. It seemed to have nothing whatsoever to do with her and I hated every moment of it.'

She pulled the ring on the can and took a mouthful of lager. He thought she was going to continue, but she started to put away the pile of crockery on the draining board.

'Lydia, you asked me a question last night, which I've found impossible to ignore. It's not something I felt able to think about, but now I think I can. But I need your help and your thoughts.'

She turned round then. 'When I saw her after she'd died, she didn't look or smell like my Gran. They'd fluffed up her hair and put make-up on her face. I wanted to kiss her just one more time, but they'd destroyed her.' Tears were trickling down her cheeks. She took another swig of her lager.

'And then it was as though we were on a roller coaster. Which coffin did we want? Which lining? Which handles? What hymns did we want, did we want flowers or donations, when should the notice go in the paper. And all the time I thought, '*This is not how she would have wanted it.*' But I didn't know how to stop it. I didn't know what other options there were. But I knew this wasn't right. I just knew.' She was crying openly now, grabbing

201

up her sleeve for a tissue.

'I'm so sorry. I didn't mean to upset you.'

She shook her head and blew her nose. 'You haven't. It's just brought back the helplessness I felt.' She looked at him directly. 'I don't want to feel that with you. I want you to have a good death. An appropriate funeral. So that if you were up there watching, you'd nod and say, *yes, that just about sums me up, sums my life up.*'

He stood up and put his arms around her and held her while she sobbed into his chest. He stroked her hair until he felt the tension go out of her, felt her start to draw away.

'Have you got anything in for supper?'

She looked at him blankly, red-eyed and then shook her head.

'Then I suggest we go and have a pub meal. Then you can tell me what my options are.'

He could not believe how calmly he was taking all this. But he did feel calm. And relieved. At this moment, he felt that there was nothing he could not face.

Simon Cayser double-locked the outside door, having made sure he had set the alarm. He headed down the steps, anxious to get to his car and get home. What a day! He reflected on his appointment with Penny Young. *Crafty bitch!* Still, she had not got the better of him. He knew as soon as she mentioned Gordon Sinclair and how he had recommended her to come to him that she was lying. He had already got rid of a reporter earlier in the week. He suddenly decided that he would charge her for the appointment, even if he was not about to draw up her Will.

Penny saw that Mrs. Wright was in her garden. She deliberately parked her car around the corner and sauntered along the road, stopping to smell one of the roses poking over the wall of Mrs. Wright's garden.

'Lovely evening.'

Mrs. Wright looked up. She was clipping back a fuchsia and wanted to get it done before dark.

''Tis, at that.' She carried on with her pruning.

'I must say, your garden's looking very good. That anonymous donation must have been very welcome.'

Mrs. Wright sighed and straightened up. She had never taken to this young woman. Bit too hoity-toity for her liking.

'Do you have an idea who might have given the money to you?'

'Nope. None at all.' And with that, she turned, put her secateurs on the bench and went inside. She waited until the woman had gone by before venturing out again.

'Evening, Mrs. Wright. Garden's looking good.'

'Evening, vicar. Yes, it's grand, isn't it? Mind you, I don't get much work done without someone stopping me for a chat.'

'Oh, sorry. Who else, besides myself has been bothering you?'

She laughed, 'Only that woman from the estate agents. Wanted to know if I knew who'd given me the money.'

'Oh did she? Well I expect she's not the only one in the village who'd like to be party to that information.'

'Well, I wish I knew. I'd really like to thank them.'

'I expect they're getting thanks enough by seeing the order growing out of chaos. The gardener's working wonders.'

'Young Lydia. She's a marvel. Took me up to the Manor

yesterday to show me the new garden she's working on. Took my breath away. And she's only a slip of a thing. Needs feeding up, I shouldn't wonder.'

Lawrence Turnball agreed, exchanged a few more pleasantries and went on his way with Mrs. Wright's words resting uneasily in his head.

He stopped off for a pint and saw Gordon and Lydia sitting in a corner. Lydia was talking animatedly, Gordon almost studying her, so great was his concentration. They were still there when he left and even he wondered at their obvious closeness.

Gordon dropped Lydia at the cottage and drove home, his mind full of thoughts. He was pleased when he saw that his mother had gone to bed. He sat at the kitchen table with a brandy in his hand and mulled over the evening. He yawned, glanced at his watch and saw it was a quarter to one. Bed, he thought, and put his glass in the sink.

CHAPTER TWENTY-FIVE

He awoke late. He could hear his mother in the kitchen and he lay and listened to the familiar sounds, the slight clunk the cold water pipe made when you turned the tap off, the click of the kettle. It was the thought of a cup of tea that made him move.

He pulled on some clothes and went downstairs. His mother was sitting at the kitchen table, a cup of tea and a half-eaten slice of toast beside her. She looked up from the paper and looked at him. He hated the way she scrutinised him like this.

'Tea?'

'I'll get it.'

He busied himself and sensed she was not concentrating on her newspaper. There seemed to be a tangible atmosphere in the kitchen this morning. He took his cup and went outside and stood on the patio, inhaling the air. He shivered, wishing he had put on a jumper, but not wanting to go inside again to get one. His tea steamed in the chilly air and he warmed his hands around the mug, looking at his garden. Lydia had done a good job. She worked very much as he would and had not imposed herself on it in any way. He wondered what she would do when it was hers and felt a small frisson of jealousy at the thought. His garden was going to be the hardest thing to give up; it was what he had put the most into. He felt that his very essence was here. He fingered an ornamental grass, its long leaves glistening with dew.

He sensed his mother behind him and turned to see her leaning on the bottom of the stable door.

'You were late last night.'

She said it as a question. He suddenly felt as though the years had been stripped away and he was a teenager being interrogated after a date.

'I needed to sort something out.'

'Oh?'

He turned. 'Why are you so interested? I do have a life, you know.' As he said it, he heard how harsh his words sounded.

'Were you with her?'

'Which 'her' do you mean?'

'The girl who gardens for you.'

He knew she had deliberately used the word 'girl' rather than woman. It was thrown down like a gauntlet.

'If you mean Lydia, then yes, I was.'

'You're old enough to be her father.'

'Oh for goodness' sake, not you too. I went out for a drink with her. We had things to discuss.'

'What on earth could you want to discuss with her?'

She had gone too far. His voice, when he answered, was sharp. 'Well, whatever it was has absolutely nothing to do with you.'

She stared at him for a moment longer, challenging him, before turning and going inside. He deliberately spent the rest of the morning in the garden, pretending to work. His chest hurt this morning and he felt breathless whenever he did the slightest exertion.

When he went in for lunch, his mother was nowhere to be seen. He went up to her room, but her clothes were still there. He had wondered for a moment if she had gone and he was not sure how he would have felt if she had. He made a couple of phone-calls and in the afternoon, set off in his car.

It was late afternoon when he returned home to find his mother's car in the drive. She was busy cooking when he went into the kitchen.

'Steak and kidney pie for supper.'

He knew this was a peace offering as it was one of his favourites. 'Sounds great, do I have time to do some work in my study?'

She nodded and he went through into his near-empty room.

She called him about an hour later. It had not taken him long to put together what he wanted to do. Satisfied, he put all the information into a larger envelope and sealed it, writing his mother's name on the front. Nothing more was said about the morning's disagreement and after watching an old episode of Frost, his mother excused herself and went up to bed.

Lydia arrived early the next morning. Gordon heard her digging while he was getting dressed. He suddenly hoped his mother was still in bed as he wanted to talk to Lydia on her own. '*This is ridiculous,*' he thought as he caught himself avoiding the stair that creaked, '*it's my own house and I'm slinking around like a fugitive.*' He quietly made two cups of coffee, one ear always listening for sounds from above. He took these outside and without saying a word, indicated to Lydia to follow him. She dug her spade into the soil and left it, wiping her hands on her thighs. She looked bemused, but followed his retreating form down to the meadow. Once more, he turned and handed her a mug.

'Bit cloak and dagger, isn't it?'

'I wanted to tell you about yesterday without feeling my mother was watching me. She's having trouble understanding our friendship.'

'No, I can see I'm not what she would have in mind for you. Shame you didn't keep up with Penny Young.'

Gordon grimaced, 'Not my type, really. Too brittle.'

Lydia grinned, 'But still good mother material.'

Eleanor was standing at her bedroom window, looking out. She had seen them walking down the path towards the meadow. They were out of sight now and she could only guess at why he had felt compelled to take her down there. She sighed. It really was none of her business, but she just did not take to the girl. If she really had to judge, she would have said, quite truthfully, that their relationship was most likely platonic, but it still disturbed her.

Later, when they were alone together, Gordon reading in a chair and she doing her tapestry, she asked him about the house sale. A mixture of emotions crossed his face. He seemed to be weighing up his answer.

'The sale's fallen through.'

'What? Then whatever are you going to do?'

'Do?' he paused, thinking. Then he got up and momentarily put his hands on his mother's shoulders. 'Trust me, it's all looked after. It'll all be OK.' He left the room and went back to his study, where he spent a long time re-checking papers.

Penny Young lay next to Mark, her hands behind her head, her eyes wide open, staring into the darkness. Her investigations as to the anonymous donor had got her nowhere. People all had theories, but all seemed to be unsubstantiated. Not one person had mentioned Gordon Sinclair. She knew she could go to the paper with her hunch, but she really wanted more evidence. She wanted to be sure. Somebody must know something. Mark stirred and flung his arm across her stomach. She pushed it away, angrily and turned her back on him.

Lydia dreamt of a woodland where the trees had arms and legs. As she and Eleanor carried Gordon's coffin through the forest, they turned and bowed. Then, the largest tree, an ancient oak, lifted one of its roots, revealing a cavern beneath. Candles fluttered in the recesses of the hole and they carefully lowered the coffin down, whereupon the root snapped back into place, hiding it from sight.

Eleanor tossed and turned restlessly, unable to sleep until, eventually, she flung her bedclothes back and got up, padding down to the kitchen to make herself a cup of tea. She really craved an Ovaltine and suddenly wished she was home. She sat down on the rocker and Billy jumped onto her lap, as if sensing her need for company. She stroked his ears and he purred loudly. Bumble was asleep beside the Aga and twitched her paw in her sleep. Thus, she sat for ages, her mind full of thoughts. She did not want it to be like this with her son. She knew time was running out and she felt that she was wasting it with her petty squabbles. Did it really matter now if he enjoyed Lydia Page's company? He always seemed to be more animated when he was with her, more alive. Maybe she was good for him. She did not need to like the girl as she did not have to spend any time with her. She really was being ridiculous. She took off her glasses and rubbed her eyes. She would try to put it all right tomorrow. She picked Billy up and put him on the floor where he sat, the end of his tail twitching slightly in annoyance.

'Silly boy,' she said and rubbed his back as she went past him to bed.

CHAPTER TWENTY-SIX

Gordon woke to see his mother putting a cup of tea on his bedside table. He smiled at her sleepily and she ruffled his hair.

Whatever was that all about, he wondered.

By the time he had gone downstairs, she had cooked him breakfast.

'Do you want to do something today?'

He looked up, still chewing. 'Do? What do you mean?'

'We could go somewhere together. Visit a garden? Have a pub lunch, perhaps?'

'Yes, that would be nice,' he agreed. 'I'm going to visit the glassmakers this morning with the vicar, but I can certainly meet you for lunch. The Jugs? At midday?'

She nodded and smiled. He was making this very easy for her and she was glad.

He set off, as planned, picking Lawrence up en route. He became so absorbed in the work in progress, that he realised he was going to be late for lunch. He also needed to go home first as he had forgotten his wallet and he did not think it was very conducive to building bridges if his mother had to pay for everything.

He dropped Lawrence off at the vicarage, before heading for home. He was just passing the village green, when he spotted his mother coming out of the newsagents. He quickly stopped the car, got out and shouted across to her. He needed to tell her he would be late, but to his annoyance, she walked off briskly in the direction of the pub. He swore with irritation and began to hurry across the green, yelling to his mother.

Eleanor thought she had heard someone call her. She turned and looked and spotted Gordon at the far side of the green. She waved to him and he raised his arm in response.

Then, as she watched, he fell. Suddenly. Hitting the grass and then lying still. She heard herself cry out a small mew of anguish and then she was running towards the prone figure of her son.

She had not seen the other two people approach him, but as she ran up, clutching her side and fighting for breath, they were kneeling over him.

'Gordon,' she gasped. One of the onlookers stood up and started to dial on a mobile phone. She dropped to her knees beside the body of her son, but she could see from his staring eyes that he was dead. A thin trickle of blood had formed at the corner of his mouth and was running down his chin onto the grass.

'Oh Gordon,' she whispered. She reached out her hand and closed his eyelids. The woman who was with the man reached out a hand and grasped hers.

'This is awful, isn't it. I've never seen a dead body before.'

Eleanor thought back to her husband's death and to others she had seen. This woman had either been very lucky or she had been very unfortunate.

'You obviously know him,' the woman was saying, watching her husband anxiously as he barked out directions into the phone.

'He was my son.' She heard herself use the past tense. 'He *is* my son. He will always be my son.' And then she was sobbing uncontrollably. The woman let go of her hand and moved away, looking to her husband for support. A small group of onlookers had gathered now, all mostly silent. A man pushed his way through them and knelt by Gordon, feeling for his pulse. Then he looked up at Eleanor and shook his head. A woman in a nurse's uniform came towards them, carrying a blanket and with a nod from Tom Lander, laid it over the body. Eleanor sat on the grass and felt under the blanket for her son's hand, which she held.

'Mrs. Sinclair?'

She realised the doctor was looking at her.

'I'm not leaving him. Not yet.'

'No, of course not.'

He started to ask the people to leave and they disbanded in twos and threes, reluctant to go. Some went and stood just a little further away.

Mike Collier saw the group of people on the green and wandered over towards the nearest group. He asked one of the onlookers what had happened.

'It's Gordon Sinclair from Rose Cottage. He's dead. Must have had a heart attack.'

It was then that Mike noticed Eleanor kneeling beside the body. He stood quite still and watched her. He suddenly knew who she was - it was as if all the pieces of the jigsaw had finally slotted into place. She, the body of her son and the doctor had formed a little tableau on the green - the crowd had moved back, were talking in small groups or were beginning to move away. Interest was raised again when an ambulance appeared, it's blue lights furiously flashing. People drifted nearer again as the blanket was pulled back and the essential checks were made for the second time. And all the time, Eleanor held

Gordon's hand.

The two paramedics chatted to Tom Lander and then spoke to her. Carefully, they lifted the body onto a stretcher. Then one of the men wrapped a blanket around Eleanor's shoulders and gave them a squeeze. She followed her dead son into the ambulance. As it pulled away, people began to move off, some to their homes, others to the pub and some to the village shop. The ripples of death were still being felt. People wanted to talk about what they had seen. Mrs. Wright went into the shop. A couple of women were already describing the events to Madge.

'Well, what a saga, eh, Mrs. Wright. Seems he dropped dead of a heart attack. Poor man.'

'Best way to go though, Madge. Probably didn't know a thing.'

The talk continued to reverberate around the village long after Gordon's body was in the mortuary and Eleanor had arrived back at Rose Cottage. She opened the door and poured herself a large whisky. The tears started to fall as she was opening a can of 'whiskas' for the cats and by the time she had put it on their plates, she was sobbing. The sobs hurt her physically and she bent over, hugging her arms around her body. She felt desolate, in the depths of despair, but she refused to push back the pain. She wanted to acknowledge it, to feel it. It was a promise she had made herself.

It was the following morning that Lydia heard the news. Lord P. came to find her in the rose garden.

'Hear old Sinclair collapsed and died yesterday. Great pity. Wonderful with roses.'

Lydia froze, her hand letting go of the fork and it fell to the ground, its prongs pointing upwards.

'Are you sure? I only saw him a couple of days' ago.'

'Oh, quite sure. It's the talk of the village. He was walking across the village green when he had a heart attack and died there and then. I say… are you OK?'

But Lydia had gone, running across the grass to her cottage. She went inside, ignoring Pounce and grabbed her car keys. Then she got into her car and drove rapidly down the Manor driveway. Half way to Rose Cottage she braked sharply. Where was she going? There was no point going to Rose Cottage, she would not have a good reception there. Her recent talk with Gordon went round and round in her mind. Had he written his last wishes down? What if he had not? What if his mother did not know what he had decided? She rested her head on the steering wheel. She had to do this for him. She had to find out. She put the car into gear and continued on her journey.

Eleanor looked at her blankly as she stood outside the kitchen door.

'May I come in?'

She nodded and Lydia stood just inside the back door. One of the cats rubbed itself around her ankles and she bent to stroke it. Eleanor had not said a word.

'I'm really sorry,' Lydia heard herself say. 'Was it awful?'

Eleanor just nodded her head. She did not feel inclined to give this woman any information. Lydia instinctively felt the hostility towards her and knew then that she would not get any answers here.

'You do know he had special wishes for the funeral?' She had the old woman's attention.

'I hardly think it's any of your business!'

'Oh, but it is, because Gordon made it my business. He

215

wanted me to be involved. Have you looked in his study to see if he had written anything down?'

She knew he was going to, but did not know if he had had the time. Eleanor had stood up.

'Get out of here. I shall bury my son as I see fit. Now get out!' She screamed the last few words and Lydia went, leaving Eleanor sobbing with grief and rage. '*How dare she!*' she kept repeating. She felt even more cross with herself because it had not occurred to her to look anywhere for any last wishes.

Eventually she rose, steadying herself against the table and went along to the study. She had never actually been in here before as it had always been her son's domain. It was nearly empty, just the desk and his chair and the fitted pine bookshelves, which were now bare of books. She could feel him in here as a tangible presence. She hovered in the doorway and could see a white envelope lying on the desk. Even from this distance, she could see it had her name on it; could recognise the shape of the word 'Mother' without actually being able to read it. She crossed to the desk, picked up the letter and almost fled back to the kitchen with it. She sat down, poured herself another glass of whiskey and looked at the envelope on the table in front of her. Bumble jumped up onto her lap and she kissed her grey ears, first one, then the other. The cat rubbed her face around Eleanor's chin, purring loudly, and dribbling with delight.

'Ugh, filthy cat.'

But she held the animal close to her, seeking solace in the warm fur, in the cat's vitality. 'Oh, what am I going to do, Bumble? However am I going to cope?'

The cat stepped up onto the table and sat down on the letter. She wanted Eleanor to play with her, to poke a pen out from under the paper so that she could bat it with her paw. Eleanor pulled the envelope away, 'You're not playing with this one, silly girl. You can sit here with me while I read it, though.'

But still she sat, not attempting to open it. Instead she traced the firm, black letters of her name with her finger and then bringing it to her lips, she kissed it, the tears pouring down her face again. She feared what the letter would contain, knowing that Lydia had had some input into it. What had she made him do? Suddenly she ripped it open and pulled out several sheets of paper. With a racing heart, she started to read.

Lydia lay in the dark wood watching the badgers. She felt cold right to her core. She had felt such a mixture of emotions driving back from Rose Cottage that she had not even been aware of her trek through the woodland. It was only when, staring into space, that the familiar face of the badger coming into her vision had brought her back to the present. She waited until the badgers had gone before she made her way back down the path. She lay awake for most of the night, watching the moon through her open window, Pounce lying at her feet. She had not realised how much she had liked the thought of Gordon being there, had not realised how much his friendship meant to her. And now he was gone.

CHAPTER TWENTY-SEVEN

Tom Lander put the receiver down. It had been the hospital confirming that Gordon Sinclair had died of a large pulmonary embolism. Death would have been instantaneous and for that, Tom was glad. Gordon had had the easy option out and so had his family, even if they did not recognise it. He had heard from his practice nurse that word in the village was that he had died from a heart attack. Well, let them believe that. They had no need to learn the truth and they certainly would not from him. He would call in to see Eleanor Sinclair later, to see if he could be of help to her. Losing a child was one of the most devastating things to face, whatever the age of the child.

But Tom Lander was not to be Eleanor's first visitor. She had heard a knock at the front door and had been tempted not to answer it, but the knock came again. She stood up, swaying a little with sheer tiredness and opened the door a fraction to find Mike Collier standing there. He was holding a small, hand picked bouquet of roses and honeysuckle and these were Eleanor's undoing. She let out a wail of anguish, clutching at her middle. Mike gently pushed open the front door, put the flowers on the hall settle and wrapped his arms around her. He held her while she sobbed, soaking his shirtfront. After a while she reached for a tissue in her apron pocket.

'I'm so sorry.'

'Don't be. Ever.' He took her elbow and steered her back into the kitchen. 'Now what have you got in the cupboards. I'll fix us some breakfast while you go and have a shower.'

She looked at him for a moment and then without another word went upstairs. When she came back down, he was putting the finishing touches to a fried breakfast. Fresh coffee sat in a pot on the table. She sat down and looked at it, feeling too weak to even pour it. He put a plate in front of her and then poured out the coffee.

'I'm not hungry.'

'No, you're probably not, but your body needs to be fuelled. Grieving and shock take up a lot of your energy.'

She was surprised to find that she ate every last scrap. He did not talk to her at all, but just ate and then sipped his coffee.

'Now where's your first port of call today? I'll run you wherever you need to go.'

She looked at him then. 'Why are you doing this?'

'Because I've been where you're at now. Someone did the same for me when Amanda died - led me through the first few days and I'd like to repay their kindness by helping you.'

'I don't deserve it.'

He shook his head and began to clear the table. 'So what first?' She did not answer and he turned to look at her. 'Do you need to go to the undertakers?'

She was holding out a letter, which he took and scanned the first few lines. 'I shouldn't be reading this.'

'I'd like you to. I can't cope with it.'

He sat again, automatically replenishing his coffee cup and he read in silence, until he placed the letter on the table.

'Sounds wonderful.'

She suddenly looked fierce. 'Wonderful? It sounds cranky to me. Why can't he just have a normal service?'

'Because it's not who he was. It's also not what he wanted. He's made that quite clear.'

She shook her head, unconvinced. 'He was talked into it by that bloody girl.'

He was taken aback by the venom in her voice. 'Tell me about her.'

But Eleanor had started to cry again. He handed her his handkerchief, caught her small hand up in his large one and waited. When she had quietened, he made a suggestion. She looked at him for a moment and then nodded. He squeezed her hand and she got up and pulled on her woollen wrap. Then they left together.

Lydia sat on her front door step twiddling a piece of rye grass between her finger and thumb. She felt aimless, only able to drift, her mind too absorbed with thoughts to concentrate on anything. She saw Lord P. coming towards her. He stopped at her gate.

'Mind if I come in?'

Lydia shook her head. This was the first time he had ever been to the cottage and she wondered what he wanted. He negotiated the gate and the dog, hurling a stick round the side of the cottage to get rid of him. He crouched down in front of Lydia.

'Wanted to see if you were OK.'

Lydia nodded. Then she shook her head, tears very near to the surface. She always found kindness difficult to deal with.

'Want to go for a walk?'

He was holding out his hand to her, but she ignored it

and stood up, brushing down her trousers. Without a word, they headed into the woods, Pounce racing past them up to a clearing.

'I wanted to apologise for my crassness yesterday. I didn't tell you in a very good way. I'm sorry.'

She had never heard such a long sentence from him. He seemed embarrassed by his apology and he strode on ahead of her on the path. She caught up with him at a stile. She was in woodland she did not normally encroach into, respecting the *Private* signs. He perched on the edge of the stile.

'So tell me about him. How you came to know him.'

Lydia flopped down onto a grassy bank. She sighed, remembering the misunderstanding over Pounce when they first met. Unused to this sort of communication, she started haltingly, her eyes wary. But as she continued, she sensed that her employer was genuinely listening to her.

'You seem to have had a very special relationship. You need to treasure that. There aren't many times that happens.'

Lydia nodded, checking back her tears, refusing to cry in front of this man. 'I shall miss the garden too, I really grew to love it; it taught me so much and I never told him.'

'Will the house be sold or go to his mother?'

'I have no idea. He was going to sell it and give the proceeds to charity.' It was then she told Lord P. about the anonymous donations.

'So he didn't die of a coronary like everyone's saying?'

'No, he knew he was dying months' ago. He had lung cancer.'

'Well, what a man! Had us all fooled. A real Robin Hood

in our midst. Who'd have thought it?'

'But you mustn't tell anyone of this.' She felt suddenly afraid.

'My dear, I won't breathe a word. Now come on, let's go and wake cook up and have some tea.'

He strode off ahead of her and she did not catch him up until she reached the Manor.

Mike Collier dropped Eleanor off late that afternoon. He sensed she wanted to be on her own.

'So what are your thoughts about it all now?'

She had opened the car door, but turned back to look at him. 'I think I'll do it just as he wanted.'

'Even though it involves Lydia Page?'

'Even though.'

'Good.' He smiled at her and she smiled back. 'You'll be OK, you know.'

She nodded.

'But you know where I am if you want me.'

'I can't thank you enough. You've managed to unscrew my head.'

'You're more than welcome.'

On an impulse, she leaned over and kissed him on the cheek before getting out of the car and closing the door. She suddenly felt exhausted, as though all the life was draining out of her body. She made her way indoors and sat huddled up against the Aga. Suddenly, she stood up, went into the lounge and got out her saxophone. She fingered the notes and rubbed at a darkening piece of the brass. *Needs a jolly good clean,* she thought.

She went to see Lydia the next morning. She had gone straight to the Manor and the housekeeper had pointed out Lydia's cottage. She drove across to it, trying to save her energy. The dog barked furiously as she pushed open the picket gate and walked to the front door. She noticed it could do with a coat of paint and that the brass knocker was dull from years of grime. The dog scrabbled frantically at the front door, but nobody came to answer it. Eleanor felt oddly exasperated. She had wanted this over and done with.

It was as she was driving through the village that she saw Lydia go into one of the cottages. She drew her car up outside and got out. Lydia was tying up a shrub in the border, but she stopped when she saw Eleanor.

'I want to talk to you.' Her voice sounded brittle and unfriendly and she cursed her sudden attack of nerves. Lydia began to walk towards her and stopped a few feet away.

'Did you find anything in the study?'

Eleanor felt a flash of annoyance at the impudence of this girl. 'Yes, I did. My son had written lengthy instructions on what he wanted for his funeral.'

Lydia breathed a sigh of relief, 'Thank God. And are you going to follow them?'

'Yes. I am.' She paused. She really did not want to ask the next question and when it came out, it sounded more like an order. 'And you'll organise a reading?'

'Oh, I'm not sure I could.' Lydia had blushed scarlet with confusion.

'I think it would be better coming from you.' Eleanor looked at this tall, thin woman in front of her and sighed. 'It's what he wanted.'

'How do you know?'

Eleanor fished in her pocket and came out with a sheet of paper, 'Because it says in the letter, *Tell Lydia she has*

223

to say something appropriate. I'll leave it up to her to choose. *She has a knack of always saying just the right thing. I know she won't let me down.*'

Lydia's eyes filled with tears, feeling panic strike. She could not possibly. What ever would she say? She realised Eleanor was waiting for an answer and heard herself croak, 'I can't.'

'You've got to. He's relying on you.'

And with that, Eleanor went back to her car. As she was getting in, she called, 'The funeral's Friday. Eleven o'clock. Can you get yourself there?'

Lydia nodded and watched the old woman drive off in her car. *What the hell was she going to do*?

She spent the next two hours in a dilemma. It was later in the day that she drove into Delaby on an errand for Mrs. Wright. She parked in the High Street and as she walked along it, she glanced in the window of the bookshop and what she saw stopped her in her tracks. Beside a book on David Austin roses was a book called *'Badger's Parting Gifts'*. It was too much of a coincidence. She went in and within five minutes, had come out with the book. It was perfect.

LYDIA

CHAPTER TWENTY-EIGHT

Friday was one of those fine autumnal days that made you glad to be alive. Which was rather an ironic thing to feel, Lydia thought, as she tried not to look at the wicker coffin in front of her. Instead, she looked at the blue of the sky and sniffed the freshness of the air, like a young animal.

She had rolled the book up into a thin tube and was not aware she had been tapping it against her leg until Lord P. put a quietening hand on her arm.

'Are you OK?' he asked, but secretly thought the question was rather unnecessary as it was obvious that she was not. He tucked his hand under her arm.

More people were making their way down the field. 'Oh doesn't that look beautiful,' one of the latecomers remarked, nodding at the rose-strewn rug Gordon's coffin was sitting on. It was hard to know what to say at funerals at the best of times, but this one made it harder.

There was quite a turnout, despite the location and the unorthodox nature of it.

The Reverend Turnball, looking slightly out of place in his black robes, was now asking people to make a circle around the coffin. Gordon's instructions had stipulated that there were to be no mourning clothes and all had concurred, although a few had on a black hat, or shoes, or gloves.

The vicar was welcoming them, explaining the

concept of this woodland burial site. 'He wanted to be buried here and help plant a woodland and a place of beauty for future generations. He loved his garden and he loved nature and it is a fitting resting place.' He turned to Lydia. 'I think you have something you want to share with us.'

Lydia could feel her cheeks burning and she was sure people would be able to see her heart pounding, it was beating so violently. *Blast this man*, she thought, *making me do this*.

She went and picked up the candle on the grass in front of her and fumbled to light a match that promptly blew out in the breeze. As she tried again, she dropped the box.

Suddenly, there were two or three people at her side, one helping to pick up the box, and one flourishing a silver cigarette lighter, which he lit the candle with.

'Good job some of us still have vices,' he said. It broke the ice. People laughed and she was so grateful to him she could have hugged him.

'Sorry,' she whispered. She started to speak, her voice quavering. Suddenly, a grey shape sped towards her, wagging its tail in a frenzy of joy. Pounce had escaped again, but as she quietened him down, she suddenly felt a calm go over her and she began to speak with more clarity. As if listening to her, the dog lay at her feet, his head on his paw, looking ahead of him.

'The first and second time I ever met Gordon Sinclair, it was because of my dog's ill manners.' She told of the occasions, trying to make them as light-hearted as possible. 'So it seems appropriate that he should have turned up now.

'I want to read a story to you about a badger who dies.'

She opened the book and with a confidence she did not know she possessed, read the story of the animal that died, but lived on in the things he had taught the other animals. As the animals shared stories about Badger, they remembered the skills he had taught them. Mole learnt how to cut paper chains; Frog how to skate and Fox how to knot his tie. It was simple and it made them all think. Alice wiped away a tear and she was not alone.

Lydia closed the book, 'He taught me how to trust,' she said, 'and I will always be thankful for that.' She looked at the vicar who nodded at her. 'So let's just reflect for a moment on what he gave you as his parting gift, and send our thanks for it.'

In the silence, a blackbird sang in a hawthorn bush. It was exquisitely beautiful. And then different notes broke out over the countryside.

All eyes followed the sound and saw Eleanor with a saxophone, the haunting melody finally breaking down even Lydia's defences. She continued to play as the coffin was gently lifted into the hole. Lydia carefully put the roses on top of the coffin and then scattered a mass of petals down onto it. Everyone there was encouraged to say their own good byes before making their way back to the cars and on to the Manor.

Lord P. had gone to see Eleanor after his talk with Lydia and had offered the Manor for people to gather after-wards.

'Oh, but I couldn't possible accept,' had been her response.

'Nonsense,' he had replied, 'it will give Cook something to get her teeth into.'

'But he wanted a celebration,' Eleanor continued, 'he'd left some money for food and drink.'

'Then we'll jolly well get some champagne. Push the boat out a bit. Got a man in London who supplies me at a very good rate. And we'll put on a real feast. And what about some music? How about we hire a band? What sort of music did he like?' And so he had gone on, planning and scheming, completely unstoppable. But Eleanor had been glad. He had access to resources she did not.

She looked round now at the lovely drawing room, its pale lemon and white stripes showing off the lovely mahogany furniture. He had done Gordon proud. Tables were covered with food and there was enough champagne to see them through to the next year, she thought. At various points in the room were simple arrangements of roses. The jazz band was audible from the conservatory and people were milling and chatting. There were a few long faces, but with the absence of black attire, it could have been a social gathering. *Yes,* she thought, *this is how he would have wanted it.*

It was some time later that she saw Lydia approaching her. She smiled thinly at her. 'It was perfect. Well done.' As hard as it was for her to admit, it had been the best funeral she had ever attended. And it was partly due to this young woman.

'I thought you were pretty amazing yourself. When did you decide to play?'

'He asked me to, in his letter. He was devious to the end, my son.'

'And will you play for us now?'

'No. I shan't play again. I'm going to sell my saxophone. I won't be needing it anymore.'

'Lydia looked astounded. 'But why? I thought you loved it. You've had it for so long.'

'Exactly. And it holds too many memories. Memories

which are in the past and should remain there. I need to let go. Let 'it' go.' She turned as members from the Jaguar club were waiting to speak with her.

Lawrence Turnball stood by himself for a moment, reflecting on the day. It had been lovely, he had to admit. He watched Penny Young smile at Toby Thomas from the garage. He decided to go and get himself another glass of champagne and as he passed them, he overheard their conversation.

'You mean he didn't die of a heart attack?'

'No, well at least he may have done in the end, but he'd been ill for months.'

'How do you know?'

'Because he told me he was dying on the way back from a rally,' Toby laughed nervously. 'In fact, the funny thing was he wanted to give me his Jaguar.'

'You're joking!'

This woman made him nervous. He regretted saying what he had said the minute it was out of his mouth. 'Yeah, well, I couldn't have accepted, could I?'

'Well, why ever not? I would have.' She thought of the beautiful car and sighed. She really had not played her cards right. She glanced over at Lydia and thought, *I wonder what he gave her?* She felt a surge of jealousy and, with difficulty, pulled her attention back to Toby. 'So, do you think the dear departed is our modern-day Robin Hood?'

He looked taken aback. 'I'd never given it a moment's thought!'

'Well think now. Don't you think it all ties in?' she realised how sharp she sounded, but he really was most dreadfully slow-witted. She moved aside to let the vicar go past. 'So tell me about the car.'

231

Toby wished he had never started this. He felt he had betrayed Gordon. 'There's nothing to tell.' He realised Penny's attention had drifted again and she was looking at a man coming towards them.

'We meet again, Miss...er...Watson?'

Toby noticed Penny was blushing furiously and excused herself. The man was holding out his hand to Toby. 'Simon Cayser. I'm Gordon Sinclair's solicitor. He left me a letter to give to you on his death and I'd be grateful if you could call in at the office to discuss it.'

It was Toby's turn to look flustered. 'Letter? I don't understand.'

'Ring my office in the morning and we'll make an appointment.' He handed Toby a card, patted his arm and excused himself. Toby watched him go over to the woman who had read at the funeral, saw him speak to her for a few minutes. He had not spoken to her himself, because she unnerved him, but then a lot of people did that. He knew he lacked confidence, but was not sure what to do about it. People like Penny Young always made mincemeat out of him and he was sure this young woman would do the same. She always looked so tough. Even today she was in trousers. He saw the solicitor hand her a card, the same as he had done to him.

People were getting noisier and noisier as the champagne took effect. Lawrence Turnball knew he should be leaving, but the conversation he had overheard with Penny Young and Toby disturbed him. He had a jolly good idea what that woman was up to and he did not like it one bit. He saw her chatting to Alice, who excused herself as he watched. It was now or never. He went over to her. She looked surprised to see him approach, but smiled at him, rather falsely he thought. He didn't beat about the bush.

'So, you've found out what you wanted to know. What do you intend to do with the information?' He was glad to see she looked uncomfortable.

'I...I don't know what you mean.'

'Oh yes you do. I've heard you asking questions. You've put two and two together and made four. Are you going to the papers about it?'

She was recovering quickly. 'Are you saying that Gordon Sinclair was the *Robin Hood of Lowesdon*?'

'Gordon Sinclair was a lot of things to a lot of people, Miss Young. But Robin Hood?'

'Oh, you've read the stories. I have reason to believe he is the anonymous donor. If I can confirm he is, then I win myself a nice big reward.'

'I never realised you could stoop so low. I'm not confirming anything.' He put his glass on an occasional table and walked out. He needed some air. That woman was poisonous.

Lydia stood making polite conversation to two women who lived in the village. They were trying to get her to come onto the church flower rota, but she was not buying. She fingered the card in her pocket - the pointed edge catching her finger. *Whatever could it all mean?*

Toby Thomas could feel the solicitor's card in his pocket. He felt such a conflicting array of emotions that he gulped down his glass of champagne, strode across the lawn and drove back to the garage. He needed to work, it would help clear his mind. Besides, he was not comfortable in crowds of people. Polite social chitchat really was not his strong point. He picked up his tools, checked the appointment book and with a sigh of relief started jacking up an old Mini Metro to change the brake pads. He was soon absorbed in his work, the card forgotten.

Alice Stamp was deep in conversation with Eleanor. 'So, there'll be no headstone, then?'

Eleanor shook her head. She felt exhausted, as though she could not answer another question. 'We're allowed to choose a tree, but it must be native to Britain and like the growing conditions.'

'Oh dear, so where will you go?'

'What do you mean?'

'Well, I'd want a grave to tend, somewhere to take flowers.'

Eleanor wondered if this woman was being deliberately thick-skinned and unfeeling. 'What Gordon chose is not for people who want a neat and tidy grave and a headstone, but for those who love birds and wildlife and who choose to create a woodland for future generations. Now, I must just go and have a word with the vicar, if you'll excuse me.'

She went off, limping slightly, her left hip beginning to ache from all the standing around. Lawrence Turnball greeted her warmly. 'Do you want to sit?' He had noticed her lameness.

'Please.'

He led her to a small upright settee where he felt they would not be disturbed. He replenished their glasses. 'Have you eaten anything?'

'No, I can't.'

He shook his head and disappeared, returning with a plate full of tempting morsels. 'We can share this - make us both feel better.'

Eleanor looked at him in surprise. She had not actually considered that today was any more than part of his

234

duties. She looked around then at all the other people present and wondered what they were truly feeling. She guessed their lives would go on pretty much as before, with one or two exceptions. Unless death was very close to home it rarely stopped you for long. One always took stock, of course. Maybe listened a little more carefully to your own body for a while.

As if reading her thoughts, the vicar spoke, 'How are you feeling?'

She looked at him blankly. She really had no idea, such was the jumble of emotions inside her. 'I'm sorry, but I don't really know. I think exhausted.'

'You've a lot to deal with. One never expects to have to arrange ones children's funerals.' He paused for a moment as if thinking over his next words. 'Did you mind how he chose to be buried?'

Eleanor liked this man. He was so direct and honest. She shook her head, 'No. I did at first. But I felt that today was truly about him. Did you mind? That he wasn't buried in your churchyard?'

Lawrence shook his head, 'Besides, we'll always have a memory of him in the church.'

'Oh, the windows. How are they coming on?'

'Fine. The middle one's finished and is absolutely stunning. It was that one Gordon and I went to see on the day he died.'

'I'm glad he saw it. Did he like it? I never got to ask him.' She was suddenly overcome. She fished in her pocket for a tissue and held it to her eyes. 'So sorry. It just comes over me at times. Nothing I can do about it.'

'Would you like to walk for a bit? Or is your hip bothering you too much?'

Eleanor shook her head and allowed herself to be

helped up by this kind man. 'Please don't neglect your duties because of me.'

'Right now, you are the most important duty I have.' He smiled at her and held out his arm, which she gladly took.

As they made their way outside, he caught sight of Lydia's face and thought, *Well, maybe not my only duty*.

Lydia woke from a restless, troubled sleep. She reached out and stroked the dog, who wriggled in ecstasy. She opened an eye and glanced at the clock by her bed. 4:30. Far too early to be awake. Her head thumped from too much champagne, but she knew she did not have any painkillers. With a start she realised it was Tuesday and she would normally be due at Rose Cottage. But there was no normality. She curled up into a tight ball clutching at her stomach and sobbed.

Toby stopped, stood up and stretched his aching back. He had been bent over the engine for what seemed like hours.

'Tea?'

His dad looked up from what he was doing. 'Thought you'd never ask.'

Toby grinned and went into the office where the kettle was. He pushed aside the clutter on the desk, leaving just enough room for two mugs, filled the kettle up and then picked up the phone. He was put through to Simon Cayser himself. By the time the kettle had boiled, he had made an appointment and had got directions on how to find the office. He still felt uneasy about the whole thing, but had resolved to see it through.

Simon Cayser put the phone down and then redialed Rose Cottage.

Lydia had forgotten all about the card until she picked up her trousers from the floor and it dropped out of her pocket. She would ring later. Right now, she was going for a walk with the dog.

It was three days' later that Simon Cayser finally got through to her. She reluctantly agreed to an appointment.

He saw Toby Thomas that afternoon. The boy sat nervously on the edge of the chair.

'Thanks for taking the trouble to come in. It's more usual nowadays, I know, to send a letter to Will beneficiaries, but in this instance I preferred to do it in person.'

Toby shifted uneasily, 'I don't understand.'

Simon Cayser opened his desk drawer and handed Toby an envelope, indicating that Toby should open it, which he did.

'I'm still no clearer.' He had pulled out a Jaguar Enthusiast Club Membership pack in his name.

'No? Well, I've only given you half the clues.' The solicitor was obviously enjoying this tremendously. He reached into the drawer again and pulled out a further bulky envelope, which he passed over. Toby found the contents included a set of car keys and the logbook for the Mark 1. It had already been sent off to the DVLC and his name was recorded as the new owner. He blushed a deep shade of red.

'But I told him I didn't want the car.'

'Then it's yours to sell. You're the legal owner and can

do as you wish with it.'

'But…'

'Whatever you decide,' the older man interrupted, 'the car can be left at Rose Cottage.'

Toby looked up. 'Won't it be sold?'

'Not sold, no. But the new owner has instructions that the garage is to be leased to you, indefinitely. In fact, until you no longer have a need for it. I shall send you a copy of the agreement shortly.' Simon Cayser stood up. 'So go and think about it. Either sell it or enjoy it.'

He held out his hand and Toby realised the appointment was at an end. He left the office in total confusion although, even to himself, he could not say what his confusion was over. He decided not to say a word to anyone about the Jaguar. It could just sit in the garage until he made up his mind.

It was the day after that Lydia found her way to the solicitors. She had deliberately dressed in her oldest clothes. She had thought they would make her feel comfortable, but when the smartly dressed receptionist confronted her, she just felt shabby and even more ill at ease. As she waited, she picked at the skin around her thumbnail and made it bleed. Cursing, she wound a piece of tissue round it, aware all the time that the receptionist was watching her.

Simon Cayser came out to meet her personally and his warmth and his lack of stuffiness immediately struck her. He could sense her unease and likened her to a wild animal in an unnatural habitat. He wondered again at the strange relationship between this girl and his client. He thanked her for coming and made her a mug of tea himself, dispensing with his secretary, as he knew instinctively that she would only make Lydia more uneasy.

'I enjoyed your reading so much at the funeral. It's such a wonderful book that I went and bought it for my daughter.'

'Thanks.'

'It just seemed so him, somehow, so well done you.'

Lydia looked down at her hands, but was secretly pleased. She believed that this man genuinely meant what he said and was not just trying to please her. Like the vicar. He had driven to the Manor expressly to thank her for her part in Gordon's funeral. He had thought it very apt, too.

The solicitor's voice broke through her thoughts, '...so he asked me to give you this. You'll need to read it here. I'll nip out - give you a bit of space. Be back in a tic.' He left an envelope on the desk in front of Lydia. She picked it up, took out a sheet of paper and began to read;

Dear Lydia,

As you know, I tried to sell Rose Cottage, but if truth be known, I could never quite part with the garden as I loved it so much. You, of all people know that. So I've decided that the only person I could bear to entrust it to is you. I guess I gave it to you months' ago when you started working on it.

Of course, the downside of it all is that giving you the garden also means I've had to give you the house. I hope it won't be too much of a burden. I've got it all up together and have arranged for a log delivery. I've left some furnishings for you, but do feel free to discard what you don't like. Your bedroom I've left as it was.

My solicitor has all the finer details and he'll go through these with you.

Look after the garden for me. Change it, do what you want with it, but leave a rose somewhere.

With great love and thanks for all you did for me,
Gordon Sinclair

He had signed himself by his full name, almost as if she would not know who he was. She put the letter down slowly, stood up and left the building.

Simon Cayser found an empty room when he returned to his office a few minutes later. Gordon's letter had fallen to the floor. He looked out of the window down onto the street, but Lydia was nowhere in sight.

She realised she was driving too fast when she nearly lost control of the rear wheels of the car as she was going round a bend. She took her foot off the accelerator and came to a halt in a farm gateway. She banged her fists on the wheel and the horn sounded, making her jump out of her skin. *'How could he,'* she kept asking over and over to herself.

Eleanor packed the last of her bags and started to load the car. She had received the letter from Simon Cayser this morning, notifying her about Gordon's Will. She had been quite unprepared for the contents of the Will, despite Cayser's warning telephone call a few days before. She had known she was not to have been a beneficiary, but she had not, for a moment, thought that he would leave his beautiful house and gardens to that girl. There was no more she could do here. She would not even dream of contesting the Will. She did not want Rose Cottage. No, the only thing to do was to go far away, back to her own cottage and her own life. Bumble was yowling in her cat carrier and kept up a steady protest as Eleanor went down the drive and headed west.

Lydia had received a letter from the solicitors that morning, enclosing Gordon's letter and fuller instructions, including a set of keys. These had a large brown label attached to them with the name *Rose Cottage* written on it. She had given a howl of anguish and had dropped them on the floor. Pounce had leapt on them and she had had to push him off and take them out of his mouth.

She had worked furiously that morning, trying to forget. She had missed breakfast and Lord P. appeared at eleven with a mug of coffee for her and one of Cook's cakes.

'You OK?' He had watched her digging furiously and had known something was up.

'Fine.'

'Only it's not like you to miss breakfast.'

'Wasn't hungry.'

'Fair do's. Well you know where I am if you need me.'

Lydia nodded, taking a bite out of the cake, 'Thanks...For this.'

He nodded and left her alone. She sat down on the seat, suddenly weary with all the digging she had done. The roses would need cutting back soon, she thought. Into her mind came Rose Cottage. Who would cut those back if she did not go? She pushed the thought to the back of her mind and went and fetched her pruning knife and secateurs.

She tossed and turned all that night, her sleep disturbed by vivid dreams of jungle-like gardens where rose-shaped faces peered from the foliage and cried for food. She was even quieter at work that morning, not saying a word to any of the other groundsmen.

By lunchtime she had made up her mind. She would go to Rose Cottage and do the garden and no more. She had a shed key so there was no need to go into the house. With a firm resolve, she drove there, Pounce leaping out of the car as soon as she had opened the door. He sat and barked outside the back door, scrabbling at it with his paws until Lydia snapped at him to stop.

She worked until dusk, aware that there was a tremendous amount to be done if she was to put the garden to bed for the winter. She had left the house keys at home, but she had no desire to go inside. Neither could she go down into the meadow yet. The swing was too evocative and she was not ready for it.

She came in every bit of spare time she could, doing half an hour here or an hour there.

Snatches of conversations with Gordon would come into her head as she pruned or dug or replanted and before long, she was talking to him as she worked. But always about what she was doing, about what she was planting. Never about the house.

On one of the days, Alice Stamp appeared around the corner of the cottage. Lydia, involved in a task, had not seen her.

'Lydia?'

Lydia jumped. What on earth was the woman doing here? She was never sure if Alice approved of her or not, but was wary of her forthright manner, unaware of how like her own it was.

'I've brought you a cake for your tea. I'll put it on the kitchen table, shall I? Put the kettle on?'

'No…I…you…I haven't…' Lydia stumbled to a halt. She showed no signs of moving from the border.

'Well, you'd better let me in then - I haven't got all day.'

Alice was holding a chocolate cake so huge it would feed Lydia for a fortnight.

'I can't. I haven't got the keys.'

Alice rested the cake on the window ledge. 'Well, where've you lost them? You'd better look for them.'

'No. I haven't got them with me.'

'Brought them with you? Whatever do you mean?'

Lydia sighed, 'I just come here to do the garden, that's all.'

Alice looked at her sharply. 'Oh. I see. Well you'd better take the cake with you then, hadn't you.'

She pushed it more firmly onto the ledge and turned and scurried off. Just before she went out of sight, Lydia called after her, 'Thank you, Mrs. Stamp.'

Alice turned.

'For the cake.'

Alice nodded and disappeared. Lydia picked up the cake, opened her car door and sat it on the passenger seat. She had had enough. She went and put the tools away and left for home.

Home? Lydia looked round the living room of her cottage, noting its threadbare carpet, the ingrained dirt and stains of previous occupants, saw where the wallpaper was peeling back from the wall over by the window, where the damp came in. She had never changed anything in here since she had moved in and she did not have any possessions as such. She went into the kitchen, pulled a plate out of the cupboard, a knife out of a drawer and cut a large piece of the chocolate cake. This she ate while waiting for the kettle to boil, before cutting herself another piece to eat with her mug of tea. For the first time, she noticed the mug was chipped. She wondered why she had never seen it before now. She had spent her life with old and chipped things. Worthless things which her father could not possibly sell for his drink money.

If she thought long and hard, she could remember a time when her mother had had pretty things. She remembered one china figurine of a girl in a ball gown, her small, perfectly formed porcelain hands clutching at her netted skirts to reveal dainty slippers. She had a trail of rosebuds in her hair and some more at her waist.

She also remembered picking up the pieces after her father's drunken arm had swept it from the mantelpiece in a fit of rage which had probably been over nothing. His rages had all been over nothing. That just made it worse. Made the fear worse until both mother and daughter would dread the sound of his key in the door. Eventually, when he had nothing else to break or destroy, he started on her mother.

She learnt to keep out of the way; had been keeping out of people's way ever since. Particularly if a person meant a man.

She finished the piece of cake and put the plate on the floor for Pounce. He leapt upon it, pushing the plate across the floor in his eagerness not to miss a single crumb.

CHAPTER TWENTY-NINE

Toby stopped outside Rose Cottage. As he did so, Lydia walked round the side of the building, pushing a wheelbarrow. She stopped short when she saw the strange car blocking the drive.

Toby got out and came towards her. 'Hi, I'm Toby Thomas.'

Lydia put the wheelbarrow down. 'What do you want?'

He was taken aback by her abruptness. It made him flustered. 'Um…oh…nothing really. Just wanted to see how the Jag was.'

'The Jag?' she had forgotten about the car, had no need to go into the garage.

'It is still here?'

'I think so, but why don't you go and see?' She picked up the wheelbarrow again and pushed it round to the small front garden, leaving Toby standing uncertainly in the driveway. He got back into his car and drove away.

Lydia phoned Simon Cayser at lunchtime. He acted as if nothing untoward had happened at their last meeting, chatting away about probate.

'Now, what can I do for you?'

Lydia paused, 'I wondered what was happening to Gordon's Jaguar? I noticed it had just been left in the garage.'

'Ah, yes, that is something I was going to get round to discussing with you. The car has been left to a young man called Toby Thomas. Now, what you need to be aware of is that Gordon has given Toby the right to lease the garage at Rose cottage for as long as he needs it. For a peppercorn rent. I can go over all this with you when probate comes through.'

She ended the call shortly and put the receiver down, her mind whirring. *What a strange man he was*, she thought. *Fancy not saying anything this morning. He was as bad as she was.* She began to laugh then. What a pair!

Her next visitor at Rose Cottage was Alice. She found Lydia standing in the meadow, looking into space.

'There's a lot of work here for one person, isn't there?'

She turned on hearing Alice's voice and nodded. It was here she pictured Gordon most clearly, here she felt him near to her.

'Have you been inside yet?'

She shook her head.

'Why ever not?'

She felt exasperated at this interfering old woman, but a look of compassion in Alice's eyes made her bite back a sharp retort.

'You loved him, didn't you?'

Lydia nodded, but then added fiercely, 'But not in the way everyone will think when they hear about the Will. We never...' she paused, '...we never slept together. There was nothing like that. I just loved him as a person. He treated me so differently, as if I was so special, but wanted nothing in return. Nobody's ever been like that to me before.' She stopped, a lump in her throat and her eyes filling with unshed tears.

'So why can't you accept his gift to you? It's what he

wanted.'

'It's too much, Alice. I don't deserve it. I'm scared of what people will think.'

'People. Pah! Let them think what they like. As to deserving it, why ever shouldn't you have it? You gave so much to Gordon in his last months. I could see that. So could his mother. That's why she didn't like you or want you here.'

'But whenever I've had anything in my life, it's always been spoilt.'

'How so, child?' Alice had sat down, pulling her coat tightly around her and patted the seat beside her. Lydia sat down and to her own amazement began to tell Alice about her home life. Alice sat and listened intently.

'So what happened to your father?' she asked as Lydia paused in her tale.

'He's inside,' she answered simply.

Alice waited.

'He finally went too far and stabbed my mother with a kitchen knife.'

'Oh my dear Lord,' Alice raised her hand to her ears as though she did not want to hear any more. But she had to know. 'Did he kill her?'

'No, but he hurt her badly enough for her to be kept in hospital for a fortnight.'

'And what happened then?'

'The police prosecuted and he got seven years. My mother came home and started to rebuild her life. She met someone else and it was clear I was in the way. I got a live-in job at a nursery.'

'You poor thing. Was Gordon aware of all this?'

Lydia shook her head, 'I feel ashamed of my past. Of my father. It's only since I trained properly in horticul-

247

ture and got taken on by Lord P. that I've actually managed to put some of it behind me.'

'Then taking on Rose Cottage is a chance to really put it all behind you. It's what Gordon wanted.'

'How do you know?'

'Because I know how miserable he was when the cottage was on the market and how his mood completely changed after making his Will.'

'But he was going to give all the money to charity.'

'And so he did, a lot of it. But he thought you were more important. Charity begins at home, you know.'

Lydia said nothing, letting all this sink in. Eventually she spoke, 'I've always found it easier to own nothing. Then nobody can take it away from you.'

'You've got him.' She nodded at the dog who was lying at their feet, watching them. He wagged his tail.

Lydia did not answer.

'I could meet you here tomorrow and we could go in the house together. If you'd like.'

Lydia looked at her and nodded. 'Yes,' she said simply. 'I would like.'

Alice was already there when she arrived the next day. She felt reluctant and deadheaded a missed plant as she came towards the back door.

Alice watched her. 'Come on, this cake's heavy.'

'Not another cake. I'll get fat!'

'Huh! There's nothing of you. Now get the door open and let's get into the warm.'

Lydia took the long-ignored keys out of her pocket and found the right one. The lock clicked back and the door opened. Pounce shot in between their legs and tore off to go round the house, barking at the top of his voice.

'Now then, let's get some heat on, shall we?'

Alice knew her way round and soon put the central heating on. Lydia stood in the centre of the kitchen watching her.

'Well, you could put the kettle on. There's some milk in my basket,' Alice called from the back of a cupboard where she was fiddling around.

Lydia set about the task of making some tea. She ignored the old rocker by the stove, not able to face looking at it. It was all just like he had left it. As if he would walk in at any moment. To her dismay, Pounce leapt up onto the rocker, bracing himself at the sudden movement.

'Pounce!' she snarled.

'Oh leave him,' Alice retorted, stroking his wiry head, 'he's just finding out where the good places to sleep might be.'

Lydia handed her a mug of tea and Alice cut a chunk of ginger cake.

'You must spend your entire life baking cakes,' Lydia commented as she bit into the moist mixture.

'Oh, it gives me something to do. And people always look pleased to see me because they know I'll have a cake with me.'

Lydia had a sudden insight into how lonely Alice was. 'Well, you've no need to bring a cake when you come here. I shall be pleased just to see you on your own.'

Alice flushed, 'Well, that's right nice of you. But I expect I shall bring one all the same.'

Lydia slid the door open on the range. 'Guess I'd better learn how to light this and keep it going.'

'Ever had one before?'

'No, never. Haven't got a clue about them.'

'Well let me show you. They've all got their little ways, but once you've settled down with each other, you'll be all right.' She bustled around showing Lydia what to do and soon the kitchen had a familiar warmth about it.

Lydia looked at her watch. 'I'd better be getting home.'

Both women looked at each other and Lydia laughed as Alice shook her head in disbelief. 'Well, it's going to take me a while to get used to the idea.'

'Don't leave it too long, that's all. Houses don't like standing empty. It makes them feel useless.'

She really is something, thought Lydia as she drove back to the Manor. She actually wanted to get to know her better. She had let Gordon and now Alice, get closer to her than she had ever let anyone before. She saw Lord P. inspecting a tyre on his car and gave him a wave. *He isn't too bad, either,* she thought.

CHAPTER THIRTY

Penny Young dressed carefully. She had had a real stroke of luck yesterday. She had bumped into the girl with the artificial leg who had been at Gordon's funeral. The girl had recognised her and had not needed any encouragement to sing Gordon Sinclair's praises. She had chatted on about how grateful she had been for the money he had sent to her appeal and although it was done anonymously, she just knew it had been him. Penny now felt she had enough firm information to go to the Observer.

She had been further fuelled after bumping into Alice Stamp as well and had no joy with getting information out of her. In fact, the woman had been openly hostile towards her.

She decided to walk to the Observer's offices, as it was one of those bright, crisp mornings she loved. She had started to climb the steps leading up to the plate glass doors of the office, when she heard her name being called. She turned and saw the vicar, of all people. She blushed deeply.

'Putting in an ad are you?' He walked up the steps until he was level with her. 'Or handing in the WI report. Or are you playing Judas?' His voice rose and he nearly spat out the name. His vehemence made her heart jump.

'It's none of your business. How dare you accost me like this.'

'Oh, I dare, Miss Young, if it's to protect a brave man's

privacy. A man of such utter decency that you wouldn't understand.'

'Decency! A man who lured me into his bed and then never gave me the time of day! A man who preferred a little trollop over me!'

The vicar blanched. He held out his hand. 'Come. Come with me. Let's talk about this. Two wrongs don't make a right. Come.'

To her surprise, she found herself taking his out-stretched hand and allowed herself to be led down the steps.

'To my house, I think, don't you?' he said, tucking her hand through his arm. 'I think that what we might be going to say might be rather private.'

Lydia had not gone back to Rose Cottage for two days. Once there, she fiddled around with the range and was absurdly pleased when she got it going again. She pottered around the kitchen, but went no further. That night, she returned to her cottage on the estate.

She was working on the large herbaceous border, when Lord P. joined her to see how progress was going. They had plans to totally replant that autumn using hot colours. It was something Lydia had not been totally comfortable with at first, but once she had drawn up the plans, she could see the impact the border would make.

'Are you OK?' he asked her and she knew he was not talking about the planting. To her surprise, she found herself talking to him about Gordon's Will.

'Well good for you. So you won't be needing No. 3 then. Good. Good. Sam Hilby's asked if we've got any spare cottages so he can have yours. Solves a problem very nicely. Wouldn't want to lose Sam.'

'But…' began Lydia.

'End of the month do you? Shouldn't think there's much to get sorted out the other end, eh?'

'No, no, there's not,' agreed Lydia. 'But…'

It was too late. Her employer had spotted a car coming along the drive and was already striding away towards it.

'Oh bugger,' she said.

It gave her eight days in total. She probably only needed half a day to move as the possessions she owned would have fitted into a large holdall. The day she moved in, she slept in the kitchen rocker. She woke, stiff and tired and made herself tea and let the dog out. He barked at someone coming up the drive. It was Alice, and Lydia discovered that she was absurdly pleased to see her.

'Saw your car here last night and thought it was time I brought you this.' She handed Lydia a parcel.

'What's this?'

'It's your house-warming present.'

Lydia unwrapped the paper and pulled out a flower vase. It was a beautifully simple shape in a dark green pottery.

'It was my grandmother's. She used to use it for daffs, but I've used it for all sorts.'

'Oh, but I couldn't…' began Lydia, but Alice was waving her hands at her.

'I want you to have it. You'll need it in this house. Never could find a decent vase to put things into.'

'Thank you. It's so lovely.'

She suddenly went outside, picking up her secateurs on the way and began to cut the remaining asters and some foliage. She arranged them deftly in the vase and put it in the middle of the old pine table.

'That's better. Looks more like home already. Probably could do with some in your room, too.'

Lydia did not like to admit she had not been upstairs yet.

'Have you seen what he's left you in the way of things? I could always lend you linen if you need it.'

She talks as though Gordon's just gone on holiday! Lydia thought, *not as though he's dead.* She watched as Alice collected up some cleaning gear from under the sink.

'What are you doing?'

'I expect it could do with a freshen up, what with you dithering and all.' She vanished out of the kitchen and Lydia heard her going upstairs. She had no option but to follow her and found that Alice had started in the bedroom under the eaves, the one she had stayed in when she was ill. She had already flung the windows open and was busy dusting the ledges. 'Have you decided which room you'll be using?'

'No, I've not given it any thought.'

'Well, best you had. That rocking chair'll do your back no good at all.' She turned and saw Lydia standing there. She sighed. 'Let's go and see.'

She bustled down the corridor and pushed open the door to Gordon's bedroom. Eleanor had cleared away all his remaining clothes and the room was devoid of personal possessions. To Lydia's surprise, it was also empty of furniture.

'Where's his bed?'

'Oh, that was collected after he died. The other furniture's gone to auction. He didn't want you to have to live with his stuff. I think his idea was that he'd just leave you enough to live comfortably with and you could then add to it when you wanted.'

She left the room, hooking the door back, and led Lydia down the passageway to the third room. Lydia had never actually been into this bedroom. It was pretty with blue walls, a single bed covered with an old antique lace counterpane and an old pine cupboard by the bed. The only other furniture was a small pine desk and chair.

'Is this where she stayed?'

'If by 'she', you mean Mrs. Sinclair, then yes.'

'Well, I won't sleep here then.' And Lydia made her way back to her small bedroom under the eaves. 'This will do me fine.'

Alice nodded, 'Happen you could do a bit of B & B when you get the other two rooms sorted.'

Lydia thought for a moment, looking around the pretty room. She suddenly did not want to share the cottage. Not yet anyway. She felt a small flutter of excitement inside her, closely followed by a feeling of fear.

'Right then. You finish off in here and I'll go down and start on the bathroom.'

'But everything's so clean already.'

'That may be so, but giving a house a good clean when you move in's a very good thing you know. Helps you settle.'

And with this, she was off. Lydia could hear her singing to herself as she worked. She sighed, picked up a duster and started to polish the already gleaming bedside table.

She opened the small drawer and saw a jewellery box in it. She was about to close it again, when she caught sight of a piece of paper by the box with her name on it. She knew without any doubt that this was from Gordon.

She opened the note.

If you've found this, then you're doing a great job. One collar as promised.

That was it. No signature. Nothing. She reached into the drawer for the box. It was quite large and she saw it came from a jeweller's workshop in Delaby. She opened the lid. Inside was a navy collar, with a beautifully chased silver buckle. On the opposite side to the buckle was a silver nametag in the shape of a rabbit. It was engraved with the word *Pounce* and a telephone number. Lydia realised it was the number for Rose Cottage.

She sobbed until she thought her heart would break. Alice heard her and quietly pulled the bedroom door to, leaving her with her grief. 'Better out than in,' she muttered and crossly brushed away her own tears.

Lydia had cried herself into exhaustion. She had lain down on the bed and slept. Alice had let herself out hours ago. It was dusk when she made her way downstairs, carrying the collar. Alice must have let Pounce in, because he was asleep in front of the range. She saw a note on the table, *Be back tomorrow to finish off. Alice.*

She called Pounce over to her and undid his old, brown collar. Then she buckled on the new one. He wagged his tail and then crouched down, expecting a game. She threw open the back door and he was gone. Wrapping her arms around herself against the cold, she looked up at the night sky and tried to make out some of the constellations. She heard Pounce scrabbling after something and hoped the creature had got away. She went back inside into the warmth of the kitchen and felt she had come home. She could sense Gordon close by and simply whispered, 'Thank you.'

CHAPTER THIRTY-ONE

Penny Young closed the back of her car on another load
of jumble. She drove to the church hall and started to
unload it. The vicar came out to help her.

'That's the last now. Guess it's sorting it out time.'

She joined a group of women emptying bags and re-
distributing it onto various tables. They had nodded to
her when she arrived, but none had spoken to her. She
put a jumper on a pile and was told it was an adult's and
not a child's. Someone asked if they wanted tea.

'Look, as I'm new and don't know what I'm doing, why
don't I make the tea?'

The women all looked at her. Then one said, 'Well that
would be very nice.'

By the time she returned with the mugs, the atmosphere seemed to have thawed. 'Best come on bric-a-brac
with me this afternoon,' one of the women ventured and
Penny nodded, happy to feel included.

It was not until they were clearing away that the vicar
approached her. 'Fancy a drink?'

'Love one. I need to get rid of all the dust I've ingested.'

He smiled at her, sensing a beginning of peace within
her. He had no idea where that morning last week was
going to lead when he had virtually manhandled her away
from the Observer steps. He had no idea if he was going
to be able to stop her from going to the Press about
Gordon Sinclair. What he did know is that he had to try.

He had not bargained for the sheer force of emotion he had unleashed, and it was not until well into the afternoon that she had left. He did not think she would be going to the paper. But he could never be sure.

They walked to the local and she insisted on buying their drinks.

'As a sort of thank you.'

'Not needed, believe me.'

'Even so.'

They sat down at a table.

'So, how're you feeling?'

'Much better, although I won't pretend it isn't hard. I finished with Mark that evening and am fighting off all my other admirers.' She gave a nervous laugh. 'It's hard for me to be without a man.'

'I know. But by being by yourself for a while, you'll find your own inner strength if you give yourself time.'

'I know, I know. But a life-time's habits are very hard to break.'

'True,' said the vicar, nodding at his pint.

Alice was questioned when she went into the village store.

'What's Lydia Page doing at Rose Cottage? Her car's been in the drive every day for a week now. Are the new owners having a garden make-over?' Madge paused for breath. The other three women looked expectantly at Alice.

'Lydia Page is the new owner.'

They all gasped and asked her questions simultaneously, but she did not say another word. She warned Lydia that evening and Lydia wailed, 'Oh, I didn't want them to know. Now they're going to think all sorts of things.'

'Well what does it matter what they think? They have to know sooner or later and the sooner they do then the sooner they'll get onto other gossip.'

'Oh, I'll never be able to face them!'

'Well don't then. Shop in Delaby,' Alice retorted.

Lydia glared at her.

'Well, I really don't see what all the secrecy is about.'

That evening, there was a knock at Lydia's front door. She opened it and saw Toby Thomas standing there.

'Wondered if it was OK if I checked on the car?'

'I would say it's high time,' answered Lydia and thought how exactly like Alice she sounded.

He shuffled on the doorstep. 'Is it OK if the car's here? Is it in your way?'

'If it is or it isn't, it's what he wanted.'

Toby nodded, 'I'll get on, then.'

She watched him through a window, taking the covers off the old Jag and running his hand down the side of it, as if he were stroking a horse. He opened the bonnet and fiddled around for a while before re-covering the car and leaving in his van.

'What a funny pair we are,' thought Lydia as she watched his van turn out of the drive. Gordon must despair of us. As if to make up for Toby's behaviour, she went into the garden and picked a few hydrangea heads. She put these in an empty jam jar by her bed. Her teddy looked at her from the chair in the corner of the room. Apart from her clothes, and she had few enough of those, there was nothing else of hers in the room. She did not even own an alarm clock. She wondered, briefly, how she could have got this far through life with so few pos-sessions. But the fact that she had did not really bother her. Just maybe, though, she would treat herself to some

259

new shoes the next time she was in Delaby.

The new shoes turned into a new dress as well. She had not owned a dress since she had to wear one for school. This one was in the window of a boutique in one of the small side streets. It was simply cut in a rich terracotta silk. It had taken Lydia an hour to pluck up the courage to go into the shop. But once the dress was on, she knew she would have to have it. She waited while the assistant wrapped it up in brown and gold tissue paper and fastened this with a gold sticker. She left with a beautiful brown and gold carrier hanging from her arm. This changed her whole outlook on shoe buying. She had already seen a red pair of Doc Martins she fancied, but they would hardly go with the dress.

Eventually, she found the perfect pair, which had been hand beaded. Low, but slim, she felt excitement rise in her as she saw them in the window. Five minutes later, she had made her purchase.

On an impulse, she went into a china shop and splashed out on a couple of cheap vases. She also saw a beautiful fruit bowl and added that to her other bits. A bone, too, for Pounce from the butchers and she decided she had better call it a day. Then she stopped and retraced her tracks. She had forgotten someone.

When she got back to Rose Cottage, she hung the tea towel and the oven gloves up in the kitchen. She took the price sticker off the bowl and filled it with the apples she had picked from the garden. Her very first purchases for a home of her own. She felt enormously pleased.

'I hope you don't mind,' she whispered. An apple dislodged itself from the bowl and thudded onto the table, making her jump and then laugh at her own timidity.

CHAPTER THIRTY-TWO

Lydia came home from the Manor, muddy and exhausted. She turned into the drive and saw the garage doors were open and the Jaguar was uncovered and the bonnet up. Damn, she could do with just collapsing into a bath. This was her little treat to herself of late. She would get in, feed the dog, make herself a large mug of hot chocolate and run a deep bath, which she would lie in for ages, letting all the dirt and grime, aches and pains, just soak away.

She let Pounce out of the car and he shot off into the garage to see who was there. She followed reluctantly. Toby was coming out from the garage with Pounce frolicking around him.

'I'd say this was a dog that had been cooped up all day on his own.'

'I'd say it was a dog that is trying to make you think that, so that you'll play ball with him. He's actually a dog who's spent all day hurtling round a park with two spaniels.'

Toby laughed and bent to stroke him and was licked vigorously in return.

'Glad to see you're working on the car.'

Toby looked embarrassed, 'Sorry about ignoring it for so long.'

'S'OK. I didn't go in the house for ages. It was only Alice's persistence that got me inside at all.' She went past and unlocked the back door. 'Cup of tea?'

'Love one. Just need to get the oil filter changed and then I've done.'

Lydia went in and pottered around, wiping up dishes, making tea and feeding the dog. She leant up against the range, warming herself through. It was getting decidedly wintry. Pounce pushed the door open, emptied his bowl and flopped down in front of the range, his back against the warm door.

'Silly dog.' She poked him with her toe and he rolled onto his back with his paws in the air so that she could rub his tummy. There was a knock on the door.

'Come in,' she called out and went to finish the tea. Toby stood in the doorway, looking awkward. 'Sink's there if you want to clean up a bit.'

He nodded and started to rub the grease off his hands. She put the mugs on the table and cut the last piece of Alice's cake into two. She had not seen Alice since she had been on her shopping spree to Delaby and she missed her company.

Well, Gordon, she thought, *here am I in my own kitchen, entertaining a young man. It's a first!'* Toby drank his tea down while still propped up by the sink.

'So, when's the car's first outing, then?'

'There's a club night next week, but I'm not sure whether I'll go or not.'

'Why ever not?'

'It just doesn't feel right.'

'What, as if you're stepping into a dead man's shoes?'

He looked astonished at her forthright manner. 'Well…yes.'

'But he would have wanted you to take it - you know he would.'

Toby was quiet. He could not get out of his head the last club night he had been to with Gordon and how badly he had behaved. He just could not cope with illness and with death - never had been able to. And he never had the courage to apologise to Gordon. He was such a blinking idiot at times. And then that woman after the funeral - he could have bitten his tongue off. He could almost see the thirty pieces of silver! But he did not want to tell this young woman all of this.

'I'll see,' he finally said, and drank back his tea, even though it was too hot. He did not want to stay here any longer - he felt uncomfortable. 'Well, I'd better be off. Thanks for the tea.'

'S'OK,' she answered, looking at him beneath her lashes and sensing his confusion.

After he had gone, she pottered in the garden, walking down to the meadow and sitting briefly on the swing.

'I'm doing all right, aren't I Gordon?' she asked out loud, but the only sound in reply was that of the wind through the trees.

Alice popped in the next evening. Lydia greeted her with a, 'Where have you been?'

Alice looked flustered, 'Well...well...I figured you wouldn't want an old 'un like me keep coming round and getting in the way. But I thought by now you'd be out of cake.' She hooked a tin out of her bag.

'Oh Alice! Whatever am I going to do with you? I've missed you.' Lydia fiddled around in the kitchen drawer and pulled out a package. It was her turn to look embarrassed. 'I've bought you something.'

'What? For me?'

'Yes. I had a little shopping spree in Delaby. Look! I

bought these and these and this ... oh, and a dress I'll show you later.'

Alice sat down. She had not seen Lydia look so animated. Or so well.

'Well, open it then.'

Alice undid the wrapping and pulled out a beautiful little antique blue and white candlestick. 'Oh, it's lovely. But how did you know?'

'Gordon told me you collected blue and white china.'

'Well, fancy you remembering. It was my birthday last week as well.'

'I wish I'd known. How old were you?'

Alice looked up, recovering quickly, 'My, but you're a cheeky one. Don't you know better than to ask your elders a question like that?'

Lydia laughed. She rummaged around in one of the kitchen drawers and pulled out a pack of birthday candles. 'Thought I'd seen these hanging around.' She began to sink them into the top of the chocolate cake Alice had brought with her. She got some matches and lit them.

'Oh, you are daft,' muttered Alice, but she looked secretly pleased.

'Wish!' shouted Lydia as Alice blew them out. Alice closed her eyes and concentrated.

'Now I think there's still a few bottles in the kitchen cupboard. Let's have a birthday drink as well.'

It was much later that the Reverend Turnball called in to see Lydia. She invited him in and he noticed how flushed she looked and less strained. As he went through, he saw Alice and then the bottle of port and the two glasses.

'Care for a glass, vicar? Get him a glass, Lydia.'

Lawrence had never seen her like this before. He looked

at both of the women before him, one holding a bottle of port and the other beaming at him.

He laughed and shook his head. 'No, thanks very much. I'm on duty. I was just driving past the cottage and I thought I'd stop and see if you were OK, Lydia. But I can see you are.' He winked at them both, 'Enjoy the rest of your evening.'

He let himself out and heard Alice cackle with laughter over something. Well, who would have thought it? Cantankerous old Mrs. Stamp and that straight faced young woman. Both drunk together, but quite happy. *'Oh his God worked in mysterious ways,'* he thought and chuckled.

CHAPTER THIRTY-THREE

Lydia was clipping the privet hedge next to the garage when she realised she had not seen Toby Thomas for a fortnight. He had obviously decided not to take the Jaguar to the last club night after all. She wondered if she ought to suggest going with him. After all, she did know how he felt. It also made her realise how far she had come since Gordon's death.

As she explored Rose Cottage, she began to realise how much trouble Gordon had gone to, to make sure that the place was left in perfect order. Although she often felt his presence, she truly felt that Rose cottage was hers to do with as she wished. He had left her exactly the right amount of furniture - just enough for day-to-day living, but giving her the potential to add her own, to the existing pieces. There were no pictures on the walls and he had even taken out the hooks and touched up the paint so that she had a blank canvas to work with. The shelves in the study were empty so that she could put in a few of her own books. Everywhere was clean and well maintained. She had not actually bought anything beyond those first few purchases, but she had started to look at the prices of things.

Her work had picked up and she now had a full week. This left her only the weekends to work in Gordon's garden. She still thought of it as his and she guessed she always would.

She started to mull over what Alice had mentioned all those weeks ago about doing Bed and Breakfast. She wanted to be able to spend more time at Rose Cottage, not less time. She asked Lord P. about that when next she saw him.

'Have you thought about what a tie it'd be, particularly as you're on your own?'

She nodded.

'And people expect en-suite now. Can you offer that?'

'Well, no.' She thought about the room which had been Gordon's. 'But there's enough space to put in a shower room.'

'Lot of expense and just so as you can fill your house up with strangers.'

Despite his reservations, the idea just would not go away. She saw herself feeding guests with eggs from her own hens. She could even keep bees. It was just where to get the money from to do the necessary improvements.

She was deep in thought one evening, when Toby appeared at the back door. She had hardly seen anything of him, although she knew that he had been working on the Jaguar, as he had left the covers off it a couple of times.

'Just thought I'd let you know I'm taking the car out for a spin. Didn't want you to think you had burglars.'

'Can I come?'

He looked surprised and she immediately regretted the impulse that had made her ask. 'Oh look. I'm sorry. Of course you don't want me along.'

'No. It's not that. I was just surprised.' He seemed to hesitate. 'We…um…we could stop for a drink if you like?' He did not know why he had said it, as she made him feel slightly uncomfortable, but the words were out now and there was no retracting them. She was picking up a coat. She pulled open a kitchen drawer and ran what looked like one of Pounce's brushes through her hair.

'Ready.'

He couldn't help smiling. She was so without artifice. What you saw was what you got. Pounce leapt up when she opened the door.

'No! Stay!'

He gave her a look and then slunk over to the range, flopping down with a huge sigh. She locked up while Tom backed the car out of the garage.

He drove hesitantly at first, getting used to the old car again. Then his confidence came back, along with his natural deftness.

'Where do you want to go for a drink?'

They had been driving for about half an hour and were in an area Lydia was not familiar with.

'I've no idea. I don't really go to pubs.'

He looked surprised. 'Do you not drink?'

'No, it's not that. I'm just not very sociable.'

He glanced at her, wondering if she was teasing, but could see she was serious. 'Me neither.'

It was her turn to stare.

'Which doesn't help with where we're going.'

'Look!' Lydia pointed. 'A sign for a village. There's bound to be a pub.'

Toby turned the car down a lane and within a few minutes they had reached a small village. Sure enough, there was a pub. He parked the Jag carefully, as far away from the other cars as he could. It was quiet inside, but tastefully done out.

In the lounge bar, a log fire put out a welcome warmth. They bought drinks and sat down at the table nearest to it. They were awkward in each other's company at first, but Lydia started to ask him about doing B & B and it broke the ice.

'I just wish I knew a builder I could trust. You hear so many horror stories about poor work and huge prices.' She took a sip of her drink. 'Don't you know anyone? You've lived in the village forever.'

He had reddened and looked slightly uncomfortable. 'Only my step-brother.'

'Is he a builder, then?'

'He trained as a plumber, but he's a bit of a jack-of-all-trades now.'

'Will you ask him to come round and have a look at the room. I need someone who could give me suggestions.'

'Oh, he'd do that, all right,' Toby answered darkly. He seemed to be making his mind up about something. 'I'll ask him to drop round, but make sure you get a few quotes.'

'Well there's family loyalty for you. OK, OK, I will.'

Toby picked up their empty glasses and they went out to the Jag and made their way home through the pitch-black lanes.

'Then you don't think I'm mad?'

'No, but I think it'll be damn hard work on your own.'

'That's what Lord P. said. But it's only one room. And I'm sure Alice would come in and help.'

He could see her excitement and was glad for her. She was quiet for a moment, looking out for rabbits on the verges. 'Toby, did you know Gordon well?'

'In some ways, yes, in others, no. Why do you ask?'

'Do you think he'd mind me doing the B & B?'

What a strange question, he thought, but knew she

wanted a considered opinion. 'He liked people, didn't he? His door was always open to visitors. So no, I don't think so. I think he would want you to do whatever made you happy.'

She seemed satisfied by his answer and when they reached Rose Cottage, she reminded him about his brother. He nodded, standing some way away from her.

''Night, then and thanks for letting me come with you.'

He smiled at her, 'I enjoyed it.' He got back in the car, having opened the garage doors. When he had put the car away, she had gone. He was half-relieved and half-disappointed.

Lydia had gone inside and had hastily closed the door, leaning against it for a moment, but then having to right herself to ward off Pounce's affections. He was much nicer that she had imagined. More sensitive and yet very practical. He was also, by all accounts, as anti-social as she was. She finished her chores and lay in bed with the intention of listening to the radio. It droned on in the background as an accompaniment to her churning thoughts.

Two days' later, just as she had got in from the Manor, a van drew up in the driveway. It was Robin Thomas, Toby's stepbrother. Lydia showed him into Gordon's bed-room, where he spent a good fifteen minutes measuring and writing things down while she hovered in the door-way.

'Well, you've enough room to do it. It's just deciding what you want. For a start, do you want a shower or a bath?'

Lydia thought for a moment, 'Oh, just a shower, I think.'

He finished a quick sketch and showed it to her. 'This

would be the best combination.' As he explained the details to her, it suddenly seemed to be a lot of work.

'How much will it all cost?'

'Well I think I can do it all myself, including the partitioning.' He gave her a price and she whistled.

'I'm going to have to think about it. I hadn't realised it was going to be so much.' Robin Thomas started justifying his quote, but she stopped him. 'No, no, no. It's not your quote. I've just never done anything like this before. The biggest item I've ever bought for a bathroom is toilet paper.'

'Well get another couple of quotes and see.'

She nodded, but knew that it would take her ages to save up to have the work done.

She found Toby cleaning the Jag a few days later. She thanked him for sending his brother round, but explained that she would not be able to afford it.

'So get a loan.'

She looked at him blankly.

'A bank loan. Go and see your bank manager. You do have one, I suppose?'

She nodded, 'But they won't lend me any money.'

'Of course they will. You own property outright. You're a woman of means.'

She had never even thought of that. But she quickly put up more objections.

Toby sighed, 'Look, book an appointment to see your personal banker and I'll get the time off and take you.'

He saw her go indoors mouthing *personal banker* under her breath. She came out ten minutes' later.

'Thursday at two o'clock. Is that OK?'

'Of course it is.'

She was a complete bundle of nerves on the way to the bank. Toby had insisted on driving her there in the Jag, saying it was a fitting car for someone about to take charge of her financial future. He had to practically push her through the door of the bank and took charge as she stood and dithered in the foyer.

'For goodness sake, it's only a small loan. It's chicken feed to them.'

'But I've never borrowed money before. Not ever. What if I can't pay it back?'

'Why wouldn't you be able to? You're in full-time work, and if you do B & B, the income from that will pay off the loan in no time. Now go on!' He almost shouted the last words at her.

He was right. They gave her a decision instantly and the whole process was extremely straightforward. She came back, smiling broadly. He was sitting, reading a classic car magazine, but could tell, from looking at her face what the outcome had been.

'Better go and look at showers, then,' he said.

She never realised there was so much choice - bath-room suites, tiles, floor coverings, light fittings, paint charts. The next few weeks opened up a whole new world to her. She was not sure what she had expected when she employed Robin Thomas for the job, but it certainly was not so much involvement and decision-making on her part.

Alice's common sense was a godsend to her. She was quite happy to discuss paint charts over a cup of tea. 'What colour are you going to do the bedroom?'

Lydia frowned, 'I hadn't thought of decorating it.'

'Well, of course you'll have to. Once the partitioning

goes up and he starts wiring, you're going to have to do the whole room. And you'll probably have to look at your floor covering as well.'

Lydia scowled, 'Can't we just have bare boards and strip them?'

'It's not very practical. It's OK in the Med., but over here it can be cold and people expect comfort now.'

She talked Lydia into looking at the room as a whole and doing it all properly. Robin started work on the Monday, but had usually left before Lydia got home. She inspected the work each night with great excitement. Now it had begun, she could visualise it all so much more easily.

She gave herself the day off during the next week and she and Alice went shopping. She had already taken Alice's advice and had ordered a bed some weeks ago. Now they needed all the soft furnishings. They came home laden with parcels. Alice collapsed in the chair.

'My feet are that sore. I'm too old for malarkies like this.'

Lydia looked worried.

'Oh, don't take on so. I'll be all right after a cuppa.'

Robin appeared in the doorway of the kitchen. 'Good idea.' He came through and sat down at the table. The cosy atmosphere changed and Alice noticed a tension in Lydia.

'How's it going?'

'Should finish the bathroom by the end of next week. Then it's just decorating.'

She nodded. She felt uncomfortable with him here and she had wanted to go through the contents of the bags with Alice. He picked up his mug of tea.

'See you two've been out spending money. Brought me

back a present?'

'You're too cheeky for you own good,' snapped Alice, 'You'd get more work done if you stopped asking daft questions and got back to your work.'

'Ooh, a real slave driver,' he drawled, but Alice could see he was annoyed. 'OK, I'm going.' He left the room but the mood had broken.

'Thanks,' was all Lydia said.

'Well, you mustn't let him get the better of you - not his sort.'

'What do you mean?'

They had both lowered their voices so that he would not hear.

'He's a sharp one, that one. Does a good job, mind, but you need to watch him. Not like his brother. Chalk and cheese they are. But then they are only half-brothers.'

'Are their parents divorced?'

'No, Toby's mother died when he was young. His dad remarried a year later.' Alice snarled her disapproval. 'Not like Edith, this one's a real hard case. Just like her son.'

Lydia took Alice's disapproval with a pinch of salt. She took against people for the strangest of reasons at times. Lydia often wondered why Alice had accepted her.

It was a few days later and Lydia was in the garden, catching the last few moments of daylight. She tried as much as possible to stay out of the way when Robin Thomas was around. He made her feel uneasy, although she could not say why. Pounce was down in the bottom meadow, so he gave her no warning of Robin coming up behind her.

'All finished, gorgeous.'

She jumped with fright, the spade fell with a clatter

and she swore violently. Robin was laughing and he casually draped an arm round her. 'You're jumpy, sweetheart.'

At that moment, Toby walked into the garden. She stiffened and pulled away. 'I'm not your sweetheart!'

'Yeah, but you could be.' He was moving towards her. She backed away and trod on a plant in the border.

'Robin!'

They both jumped and Lydia felt so relieved, her knees went quite weak. Robin was moving away now, leaving her to wipe her damp hands down her jeans and regain her composure.

'What's up, big brother? What brings you here? Not tinkering with that old car again, are you?'

Toby shook his head, 'Your mobile's switched off. The school has a problem and wants you there, pronto.'

'Damn. I was about to go and have a pint. Oh well. Beer and carnal desires will have to wait.' He leered in the direction of Lydia, who was pretending to work. Toby's hand shot out and grabbed his arm.

'Leave her alone. She's not for the likes of you.'

Robin turned to face him and laughed out loud, 'Got a fancy for her yourself, bruv?' He snorted derisively. 'She needs a real man. She'd be too much of a handful for you.' He pushed Toby out of the way and disappeared inside to pick up his tools.

'Lydia?'

She carried on working. 'Yes?'

'You OK?'

'Yes, fine. Why shouldn't I be?'

He sighed, 'I'm in the garage. If you should need me.'

She did not answer and he went and worked on a bit of the chrome bumper until he heard his brother's van start up. He heard Lydia call the dog and then the sound

of the kitchen door being closed and bolted. He regretted the day he had sent his brother round. He thought
she could look after herself, but now he was not so sure.
His brother was street-wise and persistent, with a nasty
temper. He would have to watch out for her, that was all.

CHAPTER THIRTY-FOUR

Lydia saw that all the structural work had been finished as he said. She ran her hand over the shining tiles as she looked around the shower room. It was perfect. It just needed decorating and it was done. She had got him to put in some new lighting in the bedroom and some extra sockets for a TV and kettle. If only she could get rid of the uncomfortable feeling she had about Robin Thomas. He was so unlike his brother. He felt dangerous. In fact, he reminded her of her father.

She woke up in the early hours of the morning and decided. She would pay him and finish the rest of the decorating herself. That way, she need not have him around the house any more, and she would save herself a bit of money. She would tell him in the morning.

When she woke hours later, she felt less sure of her plan. She did not relish the task at all and so one of the first things she did when she got up was to phone Alice. She could tell Alice was flustered at the early call, despite being an early riser, but she said she would be round straight away.

As it was, she only beat Robin Thomas by a few moments. He walked jauntily into the kitchen, rubbing his hands together.

'Not often I get a welcoming committee. Any chance of any breakfast?' he looked from one to the other. 'No? OK, I'll get on then.'

'No.'

The word hung in the air. He stopped, almost in mid stride and turned back to Lydia. 'Sorry?'

She could feel her resolve weakening, felt defenceless in the presence of this man. Then she remembered her father and she rallied. 'I want to settle up with you today for the work you've done. I've decided I can do the painting and decorating myself.' She was aware of Alice clattering in the cupboard. Other than that, there was silence.

'I see.' He came towards her, his eyes narrowed. 'Not happy with the work then?'

She stood her ground, facing him squarely, aware of Alice watching behind her. 'It's not that at all. I think what you've done is brilliant. I'm just running out of money and although I won't finish it as well as you would, I'm sure I'll do a good enough job.' She held his gaze for a moment longer and then moved to the table where she had a chequebook. 'So what do I owe you?'

'I'll have to go out to the van and check a few invoices.' He marched out, clearly not happy.

Lydia sighed and Alice reached over and squeezed her arm. 'You're doing fine, love, just fine.'

She smiled at her gratefully and watched Alice start to cook some bacon. She seemed quite at home in the kitchen here.

Robin Thomas appeared in the doorway and gave Lydia a hastily written invoice. 'I've included today, seeing as how I expected to work and I can't start any other job at such short notice.'

Lydia privately thought that this probably was not true, but she wrote out the amount requested and handed him the cheque. 'Thanks for everything.'

He nodded, seemed about to say something and changed his mind. 'I'll be seeing you.' He nodded at Alice and went.

It was not until Lydia heard his van pull away that she slumped into the chair with relief.

'Now are you going to tell me what this is all about?' Alice put a plate in front of Lydia and sat down opposite. Lydia told her, between mouthfuls, of the episode in the garden the previous night. 'Well, I did warn you he's a bit of a rum 'un, but I don't think he'd hurt you.'

'He just makes me feel afraid. It brings back lots of stuff for me.' To her horror, she could feel her eyes filling with tears. Alice patted her hand. The moment passed and Alice offered to stay and help Lydia with some painting.

'Can't do a lot, mind, but I can help a bit. Got a meeting this afternoon about the church windows. Apparently they're nearly ready. We just need to agree a date.'

'Wish he could have seen them.'

'Oh, he'll be able to. He's not far away.'

Lydia looked surprised. She had never heard Alice talk like that before. She liked to think Gordon was near and she often talked to him, but she thought it was just wishful thinking.

They worked in a companionable silence until Alice left for her meeting. Lydia packed up at lunchtime as she was due at Mrs. Wright's that afternoon. Her garden was really taking shape and she often spoke with gratitude about her mysterious benefactor. Sometimes Lydia wanted to tell her who it was. She wanted so desperately to talk about Gordon.

Gossip in the village had settled down now about her living at Rose Cottage and the villagers treated her just as they always had. Which, Lydia reflected, was always with a slight wariness. But she was used to not fitting in, to being different.

As she dug, she saw Penny Young heading in the direction of the vicarage. She still had not met her face-to-face since the funeral and she wondered what she would have to say about Gordon leaving her the cottage. She could imagine the rumours she would be quite happy to spread around.

On her way home, she dropped in to the blacksmith as he had telephoned to say that he had finished the sign she had ordered. He held it up and she admired the large B & B in black wrought iron.

'Got a strong man to help you hang it properly?' he asked and laughed as he saw Lydia's face. 'Never known anyone as independent as you.' He had also made a wrought iron post to hang the sign from. She felt a surge of excitement as she paid him and laid the sign carefully in the back of the car. She would get on with the painting when she got home. This was the last free time she had in the daytime, as she was at the Manor for the rest of the week.

She had rested the sign in the corner of the kitchen, yelling at Pounce, who was dancing around and threatening to send it clattering. He slunk away, his tail between his legs, and she was immediately chastened. She grabbed a sandwich and went upstairs. She had been painting for a couple of hours when she heard someone banging on the back door and Pounce barking furiously. She put the paint down and laid her brush across the top of the tin. Her arms ached from the different exercise. The pounding began again. 'OK, OK, I'm coming.'

She ran down the stairs, pulled Pounce away from the

door and opened it. Robin Thomas stood there, his hands on his hips. She shoved Pounce out of the door and stood aside to let him in. It was only then that she smelt the alcohol on his breath.

'Did you leave something?' She knew it was his brush she was using upstairs.

'Oh, yeah, but I've come to claim it now.'

He moved forward, grabbed her, forcing her back against the wall and kissed her, thrusting his tongue into her mouth. She recovered quickly and pushed him far enough away to be able to turn her head away.

'Get out!' It came out as a croak and she coughed.

'Oh no, I want what my brother's been enjoying all these weeks.' As his head came towards her, she shoved him with all her strength. It seemed to incite him, because he grabbed her arms and pinned them at her sides, holding her against the wall with the bulk of his body. She could feel his erection against her stomach. His mouth forced hers open and he moved suddenly, letting go of one of her arms and struggling with the zip on his jeans. It was now or never. She raised her free arm and punched him on the side of the head. It was the only place she could reach. He grunted with surprise, raised his hand and hit her across the face, hard enough to send her flying to the floor.

'You like it rough, eh?'

She was dazed, had thought it was just a saying that people used about seeing stars. Something primal erupted in her. She heard herself yell, 'No!' her feet slipping on the tiled floor as she tried to get up. Her hand touched something on the chair. It was Pounce's silver collar, still with his lead attached to it. She was on her knees now and with a desperate haste, she grabbed the harness and swung it with all the force she could muster. It caught him across the face and he screamed in agony as the buckle tore into the soft flesh beside his eye. The blood flow was instant and blinding. He was whimpering now in pain, his hands over his face. She got up, ran to the back door and fled down the garden into the meadow, where she hid, knowing he would never find her there. She spat into the bushes, trying to rid her mouth of his taste. Pounce came into view and she called him over, softly. She pulled him near to her and told him to lie down.

Toby had got home late as he had had to finish a service on a car. His stepmother put his dinner on the table in front of him.

'Robin not in?'

Mealtimes were always more harmonious when his brother was out.

'No. Had to go round to that job he's doing at Rose Cottage. Said he had unfinished business there.'

Toby put his fork down slowly, his mouth full of food.

'Did he take the van?' he heard his father ask.

'Course he did. How else was he going to get there,' his stepmother snapped.

'Well, he'd had a few drinks when I saw him in the pub earlier. How he doesn't get stopped, I'll never know.'

Toby stood up, and pushed his chair back with such a force it clattered on its back. He ran out of the door and got into his car, ignoring their startled looks. He knew. He just knew.

He drove fast and passed his brother in his van at the T-junction just before Rose Cottage. He pulled into the drive and was out of the car almost before the engine had stopped. He ran to the back door, calling her name. It was locked. He banged on it. 'Lydia! It's Toby! Let me in.'

There was silence.

'Lydia, if you don't let me in, I'll break the door down.' Panic sounded in his voice. He had to know if she was OK. 'Lydia!'

The door opened and he rushed in, banging it against the wall in his haste. She had her back to him. The dog rushed over to be greeted.

'Lydia.' He walked over to her and touched her arm, trying to turn her round.

She spun round, shaking him off, 'Don't you touch me.'

'Jesus.'

Her cheek and eye were swollen and there was a red weal over her cheekbone.

'What else did he do?'

She closed her eyes and sat down on a chair, all the fight gone out of her. He saw the dog lead and collar on the floor, saw the blood.

'Lydia, you must tell me what else he did.'

She was silent. He went to her freezer and got out a packet of peas. He wrapped a tea towel round it. She eyed him suspiciously. 'What are you doing?'

'Hold this on your face. It'll help. I'm going to call the police.'

'No.' it was a desperate plea. 'No,' she repeated. 'This is all he did. I hit him with the dog collar.' Her voice broke and he went to comfort her, but she shrunk away from him.

'Lydia, it's OK.'

She was shaking her head. 'No, it's not. Now I'd like

283

you to go.'

'I can't leave you like this.'

'Like what? Abused by a man. It seems normal to me.' The venom in her voice shocked him.

'We're not all like that.'

'Well right at this moment, that's how it seems.'

He looked at her for a moment and then went out of the back door. She heard his car start up. Pounce came and sat in front of her, nuzzling her with his nose. She wrapped her arms around him and sobbed into his coat.

Robin Thomas opened the back door. His head, newly stitched, throbbed unbearably. He belched loudly. Damn, they had turned the kitchen light off. He tripped over a chair leg as he fumbled his way across to the switch, swore, found the light and flicked it on. He saw Toby immediately, leaning against the cooker. He looked at him and saw the hatred in his eyes.

'What the…'

It was all he got out before Toby's fist slammed into his face, breaking his nose and sending him crashing to the floor.

CHAPTER THIRTY-FIVE

Lydia inspected her face in the mirror and decided that she could not face meeting people. She rubbed some arnica onto it and went up into the bedroom. She had already cleaned up the kitchen and had washed Pounce's collar, closing her eyes as the blood swirled down the sink. She felt shaky, but also full of resolve. She would cope. And she would do it on her own.

She took the rest of the week off - lying by telling Lord P. that she had 'flu. Alice arrived the next day and exclaimed with horror when she saw Lydia's face. She also saw the shutters go up and knew that she would not push for any information, which was not forthcoming. She accepted Lydia's story of a scrape with a tree branch, but knew it was far from the truth. She went out, at Lydia's request and got her some shopping. When she got back, Lydia was hard at work upstairs. Alice worked away in the kitchen on her old sewing machine, shortening the new curtains they had bought for the room. She had to make Lydia stop for a lunch break, but she was back painting soon after. It was as though she was exorcising demons through sheer hard work.

By the end of the week, the decorating was complete and it just needed the finishing touches. The carpet was laid on the Monday and on Tuesday evening, Lydia and Alice hung the curtains and put the new bedding onto the bed. Positioning and hanging the pictures took longer than either of them had anticipated. Soon bedside lamps were in place, toiletries and thick fluffy towels were arranged in the bathroom. Lastly, Lydia brought in the small television she had bought and the tea- and coffee-making facilities. She straightened the mohair throw which was draped over the bottom of the bed and admired their handiwork. The walls glowed a rich cream, the lamps were the same soft blue as the carpet. Both set off the old pine furniture.

'It's perfect,' Alice commented.

'Yes,' said Lydia, it is. I shall put some fresh flowers in the room tomorrow.'

'Should we declare it officially open, do you think?'

'Not yet. There's still one more thing to do.' She beckoned for Alice to follow her downstairs and pointed to the heavy wrought iron B & B sign resting in the corner of the kitchen.

'But it's dark. And surely it's a man's job?'

Lydia flashed her a look of such scorn she could have bitten her tongue out. No mention had been made of Lydia's face and the bruising had faded to a sludgy green colour. But Alice could sense how tense Lydia was and hoped that the girl would be able to come to terms with whatever it was that had really happened to her.

With Alice holding a hurricane lantern, Lydia forced the stake into the ground and hung the heavy sign. She was open for business. She stood with her hands on her hips looking at her handiwork.

'Now we can open that bottle.'

Lydia's phone went two days later when she was working at the Manor. Because she was out so much of the time, she had a small plaque fixed to the B & B sign. It said *For bookings telephone* and gave her mobile number. Until the business took off, she had to combine both jobs. Lord P. was totally flexible about when she worked her hours, so there was no problem if she had to dash off to show someone the room. It was not perfect, but it would have to do. A Tourist Information officer had visited the previous evening and seemed very satisfied by what he had seen and took all her details. It was the office on the phone now asking whether the room was available tonight.

'No,' she said, in a complete panic, 'No, I mean yes.' She suddenly felt a wave of nervousness come over her. She made a mental note of the peoples' names, shouted to Sam, her co-worker, that she had to go and raced back to the cottage. She shut Pounce in the kitchen and ran upstairs to make sure the room was OK, even though she had only checked it that morning. She put a small vase of greenery and berries on each of the bedside tables. As it was getting dark, she drew the curtains and rearranged the throw for the hundredth time. Then she caught a glimpse of herself in the mirror.

'Oh my goodness.'

No time to shower, but she changed quickly, wiped the mud off her face and as a last minute thought, put on a bit of lipstick.

'Oh Alice, I wish you were here,' she cried. She heard a car hesitate in the road outside and turn into the drive. She raced down the stairs and opened the front door, ignoring Pounce's furious barking. She greeted the couple and showed them to the room.

The woman looked around, 'What a lovely room.' She turned to Lydia, 'We'll be very happy here.'

Lydia beamed at her, and showed them where the

dining room was. Pounce was now scrabbling frantically at the kitchen door.

'Why don't you let him out? We love dogs.'

'Well, if you're sure.'

They fussed over Pounce before going to get their bags. Lydia was constantly aware of their presence in the house and was glad when she heard them go out. She phoned Alice who promised to come round and cook breakfast.

She was really grateful for Alice's help. She still felt as though she had two left feet. In the end, Alice shooed her away from the cooker and told her to concentrate on serving her guests. As far as possible, she had bought all organic produce and was using one of Alice's homemade marmalades.

The guests left just after ten o'clock. Lydia stood in the hall holding the money they had paid her. She smoothed the visitors' book, reading the very first comments in it before going back to the kitchen.

'We did it!'

'No, you did it.'

Lydia shook her head, 'I couldn't have done it without you, I really couldn't.' On impulse, she leaned forward and kissed Alice's cheek. Then she put a £20 note on the table. 'That's for you. For all your help.'

Alice had flushed a bright red, 'Don't be daft. I don't want any money. I thoroughly enjoy helping. I enjoy feeling needed. It's not something that happens very often when you get to my age.'

'So can I ask you again?'

'Of course you can. Now let's go and get that room cleaned, in case it's needed again tonight.'

It was after lunch when Lydia arrived at the Manor. Her phone was quiet and she managed to make up some time by working until after dark.

She felt exhausted when she got home and she was glad she had no visitors. She heard a car in the drive and fear coursed through her. She made sure the door was locked and bolted. But it was only Toby. She watched from behind the curtains in the hall and saw the tail lights of the Jaguar disappear down the road. He had not been near Rose Cottage since that night and perversely, she had missed him. She wanted to share with him the news of her first guests. But Toby was linked to that awful night as Robin was his half-brother.

She had half-expected another visit, but then images flashed back of the flailing collar and lead, and of his anguished cry and the surge of blood. From what Alice had hinted at, he had been known to be violent in the past, but maybe not persistent. Maybe she really had seen him off. She shivered suddenly. She had allowed him to grow large in her thoughts and she realised he was still affecting her life as much as if he was in the kitchen before her. She suddenly wanted to know where he was and what had happened that night after she had hidden in the meadow. She needed to get a grip. She would not allow fear to dominate her life again as she felt tired of being a victim. She looked around her, at the mellow walls of the kitchen and thought '*I've got all this now.*' It made her feel safer, somehow. It was as if Gordon had known how it would help heal her.

The thought of him made tears well up unexpectedly. She missed him more than she would have thought possible. She had actually allowed herself to connect with him. She felt safe with him and would have trusted him with her life. Now there was just Alice. An image of Toby came into her head. She had started to trust him, until his half-brother had spoilt it all. She pushed him out of her mind and turned the radio on to drown out her thoughts.

Alice bumped into Toby coming out of the DIY shop the following morning. She took his arm, 'I want a word with you, young man.' He looked immediately anxious, blushing slightly as Alice led him to a seat on the pavement where they could talk in relative peace.

She was surprised when he spoke first, 'How's Lydia?'

Alice looked at him sharply, 'So you know, do you?'

Toby looked down at his hands, not sure how to answer. He ignored Alice's question, 'Is she OK, though?'

'Aye. She's OK. But no thanks to your brother, I'll be bound.'

'It won't happen again. He's gone.' It was as good an admission as she was going to get. He got up, 'I've got to go. Tell her...tell her I'll be seeing her.' And he was gone, leaving Alice sitting on the bench. So it had been Robin Thomas, as she had expected. She gave a little shiver. Nasty piece of work. Look at that last girlfriend he had. Twice she had seen her with cuts and bruises. They all should have done something then. She only hoped that Lydia had escaped with a cut and bruised face. She stood up and saw the vicar walking along the pavement with Penny Young. She nodded to them and scuttled off. She could not leave this where it was. She had to know.

Reverend Turnball looked after the old lady, 'She seemed very pre-occupied. I hope she was all right.'

Penny, who might had brushed his remark aside in the past, said, 'Maybe you can call round and see her later.'

He nodded, smiling at her, 'I'll do that.'

Alice knew that Lydia was at the Manor. She walked

up the long drive, glad that she had no more than a loaf of bread in her basket. She saw the dog first, lying down, his head resting on his paws. He scrambled up and raced over to her, delighted to see her.

'Pounce!'

She could hear Lydia calling. Then she appeared, coming out from behind a yew hedge.

'Alice! Whatever's wrong? What's happened?' She covered the distance between them rapidly. 'What is it? Are you ill?'

'No, don't fuss. I'm perfectly all right. I just wanted to talk to you.'

'Well, it must be important if you've walked all this way.'

'It's about that night.' She looked at Lydia darkly. 'I want to know what happened. All of it, mind, not an edited version suitable for a silly old woman.'

'Oh. I see,' Lydia ran her fingers through her hair and rubbed the side of her head. 'Alice, whatever brought this on?'

'Because I should have put a stop to his funny business years ago. We all should have, but we all turned a blind eye. That poor young girlfriend of his must have gone through hell.'

'But it's easier not to get involved. I know that.'

Alice nodded, 'That's as maybe, but I'm getting involved now and I want to know if he...you know...'

'Raped me?'

Alice could not meet her eyes, but she nodded.

'No. He didn't.' She saw tears come into the old woman's eyes. 'Oh Alice.' She put her arm round her bony shoulders and gave her a hug. 'He would have done, probably, but Pounce's silver collar won the day.' She was being light-hearted about it, which was something she did not really feel when she allowed herself to think of Robin Thomas.

Alice had regained her composure, 'I saw Toby Thomas in the village, you see.'

'Oh?'

'I asked him what had happened.'

'Oh Alice, you didn't!'

'He wanted to know how you were, so I asked him. He said his brother's gone. He also told me to tell you he'd see you.'

'Gone? But where?'

'I've no idea. He seemed a very grim young man.'

Lydia could not see Toby as grim. 'Yeah, well, I've no wish to see him.'

'Now that's no line to take. He's a nice young man and quite unlike his brother. You can't shut yourself away forever.'

'Alice! Are you match-making, by any chance?'

'Well, you could do worse than Toby Thomas. It's time you got out a bit more, had a bit of fun.'

'I'm quite happy as I am, thank you. I haven't got time for fun. Now go and bake us a cake or do anything useful, which will stop your meddling!'

Alice sighed and Lydia laughed at her. 'Bloody interfering old woman.'

Alice looked at her sharply, saw her grinning and laughed as well. 'Well, I'm glad my worst fears were wrong, anyway.'

'So am I. Now go!'

She watched Alice walk down the drive. Halfway down, she turned to look back and Lydia waved. '*Incorrigible,*' she thought and laughed out loud.

CHAPTER THIRTY-SIX

Penny Young looked up from the small desk in the rectory office as Lawrence appeared, carrying a mug of tea. She stifled a yawn.

'Isn't it time you stopped? You must be exhausted.'

He put the tea on the desk and Penny promptly picked it up from the polished surface and put it on a mat. 'I'll just finish this file and then I'll be off.'

He nodded, 'Fancy a drink afterwards?'

'Thought you'd never ask.'

She had been helping him with his accounts for a month now, as his usual secretary was on holiday. She liked coming here in the evenings. Her life had changed so much since that fateful meeting with Lawrence on the steps of the newspaper offices. He had made her realise how deeply unhappy she had become and had got her involved with village life. A year ago if anyone had told her she would be on the church flower rota, she would have laughed her head off. But when it had been her turn a week ago, she had got a deep satisfaction from arranging her chosen blooms in the peaceful old church. In a couple of weeks it was going to be all hands to the deck as the new windows were going to be installed and a special service held to bless them. The church was due to be cleaned from top to bottom in readiness.

It had involved more work that she could ever have imagined, but again, she had enjoyed being a part of it.

In the two years she had lived in the village, she had never joined in anything, believing happiness centred solely round a man.

She closed the file, drank her tea and stood up. She called out to Lawrence and after he had locked up, they walked over to the pub.

Lydia took a booking that evening from a couple who wanted a room for three nights. They arrived late, having had a long journey and they both looked exhausted. Lydia put a pot of tea and some of Alice's cake in the sitting room. She had already lit the fire and drawn the curtains and it looked very welcoming. She had bought a few bits for it when she was looking for bedroom furniture. A new pine coffee table sat in front of the sofas Gordon had left her. She had also purchased a couple of lamps and had bought a mirror for over the fireplace. She lit the candles in front of it and turned the main light out.

She heard Mr. and Mrs. Davidson coming down the stairs and showed them into the lounge. They expressed their gratitude to her and she spent a few minutes answering their questions.

By the end of the three days, she was exhausted. The minute they left the house each day, having found out what time they would be back, she dashed off to the Manor and on the last day, over to Peggy Wright's. She had got home half an hour before they got in each evening. It felt strange having people in the house, but she thought she would probably get used to it.

It was late the next week that she saw the workmen at the church and knew that the windows were being put in. That afternoon, she left Pounce at home and drove to the woodland burial site. She walked through the grounds and made her way over to Gordon's plot. A small sapling had been planted over his grave and she reached out and fingered its fragile leaves and then squatted down and put her hand over the soil where he lay. In the spring it would be planted with wild grasses and wild plants, scabious, poppy, clover, primroses and cowslips. She wanted to talk to him, but she did not know what to say. She thought he probably knew all her thoughts anyway. It was funny, but this was not where he was, it was just a symbol of his life on earth. A statement as to who he had been. She looked around at the other more mature trees and walked among them for a while. It was so peaceful here. The site owners had put benches in various places - all individually made out of different timbers. A tree seat encircled one of the old oak trees and it was here she went and sat, watching a woodpecker for a few minutes. There were no plaques or flowers allowed to spoil the naturalness of the site. She was glad he was here. Glad his body was in a special place.

The sun was beginning to set and she made a move as the cold was getting to her. She wondered who else came to sit, if any of the villagers had been up to see if a tree had been planted. *We all touch peoples' lives in different ways, but we seldom know we do.* She wanted to be able to tell him how he had touched hers. How he had transformed hers. And he had done it with no thoughts of what he would get in return.

'Thank you, Gordon,' she whispered as she stood by his graveside again, 'thank you so much.' The wind whistled through the trees as if in answer.

Toby was busy getting the Jaguar ready for the winter.

Apart from the occasional outing when the weather conditions were absolutely right, he planned to drive her only to keep everything ticking over. Since that night he had avoided Lydia, taking the afternoon off work to go and work on the car when he knew Lydia was at the Manor. He did not know why he felt he could not face her, but he felt that he had let her down in some way. Firstly by mentioning Robin in the first place and then by not coming round to see how she was.

He was surprised to hear her car pull up in the driveway much earlier than normal. Pounce raced into the garage to see him and he wiped his oily hands on a rag before fussing him.

'Hi.'

She was standing by the garage door.

'Hi.' He stood up and Pounce jumped up at him.

'Pounce! Get down!'

'It's OK. He's hardly going to make me dirty, is he?' He nodded towards his dirty overalls and she laughed. It was unexpected and it made him laugh with her. 'How are you?' He walked over to her and stood looking at her, his eyes a clear, piercing blue.

'I've just been to see Gordon's grave.'

He did not know what to say and he felt cross with himself. She saw his discomfort.

'They've planted the tree now. It's so peaceful up there. Have you been?'

He shook his head.

'No, I suppose there's no reason why you should have. Oh well, I must get on.'

She went out of sight and he swore to himself. Whatever was the matter with him? He was acting like a tongue-tied teenager. Whatever must she think of him?

Lydia fed Pounce and put a saucepan of milk on the stove. She felt chilled all of a sudden. There was a tap at the door, which aroused the slight feeling of fear she always seemed to live with.

'Who is it?'

'It's me, Toby.'

She unlocked the door and looked at him.

'Next time you go up there - to the grave, I'd like to come with you.'

'We can go anytime, but yes, I'll let you know.'

He nodded and turned away. She was just shutting the door when she heard him call her.

'Yes?'

'I'm so sorry about what happened.' He had coloured up, in his embarrassment.

'I know,' was all she replied before finally closing the door.

The envelope arrived a week later, addressed to Miss Lydia Page. She opened it and drew out an invitation to a service at the church on Sunday week, which would consecrate the windows. Her initial reaction was not to go, but then she changed her mind. She phoned Alice and asked if she could go with her.

She had a busy ten days. Her room was let for all but two of the nights and she still had her gardening to fit in. She knew she was going to have to talk to Lord P. about cutting down her hours, but she did not want to do it in the winter as she was bound to get fewer and fewer guests. She had already been asked if she was open over the Christmas period and had looked absolutely blank because she had not given it a thought. Well, she supposed she had nowhere to go. Last Christmas she had spent walking with Pounce. She had had a token present from her mother and a new fleece from Lord P., and that was it. She had not bought a single present for anyone. But this year it would be different. Now she had a proper home and people who wanted to stay in it. She had agreed to let the small single room as well, as it was to a member of the same family and they could all use the same bathroom. She would have to furnish it as it only had a bed and the desk in it, but it would not take much to do and if she could let it occasionally, it would boost her income.

She dressed warmly on the Sunday as she guessed the church would be cold. She picked Alice up on the way and they were both surprised to see the church was nearly full. Alice grumbled about having to sit near the back and by the time eleven arrived, it was standing room only. It was a huge turnout. Lydia spotted Toby with a woman she took to be his stepmother.

The service began and before long, Reverend Turnball had stepped down, allowing the Bishop to begin the unveiling.

The makeshift curtain in front of the window was removed and as if rising to the moment, the sun streamed through the stained glass, lighting the congregation with colour. '*They are stunning,*' Lydia thought as she listened to the blessing. She knew she would have to come back into the church and examine them closely. The service ended with prayers and a hymn and then the congregation started to leave.

Lydia waited for Alice, who was talking to the woman next to her.

An old woman in a wheelchair was being pushed up the aisle. Lydia realised it was Eleanor Sinclair.

CHAPTER THIRTY-SEVEN

'Mrs. Sinclair!' Lydia exclaimed in shock, stepping out in front of the wheelchair. The young woman pushing it smiled at her, but Eleanor's face was stony.

'Enjoying my son's house, are you?'

Lydia gasped, 'I'm...sorry?'

'Oh, you might look all innocent, but I know you set out from the beginning to get what you could from him.' She coughed and spittle ran down her chin. She wiped it away awkwardly. Lydia could see that she had virtually no movement down her left side.

'That may be what you think, but I can assure you you're absolutely wrong.' The voice was loud and clear. Alice had stood up and was moving out from the pew.

'Alice Stamp. And what would you know about it?'

'Actually everything. I knew your son's plans and I also know that Lydia didn't have any idea she was going to be left the house. It was something that took a lot of adjusting to.'

'Oh I bet it did.'

The sarcasm in Eleanor's voice was obvious. Lydia shook her head, 'I...I can't believe you could be so bitter and twisted...'

She stopped and fumbled for a tissue. People were looking at their little group with mounting curiosity. Lydia could see the Reverend Turnball moving down the aisle towards them and she turned and hurried out of the church. Toby, who had seen the altercation and had heard some of it, went out after her. He caught up with her as she pretended to look at one of the gravestones.

'Hey, it's OK.' Without thinking, he put his arm round her. He felt her stiffen against him and then she broke into a fresh paroxysm of sobs.

'It's so bloody unfair!' She turned towards him and he held her whilst she wept, muttering nonsense words to a place over her shoulder. He was acutely aware of the proximity of her.

She pulled away and wiped her eyes, 'I'm sorry. You must think me very stupid.'

'Not at all. It's been a pretty emotional morning, one way and another.'

Eleanor appeared outside the church door in her wheelchair. Mike Collier skirted round it, head down. He had seen Eleanor and had been shocked to his core at this remnant of the vital old woman she had been. He did not want to stop and talk to her, felt a mounting panic as he tried to get past her chair without being recognised.

Her clear voice rang out, 'Bet you're glad you didn't take up with me, aren't you, Mike Collier. Look at what a heap of old bones you'd have been left with.' She laughed harshly. Mortified with embarrassment, he turned and semi-bowed to her before hurrying down the path. She was right. He was glad.

Her helper was pushing her down the path, obviously glad to be on the move. Toby, with his arm still round Lydia, watched them go. Alice wandered over to them, limping slightly. The last few people were leaving the church.

'Who'd have thought she'd be so vindictive? Still, they do say a stroke can make people very aggressive.'

'Is that what she's had?' asked Toby, letting go of Lydia.

'Yes. Apparently she had virtually no mobility at all, but slowly she's recovering some movement.'

'You found out a lot in a short space of time.'

'It's what the care helper told me. Said she had the stroke almost as soon as she'd returned home.'

'And none of us knew,' mused Lydia, 'it doesn't seem right, somehow.'

'Well, how could you know?'

'Maybe I should have kept in touch - phoned her or something.'

'She seemed to want to wash her hands of us. It was her choice to go back,' interjected Alice.

'But we're all caught up together, aren't we? We're all linked by Gordon's death.' She rubbed her face as though she were tired. 'I couldn't see it before today, but now I can. When he died, he had very skilfully intertwined our lives so that we're all somehow…connected.'

Toby and Alice exchanged glances.

'I think we all need a drink,' Alice suggested.

Toby nodded, 'Come on then. Pub's open."

They walked off, trusting that Lydia would follow them.

It seemed that most of the congregation was in there.

'Wetting the windows' head,' quipped the landlord. To Lydia's horror, the vicar came through the door accompanied by Penny Young. Toby saw the look of horror cross her face, 'Hey, you're with us. We'll look after you.'

She smiled at him, suddenly very grateful.

'You go and sit down with Alice and I'll bring the drinks over.' The two women went over to a table by the window.

'Well, what a to do,' Alice said.

Lydia nodded, 'I can't help feeling I should have challenged her. Should have made her listen. I feel like a victim again and I don't like it.'

Toby brought their drinks over and Lydia almost drank hers in one go.

'Another one?' he asked and she blushed as she realised how swiftly she had drunk it.

'No, I mustn't.'

'Why ever not? It's Sunday. You've no guests staying. And it's nearly Christmas,' he added as an afterthought, to add weight to his argument.

'It's six weeks away!'

'Yes, well, you need to get your liver acclimatised long before it's upon you.'

They all laughed and he went to get Lydia a further drink while she went to the Ladies. To her horror, Penny Young intercepted her, 'Lydia, I'd like a word.'

'Well, what is it?' she could not hide the hostility in her voice, but was surprised when Penny reached out and touched her arm.

'I just wanted to say sorry. For everything. I was wrong and I don't mind admitting it. I was jealous of you.'

'Of me?' Lydia asked in astonishment.

'Yes. I wanted Gordon to feel about me, as he seemed to about you.'

'But we were only friends.'

'I know that now. And I know that what you two had was very unusual and very special.'

Lydia could only nod.

'Anyway, I'm desperately sorry for all the trouble I caused you.'

Lydia looked up and met her gaze, 'It's OK. It's all water under the bridge. We've all moved on, that's the main thing.'

She carried on past Penny and stood for a few minutes in the relative peace of the toilets. What a day of surprises it was turning out to be.

CHAPTER THIRTY-EIGHT

The meeting with Eleanor Sinclair still rankled Lydia over the next few weeks. She had just spent the day in town with Alice buying Christmas decorations. As she was having people to stay, she thought she ought to make a real effort. Plus it was her first Christmas at Rose Cottage. They were lugging bags of shopping back to the car.

'Did Gordon decorate very much?' Lydia asked.

'Gordon?' Alice snorted. 'He stuck a few sprigs of holly behind the pictures, if you can call that decorating.'

'So he didn't have a tree?'

'No. Not once.'

'Well, I'm going to have the largest one I can get.'

'Good for you!'

Alice had already made puddings and a cake and was feeling unusually festive. They were sitting round the kitchen table when they got home, examining their purchases when there was a knock on the door, which they discovered was Toby. He had been around more since the church ceremony and seemed to have lost his awkwardness when he was with Lydia.

'It's the witches' coven,' he greeted them.

'Cheeky. Don't give him any tea, Lydia.'

Lydia smiled at him, 'Car put to bed?'

He nodded. She poured him a mug of tea. He kept glancing at Alice.

'Cat got your tongue?'

He took a mouthful of tea and pulled a face at her. 'No, I wanted to ask Lydia something.'

'Oh and you want the old 'un out of the way.'

'Alice, don't you dare go,' Lydia said. 'Now, what is it Toby?'

'Well the Enthusiasts' Club are having a Christmas dinner and dance and…' he came to a stop.

'And…' both women said together.

'Oh you two are incorrigible,' but he laughed all the same. 'I wondered if you'd go with me, that's all.'

Lydia immediately thought of the silk dress that she had bought just after Gordon had died. And the beautiful shoes. As if reading her mind, Alice said, 'Well at least you can't say you haven't got anything to wear.'

'Look,' said Toby, 'I quite understand if you'd rather not.'

'No. I'd love to. When is it?'

'Would you really? It's the 18th December at The Grange in Mapleton.'

'I'll put it in my diary now.' She smiled at how relaxed she felt with him around.

When he had gone, Alice clapped her hands together, 'Well, it's about time.'

Lydia glared at her.

She roped Toby in on the tree-buying expedition. She knew he and his father shared a van and he had said she could borrow it. She roamed around the nursery, picking up trees, putting them back, and running over possibilities.

'I'll know it,' she said, 'I'll know the one which will want to come home with us.'

Eventually, she found it. She made Toby hold it apart from all the others as she encircled it. She nodded, 'Yup. That's the one.'

They bought a base for it and Toby carried it to the van. He could just close the door on it. 'Are you sure this will go in the house?'

They drove back to Rose Cottage and she helped Toby manoeuvre it into the hall.

'Where's it going to go, Lydia. Have you thought?'

'In the lounge.'

'But you never use the lounge.'

'Well, I'm going to over Christmas. Pounce and I shall go on holiday and leave the kitchen for a whole week.'

She fiddled around, moving furniture until the tree was in the right place.

'Now then, I'm going to go and make some mulled wine, put some mince pies in the oven and then we can decorate it.'

The wine got them into the Christmas spirit and soon all three of them were thoroughly enjoying themselves. Alice took out the mistletoe she had secretly purchased at the nursery and hung it over the kitchen door. Lydia came out into the kitchen just as Toby was coming in from the back door. They met under the mistletoe and time seemed to stand still.

'May I?'

She nodded and he reached down and kissed her softly and very gently. 'Thank you.'

He picked up the log basket and continued through to the lounge, leaving Lydia gawping after him, her heart racing.

'Alice,' she yelled.

'What is it?'

'Thank you.'

Alice smiled at Toby and threw a log onto the fire causing sparks to fly up the chimney. 'Just thought you needed a helping hand.'

Lydia brought in some more mulled wine. She suddenly felt gauche and ill at ease, but they both took no notice of her as they were busy trying to fix the fairy on top of the tree. Eventually they stood back, both satisfied.

'Well, I've done the lights. Shall I try them?'

'No,' Lydia replied, 'let's do all the rest first and then when we've finished, we'll turn them on.'

It took another couple of hours to finish completely.

'I'll have to go and buy some more for the hall.'

'No, we'll use greenery and berries,' Alice scolded, 'you'll have to keeping adding to your decorations each year. Otherwise it'll cost you a fortune.'

Lydia put candles on all the flat surfaces and lit them.

'Shame I haven't got a CD player. We could do with some carols.'

'Well, you've got a voice, haven't you?' And in a beautifully clear voice, Alice started singing *Silent Night*. Toby went to the light switch and turned off all the lights before turning on the tree lights. It was so pretty, it made Lydia want to cry. Alice was still singing and Toby had joined in too and she felt a moment of pure happiness. She knelt down and hugged the dog. 'Happy Christmas, Pounce,' she whispered in his ear. Then she got up and hugged Alice as tight as she could. 'I love you,' she said and was not sure if Alice had heard until she felt the wetness on Alice's cheek.

'Well, I don't know about you two, but I'm starving.'

'Toby!' both women admonished.

'Guess I'd better rustle up some supper then' and Alice limped out into the kitchen. Soon she was dishing up platefuls of food. It had been a perfect evening, Lydia thought as she made her way to bed much later. She had tried not to think of Toby's kiss. She was saving it until now, when she could take it out and look at it. See how it made her feel. Good, was her conclusion.

Over the next week their relationship progressed gingerly. It took Toby a whole two days after the tree decorating to suggest they went out for a walk on the Sunday. He knew she would feel more comfortable if she had the dog with her.

They set off early. The ground was frosty and their boots left imprints on the grass. Pounce was wild with the scents, dashing off to either side of the path. They found each other easy company, chatting quite naturally. As they were walking back to the cottage, Lydia slipped her hand through his arm and he squeezed it to his side. He felt he had to go slowly, that a false move would send her running. But that was fine by him. He was a patient man.

Toby took her to the pub when they got back and insisted on buying her lunch. He dropped her back to Rose Cottage afterwards.

'Are you still OK for Tuesday?'

She nodded.

'Pick you up at seven, then.'

'OK.'

He leant over and kissed her very softly on the lips, 'I've enjoyed today.'

'Me, too.'

They smiled at each other and she let herself out of the car, waving as he drove away down the lane.

She spent an unusually long time getting ready on the Tuesday. She had gone into the village hairdresser and had her hair put up. Then she had spent ages in the bath, before carefully putting on her make-up. She slid her dress on, stepped into her shoes and looked at herself from every angle in the mirror. She felt excited and apprehensive at the same time. She heard Toby's car pull up in the drive and ran downstairs and out of the house. She suddenly did not want him looking at her in the bright lights of the kitchen. This was all too new for her. As she rushed out, she heard a voice in her head saying, *'you look beautiful - relax.'*

'I'll try,' she whispered back.

Toby wolf-whistled her anyway, although he could not see her very well in the dark. He had borrowed his dad's car to drive them in, which was a bit more comfortable than his.

'Can't see why you can't take the Jag. After all, it is a club dinner.'

'Oh, I can't take her out of her mothballs. It's far too cold for her.'

They both laughed and the slight awkwardness dissolved.

The Grange looked magical, with hundreds of tiny fairy lights adorning the trees and bushes near to the entrance. A huge log fire roared in the fireplace and the place was exquisitely decorated. They were given a glass of champagne on their arrival and Toby introduced her to a few of the other club members. He was very careful to say, 'This is Lydia Page,' and no more. He felt it was presumptuous to call her his girlfriend.

Lydia, who usually avoided social gatherings, found

309

them all very down-to-earth and easy to talk to. She was soon deep in discussion with someone about her garden. In fact, she did not really talk to Toby again until they were called in to supper. But despite their lack of verbal communication, he was never far away and whenever she looked up, he was always looking at her and would mouth, 'OK?' She spontaneously took his hand as they were going through into the restaurant.

'I'm having a really good time.'

'I'm glad.'

He looked as pleased as punch. They had a wonderful meal accompanied by a string quartet playing on a small raised dais in one corner. Afterwards, there was dancing in another room.

'Do you want to dance?'

She shook her head, 'I've got two left feet.'

'So have I. Thank goodness for that.'

As it neared midnight, a guest came in through the front door. 'It's snowing!' People rushed outside, looking incongruous, standing in the cold in their party clothes. Sure enough, it was snowing quite heavily and lying where it settled. People began to get ready to go as they could see that driving conditions were going to be difficult.

'Let's go home, get changed and go out and walk in it,' Lydia suggested. Toby looked at her expectant face and nodded, 'I'll have to stop off and pick up some things from home.'

They said their goodbyes and Toby drove slowly home.

'He won't be there, will he?'

Toby glanced at her. He reached across and took her hand, 'No, he's gone for good.'

She seemed relieved. She was quiet for a few minutes

and then asked, 'Was it because of me?'

'Yes. And all his other girlfriends he's treated badly.'

'How did you make him go?'

'Oh, I can be pretty persuasive when I want to be,' Toby said darkly, 'I don't think he wanted me going to the police. I knew too much.'

'And would you have done?'

'Of course.'

She nodded, feeling warm inside.

'I'll just go and grab some gear. And we'll take my car - I don't want to end up sliding Dad's into anything. Won't be a moment.'

He dashed up to the door and returned minutes later, having changed and grabbed his car keys. They drove back to Rose Cottage. Lydia opened the door and Pounce dashed out, barking frantically at the snowflakes. She ran upstairs and pulled on some warm clothes.

They put Pounce on his lead and started walking along the lane to the fields, where they let the dog go free. Toby was looking at the far slope.

'Do you have any tea trays?'

Lydia nodded, 'Why?'

'Fancy going down the hill on one. The snow's easily thick enough.'

'Brilliant.'

She gave him her keys and he made his way back to the cottage. It felt wonderfully warm inside the kitchen and he quickly made a flask of chocolate, rifling through Lydia's cupboards until he found everything he needed. Then he grabbed the trays and set off down the lane to find Lydia building the body of a snowman. She was shivering and her teeth were chattering.

'Do you want a hug or some hot chocolate to warm

you up?' He held out his arms with the flask in his hand.

'Oh definitely the chocolate,' and she snatched the flask from him, giggling. They played for an hour or so on the trays, speeding down the slope and often going flying when the tray hit a hummock of grass. Pounce must have run for miles, as he tore up and down with them, narrowly missing getting bowled over.

'OK. One more time. A serious race this time.'

They treked to the top of the hill.

'Get, set, go!'

They flew off. Lydia took the lead as she was lighter, but suddenly she hit a bump and fell off her tray. Toby's tray collided with hers and he landed in a heap beside her. She was laughing uncontrollably. He suddenly pulled her close and kissed her longingly. She responded with a passion that was new to her. Pounce suddenly trampled on them, trying to lick Lydia's face. Toby stood up and held out his hand.

'Come on, it's too cold to stay out any more.' He pulled her up and they collected their trays and walked back, hand in hand.

Lydia made huge cheese and pickle sandwiches when they got home, as they realised they were ravenous. It was nearly four o'clock in the morning.

'I'd better go,' Toby said, getting to his feet.

'No, stay.' She got up and took his hand and led him through the kitchen door. At the foot of the stairs he stopped her. 'Are you sure?'

'Quite, quite sure,' she answered.

CHAPTER THIRTY-NINE

Alice knew as soon as she set eyes on Lydia. She just looked radiant.

'Good evening?'

'Wonderful.'

Lydia proceeded to tell her all about The Grange, but did not mention them playing in the snow. Lydia's guests were arriving today and so both were busy, making sure the house was sparkling. They then went out and did the food shopping, although Alice seemed to have been baking for weeks. She made up her mind when she caught Lydia with her hands in a sink of soapy water staring out into the garden.

'Penny for them?'

'Oh,' Lydia blushed a bright red and carried on with the washing up. 'I was just thinking about inviting people in on Christmas Eve for a drink.'

Alice knew she had not been thinking of that at all. 'Well, you'd better get a move on, you've only got a few days.'

'Will you stay Christmas Eve so that you're here Christmas morning?'

Alice took a deep breath. It was now or never.

'Actually, I've decided to go and stay with my sister in Cornwall.'

Lydia spun round so quickly she shot water over the floor. 'Whatever do you mean?'

Alice looked at the floor. 'Well, she's on her own unexpectedly.'

'Can't she come and stay down here?'

'No, she doesn't travel well. No, we'll be fine.'

And she bustled out of the kitchen, leaving Lydia standing, staring after her. It had really knocked the stuffing out of her as she did not want to spend Christmas without Alice. But Alice would hear no more on the subject and by late afternoon, Lydia's guests had arrived. She showed them to their rooms and then served them hot chocolate and mince pies in the lounge. They complimented her on the decorations and she would have felt deeply satisfied if it had not been for Alice.

Toby had drifted through the day. It was nearly eleven o'clock before he had got into work and then he had to put up with wisecracks from his father for the next hour. He could not concentrate on anything, he was so tired from lack of sleep, but also stunned at the way the night had unfolded. It had been absolutely magical and beyond his wildest dreams. He had never dreamt that Lydia would have asked him to stay. But she seemed to suddenly drop all her barriers and it had been wonderful.

He decided to go home, change and nip round to see her. When he got there, he could tell there was an underlying tension in her. He guessed she was probably starting to regret them sleeping together. She seemed to have a house full of people and was distracted with them as well. He could feel his spirits sinking. He scratched Pounce's belly and drank the mug of tea she had put in front of him. He had to say something. He had to know if it had all gone wrong. He only hoped he could salvage something. She dropped a spoon on the floor and swore.

'Lydia?'

'Sorry. I didn't mean…'

'I'm sorry about last night. I guess it should never have happened.' It had come out all wrong. He was not good at expressing himself.

She turned on him, 'Oh, so that's why you're so fidgety, is it? Like a cat on a hot tin roof. Well, you clear off as well, then.' She was yelling at him now.

'Lydia, your guests.'

She slammed the kitchen door shut, 'Get out of my house. Go on. Get out!'

He went. He could not cope with her like this. She slammed the door behind him. So he had only been using her. He had not really wanted her. He had just gone along with her.

Luckily, the guests were making a lot of noise and so had not heard her outburst.

She did not sleep at all that night. She spent most of the time looking out of the bedroom window. At dawn, she wrapped up and took the dog out. It was bitterly cold with a biting north wind. There would be more snow today, she thought.

Alice came in to help her with the breakfasts and found her totally uncommunicative and wished she could undo the damage she had done. She left after she had washed up because Lydia had made it clear she did not want any help with the rooms. She bumped into the Reverend Turnball on her way back through the village.

'Think it'll snow again today, Alice?'

Alice looked up at the sky, 'Aye, I reckon it will.'

'Still, at least you've not got to travel over Christmas.'

'Well, I'm probably going down to my sister's in Cornwall.'

'What? Not going to Rose Cottage?'

'No. Lydia's taken up with young Toby from the garage. It'll be their first Christmas together and they won't want an old 'un getting in the way.'

'I can't see Lydia agreeing with that.'

'No, well, I've not given her the choice. I've told her I'm going to my sister's and even if I don't get there, she's not to know.'

'You can't spend Christmas on your own.'

'Why ever not? I have done lots of times. There's always plenty on the television to keep me occupied.'

He shook his head, 'Why not come round to the vicarage and have lunch with us.'

'No, no. I'll be fine. Thanks for the offer.'

And with a wave of her hand, she had gone.

It was hours later when he went down to the church. He had emptied the prayer box and had put the pieces of paper in his pocket to include in the next sermon before he realised that there was someone sitting in the church. He heard a noise, which sounded like a sob. He always had a silent argument with himself over whether to interfere. He was never sure whether he should just leave people in peace or whether he should go and offer his help. The woman moved slightly and he could see by her profile that it was Lydia Page. She was fumbling for a tissue and blew her nose loudly. He made up his mind. He walked towards her, deliberately making a noise so that she would hear him. She looked up just as he sat down on the pew in front of her. He handed her his large white handkerchief to replace her crumpled, sodden bit of tissue.

'Now suppose you tell me what this is all about.'

She looked at him and fresh tears appeared, 'I just want Gordon back,' she sobbed.

He knew now why she had come back here and had sat beneath the windows.

'You know that's not possible, Lydia.'

He saw her nod.

'What's happened that's made you so unhappy?' He waited until she had caught her breath and her crying was quieter.

'I feel so alone.'

'Why do you? You've got Alice…'

He had not finished the sentence when she started crying again with a vengeance. 'Alice doesn't want to spend Christmas with me.'

So this was it. It all fell into place. He wondered if what Alice had told him could be classified as being confidential. He made a decision. 'I saw Alice this morning. It's not that she doesn't want to be with you, it's that she thinks she'd be in the way.'

Lydia looked up, 'In the way?' Why on earth should she think that?'

'Oh well, in for a penny,' he thought.

'She thinks that you and Toby would want to spend Christmas on your own, without her around.'

'There is no Toby,' Lydia said flatly.

'But I…I'm sorry. I must have misheard her.'

'No, you didn't. Toby only wanted what all men want.' She said this with such bitterness it made him recoil. He thought of Toby Thomas and somehow knew that this was one huge mix-up.

'Lydia, I think you should go and talk to Alice, explain to her how much you really want her to be there. Because no matter how much you want Gordon, nothing can bring him back.'

She looked as though he had slapped her in the face. He reached out and touched her arm.

'I'm sorry. That was most insensitive of me. It's just it's nearly Christmas and I really do want to see you get this sorted out.'

'So do I,' she whispered.

'Then go and see her.'

She nodded, 'I will. I just want to sit here for a bit longer.'

'That's fine. If you need to talk to me again, then you know where I am. Anytime. Night or day. And if you do find yourself on your own, then come and have Christmas lunch at the Rectory. Not that I think you will,' he added hastily.

He got up and left her, deep in thought. He wondered how many other people there were in the village who were also dreading the Christmas period. Perhaps he should open his door to them all. And why not, he thought. The trouble was a lot of the lonely ones probably did not even come to church and it was very late to try and find out who they were likely to be. But not too late. When he got back to the vicarage, he found Penny waiting in the study.

'I've had an idea,' he said.

Penny thought she would drop from exhaustion by the end of the next day. Notices had gone up in the village shop and with the help of the postman and Maisie, invitations had been put through people's doors. Having no idea how many people to expect, Penny had come back absolutely loaded with food. She had then spent the whole day cooking two turkeys, a ham and lots of other things suitable for a cold buffet. Lawrence had wanted a hot meal, but she had talked him out of it, particularly as they did not know if they were going to get one, or fifty people. Personally she thought that people would not like to just turn up, but she hoped she was wrong. Peggy Wright, who always spend Christmas with her sister who lived a few miles' away, had already said she would love to come as neither she nor her sister fancied driving with snow-covered roads. Her sister had family nearby, so she was going to be OK.

'Just pass the word on, Peggy, that's all. The more the merrier!' Goodness knows how much this was going to cost him, thought Penny, but he seemed unperturbed when she presented him with the supermarket bill.

It was the 23rd December and Lydia had not been round to see Alice and it was not one of the days she could help with breakfast. It was the Christmas lunch at the Manor today, but Lydia did not feel in the least like going. But she knew she had to.

Lord P. always put on a wonderful lunch with limitless champagne. He and his wife always bought his staff individual presents, which were taken from beneath the Christmas tree, just as though they were proper family. There were twenty-five staff that year and despite Lydia's despondency, she could not help but enjoy herself.

She was handed her gift and opened it, as was expected of her. It was a beautiful, soft cashmere cardigan in a perfect shade of pink. 'Oh it's beautiful.'

'Thought it was you, dear,' Lady P. beamed.

To her consternation, she felt her eyes fill with tears and she pretended to wrap the cardigan up again.

Soon it was time to leave. Lydia had brought her boots with her and she strode off across the fields, far too full of champagne to have driven her car.

As she walked up the front path of the cottage, she could see her guests were in the sitting room. She had laid the fire before she had left and this was blazing away. She opened the back door and came face-to-face with Alice.

She just held out her arms and Lydia ran to her and they hugged fiercely.

'I'm sorry! I'm just a silly old woman who wants locking up.'

'So you'll be here for Christmas?'

'Of course I will. I should have known you better than to imagine you and Toby wouldn't want me around.'

'There is no me and Toby,' Lydia said flatly.

'What on earth do you mean?'

'He doesn't want me, Alice.'

Alice shook her head and sat down, 'Well, I just don't believe it. The boy's been mooning after you for months.'

'Well maybe he didn't like the goods after he'd unwrapped them.'

'Lydia!'

'Well, why else would he suggest it had all been a mistake?'

'I have no idea.'

'Well, anyway, it'll be just us, which is fine by me.'

But Alice knew she was putting a brave face on it.

'Why don't you get your sister to come over as well?'

'She's not keen on travelling when the going's a bit difficult. She'll be OK - she's got lots of friends who've invited her.'

The sound of laugher filtered through from the lounge.

'I'd better go and see if they've got everything they need before they go out again.'

Alice left, promising to be there at breakfast time. She had a visit to make.

CHAPTER FORTY

Christmas Eve dawned and Lydia awoke to a further heavy fall of snow. She got up and let the dog out. She had an hour before they would be down to breakfast. There was no sound from above and she had already set the table the night before. She had time to wrap Alice's gifts and put them beneath the tree. Then one for Pounce, wrapped just as carefully.

The post arrived and with it a card from her mother with a £5 note inside. She tossed it on the side. At least it would have eased her mother's conscience. She would put the money in a charity box.

She heard Alice arrive, stamping her boots on the doorstep.

'Boy, it's freezing out there.' She went and stood by the range. Lydia handed her a mug of tea, which she wrapped her cold hands round.

'I've asked Sid and Maisie round tonight. The guests will be here for the beginning of the evening as well.'

'I'd better get baking, then.'

'Alice, you've baked enough to feed half of England!'

The day passed in a succession of chores. They shopped for lunch and afterwards, Lydia took Pounce to the meadow for a game. She needed to get some air, however cold it was. She wrapped her arms around herself. She felt bruised inside, bruised and battered. Thank goodness she had Alice, otherwise she could not have coped. But Alice, as much as she loved her, did not fill that emptiness inside her that Toby had filled. She called the dog, but he was too busy scrabbling in the hedgerow to take any notice of her, so she left him and went back into the warm.

They set the coffee table up with festive nibbles and opened the champagne Lord P. kindly gave the staff each year. Sid and Maisie arrived and soon everyone had full glasses. It was a very jolly gathering, but the guests had a family do to go to and Sid and Maisie wanted to go to ring their daughter so it all ended after a couple of hours. Lydia caught Alice looking at the clock several times.

'Alice, you won't miss midnight mass, so don't worry. I won't let you get that drunk.'

'Cheeky madam.'

Lydia jumped as the back door knocker rapped on the back door, 'Must be next door. Have they forgotten something?'

Alice blushed. Lydia went and opened it and did not notice Alice vanish. All she saw when she opened the door was a huge bouquet of flowers.

'What…?'

And then she saw Toby. She took the flowers and then watched as he dropped to one knee in the snow.

'Lydia Page. I can't live without you for another second. Please will you marry me?'

He was holding out a box and she caught the glitter of diamonds in the moonlight.

'Marry you?' She was open-mouthed with shock.

'Lydia, it's freezing down here. Could you make up your mind one way or the other?'

'Yes. Oh yes. I can't think of anything I'd like better.'

He leapt up and grabbed her as though he would never

let go of her again. They almost fell into the kitchen, kissing and hugging.

'Shall I put this on?'

He held out the ring and took her hand. It was beautiful; a band set with diamonds. He slid it on her finger.

'I think,' said Lydia, 'we may have champagne left.' Then she burst into tears.

Lydia seemed to have a huge smile on her face on Christmas Day. She cooked breakfast in a dream. She and Alice exchanged presents and she had also put a small novelty gift by the plate of each of her guests. They had Buck's Fizz for breakfast and then Alice went off to church, leaving Lydia on her own for an hour or two. She put the turkey in the range and called the dog. She had somewhere to go.

The girl and dog were stark against the landscape. The only colour in the monochrome world was a single red rose lying on the snow over the grave. She talked for a while and then called the dog and went back to the car. It was too cold to sit today. But she had to come. He needed to know.

As if he did not already.

When she got back, the first thing she noticed was a lack of cooking smells. She went to the oven and it was stone cold. She let out a wail of despair. It could not possibly pack up.

Alice and Toby arrived together. Toby had spotted Alice walking as he had driven towards Rose Cottage. They fussed around Lydia and Toby declared the range needed a new part.

'But whatever are we going to do?'

'I have the perfect answer,' Alice said. 'We'll go to the vicarage.'

It seemed to be full of people when they arrived. Toby had made quips about not being sure he wanted to marry her if she could not even manage to dish up a decent Christmas dinner. They were welcomed by Penny, who was more than a little merry. As, it seemed to Lydia, was everyone else.

'What a wonderful idea,' Alice enthused, but Lydia was not listening. At the end of the room, she had spotted a wheelchair. It was Eleanor Sinclair.

'How on earth…?'

Lawrence was beside her, 'I arranged it. I couldn't bear the thought of her in a nursing home. She arrived yesterday. Go and talk to her. I think she wants to see you.'

Lydia took Toby's hand.

'It's OK. I'll come with you.'

They made their way across the room. Eleanor looked stronger and she balanced a glass of wine on her lap.

'Lydia.'

'Hello. Um…Happy Christmas.'

'And to you. I'm glad you're here as I have something for you. Can you get it? It's in my bag on the back of the wheelchair.'

Lydia pulled out a slim parcel, wrapped in Christmas paper.

'Well, open it then.'

Lydia pulled off the paper and took out a silver photo frame. In it was a picture of Gordon, taken in Eleanor's garden, a glass of wine in his hand. He had a large grey cat on his lap.

'Oh…' She was overcome with emotion.

'I knew you didn't have one and I thought you'd like one as I know how fond you are of him.'

Lydia handed the frame to Toby and put her arms around the old woman's thin body.

'Thank you,' she whispered, 'it means the world to me.'

The old woman's frail arm went around Lydia and hugged her back, 'You're welcome,' she said, 'You're welcome.'

EPILOGUE

The sun streamed through the windows coating the congregation with jewel-like colours. The womens' hats were of every shape and size. Lydia saw Pounce first, sitting at the back of the church, his silver collar shining. He barked when he saw her and she laughed. Alice, who was holding him, looked embarrassed, but Lydia just winked at her as she walked slowly down the aisle with Lord P. holding her arm. She was aware of a slight pressure on her other arm and knew that he was there too, knew that Pounce's delight wasn't just for her.

The old woman began haltingly at first, but as the first notes wafted into the air, she closed her eyes and the richness of the saxaphone filled the church. Toby watched Lydia coming towards him and smiled into her eyes as she joined him.

Then he whispered, 'I will look after her,'

'I know you will,' Lord P. whispered back.

But it wasn't to him Toby was speaking. There was an almost immeasurable sigh and then Reverend Turnball began.

'We are all gathered here together...'

Sally Petch is a Reflexologist and healer. She lives in West Sussex, mostly in a house, but sometimes in a Tipi. Her passions include her partner, animals, Brighton and Hove Albion Football Club, walking, her cat Rosie and her pet hens, although not necessarily in that order! She drives a battered Jaguar held together with rust and a prayer. This is her first novel.